WINDOW of Peace

The Stained-Glass Legacy ⬦ Book Two

Regina Rudd Merrick

To Kathy Cretsinger.

Her wild idea of our small local writing group hosting a retreat—and then a few more—was the impetus for creating a series like none of us had ever read, much less written. Thank you.

Published by Scrivenings Press LLC
15 Lucky Lane
Morrilton, Arkansas 72110
https://ScriveningsPress.com

Printed in the United States of America

Paperback ISBN 978-1-64917-289-1

eBook ISBN 978-1-64917-290-7

Editors: Elena Hill and Linda Fulkerson

Cover by Linda Fulkerson www.bookmarketinggraphics.com

Acknowledgments

A few years ago, three other terrific authors and I brainstormed a series as an assignment at a writing conference. Since the four books needed to cover 100+ years of time, Heather Greer, Amy Anguish, Erin Howard and I knew that two of us, in order to cover the time periods, would have to sneak from contemporary romance to historical romance. Heather and I took it on.

Window of Opportunity, by Heather Greer, gives us the Dunne family's origin story, taking place amidst the flappers and prohibition-era mobsters of the 1920s. This book is fifty years later, in the Vietnam War era of 1970. Amy Anguish's *Window of the Heart*, releasing in August 2023, is in the current time, and Erin Howard's *Window of Time*, releasing in December 2023, takes place in a dystopian future.

The unifying item? A stained-glass window, passed down from generation to generation, reminding each of the love of family and the hope of Christ's love for each of us.

So, all that to say thank you, thank you, thank you to Heather, Amy, and Erin for believing that we could do this, and to the members of the KenTen Writer's Group for providing support and the time and place to brainstorm an off-the-wall idea that eventually saw the light of day. The four of us have stayed in contact continually – especially when the family tree received corrections

Thank you, Linda Fulkerson, our publisher with Scrivenings Press, for your encouragement to push ourselves to create an unusual, continuing story that spans over 100 years.

Special thanks to fellow author Susan Lawrence for interviewing a friend of hers who, the day I asked a question about VA healthcare in the Vietnam-era, just happened to be planning a lunch with a Vietnam veteran, and offered to interview him for me. That information was invaluable.

To our editors, Elena Hill and Linda Fulkerson, thank you for helping us make these the best they can be.

To my readers, thank you for your patience as I go off on a tangent! Let me know if you want more historical from me! ☺

To my family, thank you, also, for your patience. 2022 was a rough year for us, but we survived, and God will make us stronger for it. I have faith.

To my amazing God – Father, Son, and Holy Spirit – thank you for the lessons I've learned, and continue to learn. Thank you for peace in chaos, for my salvation, and for giving me examples of families that stand the test of time.

Chapter One

February
Vietnam, 1970

The occasional flash from too-close mortar rounds provided the only light in the dark jungle. Lieutenant Michael Connor "MC" Dunne's eyes had long ago grown accustomed to seeing at night, making the flashes of light a detriment.

Gunnar stopped.

"What is it, boy?"

MC knelt next to his K9 scout. The dog had instincts that couldn't be taught. Instincts he was born with.

Those instincts had never let the unit down.

"What do you see?"

MC crouched, gazing all around him, waiting for the intermittent light to reveal any Vietcong guerrillas hidden in the lush undergrowth. His unit had made it through the swamp, but suddenly, it was too quiet.

Too peaceful.

Frankie's moan drifted toward MC. The soldier had to keep quiet, or he'd alert the enemy to their position. Gunshot wounds to both legs sustained while taking point during the last altercation would kill

Frankie if they didn't make it to the pickup spot. As it was, he'd soon receive his fourth Purple Heart, and most likely a ticket home.

Sal, the unit's medic, gave him a shot of something. MC didn't care what it was—at least it got him quiet. It took two men to carry the wounded man, and now he was even heavier—dead weight.

They made it to the outskirts of an area that had once been a temporary base. The tents that housed personnel had long been dismantled and moved to another site.

MC and his men reached a clearing. A church stood in the center, shining in the moonlight—a small chapel, rustic in nature, with a short white steeple. Left behind when the unit vacated the area. It reminded him of his Grandpa Brendan's chapel on Dunne Farm back in Tennessee.

He heard rustling, and Gunnar emitted a low growl from his throat. The small building would either become a great hiding place. Or a trap.

MC made the decision and used hand signals. Hiding place. They had to stop in order to deliver Frankie to the pickup zone alive.

Using stealth movements, as they'd learned when guerrilla warfare became the norm, they made their way to the building.

Gunnar remained quiet, but MC could feel the dog's raised hackles. He never let down his guard.

Maybe they could rest here tonight, but someone would have to stand guard duty. In the jungles of Vietnam, no one could be trusted.

The enemy could be an old lady in the marketplace, a child harvesting crops in a field, or even a nursing mother. Anyone could be a Vietcong plant.

As they settled into the small structure, MC whispered, "I'll take first watch." They'd been so quiet, his whisper sounded loud.

Pulling out of his pack a collapsible bowl, he poured water in it for Gunnar, who, even as he drank, kept his ears at attention.

Looking around in the dim light, MC took in his surroundings. The room was about the size of the chapel on the farm. In fact, on one end, where the pulpit would have stood, was a stained-glass window, much like the one that meant so much to Grandpa. The Dunne chapel's window had survived the trip from Ireland to Chicago, then from Chicago to Tennessee. Home.

The window before him probably wouldn't survive this war, if it even made it through tonight.

Are you there, God? We're in trouble here.

He looked over his comrades, fitfully sleeping, a few snoring. Sleep was the last thing on his mind. He had to figure this out. Grandpa would say to wait, to trust in God's timing, but Grandpa wasn't here, in the thick of battle.

A blaze of light through the stained-glass window alerted him, but too late. As if in slow-motion, shards of glass flew toward them. Being awake, MC had time to shield his face with his arm. The glass bounced off of Gunnar's thick German shepherd coat.

His unit scrambled to safety, each man picking bits of glass from what little of the uniform they could stand to wear in this heat. Some of the bits stuck to their sweating bodies, driving the glass in just far enough that small rivulets of blood dripped down. These surface wounds wouldn't slow them down.

MC turned toward Frank Wallace.

Frankie.

He wasn't sure if the red he could see was blood, or a piece of glass the same color. Whatever it was, whatever color it was, it had hit its mark, deeply piercing his neck.

Frankie was dead. Not from gunshot wounds, but from being in the wrong place at the wrong time.

When MC reached him, he saw Sal, next to the body, eyes staring straight ahead, and a bullet hole in his forehead. He wanted to be sick, but there was no time to grieve.

Not now.

The enemy was close. Between them and the pickup zone.

MC drew his rifle out, still dazed at the sight of his dead friends. There weren't the first deaths he'd witnessed, but Frankie and Sal? They'd died on his watch. He turned when he heard a guttural male scream rushing toward him. The enemy.

He couldn't tell where the gunshot came from. Gunnar barked, and tugged at him. He felt Gunnar knock him to the ground as he pulled his trigger. A heart-wrenching yelp came from his partner, followed by pain searing through his shoulder. After that, MC was in and out of consciousness, seeing only flashes of activity around him. The last thing he remembered was sunrise coming through what was left of the window, then the medivac lifting him out of the jungle. Without Gunnar.

Where was God, now?

~

March
Tokyo

Dear MC,

We made a lot of promises to each other before you left for Vietnam. Promises that I can't keep.

I loved you so much …

Loved? She didn't know the meaning …

I met somebody. His name is Clint.

I can't begin to tell you how sorry I am. It's cliché, isn't it? The war hero and the flighty nursing student. I guess I'm a cliché.

The idea that I promised to wait for a soldier who, statistically, wouldn't come back, was too much for me. I need more assurance than that.

Please don't hate me. I hate myself enough for both of us …

The nurse who had attended to him for the last few weeks interrupted his thoughts.

"Lucky you, heading home."

MC looked up, his emotions roaring.

"Lucky me."

She didn't deserve that. He closed his eyes and took a few deep breaths. "I'm sorry, Carol. I didn't mean to take out my problems on you."

Nurse Carol, Captain Dryden to those she outranked, like him, nodded, then placed a clean uniform on the bed. She didn't mention his verbal slip. "Nothing I haven't seen before." Tilting her head, she frowned. "I hope things go well for you at home."

He nodded, then looked down at the paper in his hands. His attention back on that, he folded up the tattered letter and shoved it into his duffel, feeling the anger well up inside him. The smart thing would be to throw it away. He couldn't. He'd read and re-read the fine script so many times, he had it memorized.

He'd received the letter six weeks after he arrived in Vietnam. After his first skirmish in-country.

His Commanding Officer had tasked one of the men in his platoon to pack up what little personal effects that belonged to him and had them sent to the hospital. Now, going through the bits and pieces of his recent life, he wished it had all been destroyed, especially Rebecca's letter.

Maybe when he got home, he'd burn it.

Home. He should be celebrating. Instead, he wished he'd died along with his platoonmates. And Gunner, who took the bullet meant for MC.

I ended up with a flesh wound, and Gunnar ended up dead.

Why would a God who loved him make him endure such loss without easing him into death, especially when he'd begged for it?

Glimpses of war, of jungles, of friends lost, of desperation—of horror—consumed him. Now, he'd have to navigate another land as foreign to him as the place he'd just left—home.

Chapter Two

After a month in a Tokyo hospital, MC Dunne soaked in the sights. The Pacific Ocean. The Rocky Mountains. The Great Plains. Finally, he began his trek home, traveling through Illinois to the Mississippi River and a six-hour bus ride to Clarksville, Tennessee, the closest station to Park Haven. Home.

He'd spent much of Illinois and Kentucky taking fitful naps borne of exhaustion and unrelenting pain. Now, familiar spring sights scrolled by the bus window.

The closer MC got, the more he perversely wanted to delay seeing the people he loved. After experiencing the disregard many Americans had for their veterans, MC wondered if it would be the same here in Tennessee.

Surely not. He remembered the send-off and prayer circle at church before he left. He'd received a few cards and letters. Grandpa Brendan wouldn't let anyone forget to pray for him.

Hopkinsville and the nearby Fort Campbell, home of the Army's 101st Airborne Division—Screaming Eagles—came into view. A flutter of excitement filled MC, as well as a gnawing of dread. The bus hit a pothole, and a small child behind him screamed. His surroundings blurred, and he put his hand down to comfort Gunnar.

Nothing there. His scout dog was one of the thousands of military dogs sent to Vietnam, saving countless lives in combat.

He wasn't over the loss yet. After MC's injury and the decision to send him home for additional treatment, it was as if the dog had never existed. But he would always be with MC.

How do the powers that be think you can eat, sleep, train, play, and go into combat with a dog and the animal not become a part of you? While in a drug-induced haze, he overheard someone at the mobile hospital say that military dogs were classified as "equipment."

What would happen to that type of "equipment" after the war? Provided it ever ended.

Gunnar died saving his life. No question about him being deserted like so many other dogs who had done just as much.

MC shook the cobwebs out of his head and peered at the people gathering their things, preparing to exit the bus as if nothing had happened.

Nothing *did* happen. Not here, anyway.

Taking a deep breath as the bus slowed to a stop, he stood and waited for the passengers in front of him to exit the bus. His balance was still off, his left arm in a sling, and his ankle stiff after riding so long.

Why couldn't he just slide back into real life as if he'd never been gone? Why couldn't Rebecca be waiting for him at the bus station, a ring on her finger? Why couldn't he erase the last two years—two tours of duty minus pain and anxiety? Just make them disappear.

"Son!" Dad's voice boomed across the busy lobby.

MC and his dad stood taller than many of the people between them. MC raised his hand and met his father's tearful gaze.

Please, God, not that. Can't handle tears from Dad.

MC glanced around at the crowd. If he'd dreamed of Rebecca coming to meet him, he was disappointed. Just an invisible soldier getting off the bus. No fanfare, no welcome home. Along the way, he'd seen sideways glances at his fatigue jacket, upturned noses, and mothers pulling their children closer to them, protecting them from the unwanted, unloved Vietnam veteran.

But his family, if not his country at large, loved him.

Was it his imagination that the crowd parted, enabling Dad to get to him quickly? Almost instantly, he was in his father's arms, and both of them cried. The pain in his shoulder was nothing compared to the pain he'd been through to get here.

They each stepped back, and MC had a hard time meeting his dad's eyes. But then, his dad wasn't faring any better.

In 1970, men were somewhat better at expressing their feelings than in the past, but crying in public? Not cool.

And yet, it was cathartic.

In the parking lot, MC's attention turned to an altercation.

The girl … he recognized her, but he couldn't remember how. The guy she spoke to was no stranger, however. Bert Conway. MC's lifelong rival.

They'd always wound up in competition, whether it be for a position on the basketball team, a pretty girl, or class standing.

MC bit the inside of his cheek. The race for class valedictorian had been their last challenge—one MC won.

As if feeling MC looking at him, Bert glanced his way, and their eyes locked. The young lady followed his gaze but quickly turned back to Bert.

Bert was clean-cut and neat. A jolt of unwanted realization hit him. MC could feel the comparison between his scruffy self and Bert in the girl's eyes.

Competition lost.

Dad stopped at a strange vehicle, and MC put the irritation behind him.

"New truck?"

The shiny blue Ford F250 had the family's construction company logo on it. "Dunne and Morgan Construction: Get it Dunne Right."

He chuckled, remembering the family discussion to add the punchline.

"Contractor Special. Beaut, isn't she?" Dad patted the bed of the truck much as MC had attempted to pat his invisible dog on the head. With love and affection.

"Very nice." MC took in the bumper sticker. "We Support Our Boys in Vietnam." Dad never approved of what he considered tacky decorations on his vehicles. He'd made an exception.

Dad nodded quietly. He was a mind-reader.

"It's the only sticker I'd put on my truck, just so you know."

MC nodded, unable to say anything. He'd seen a few stickers on the bus ride from St. Louis to Clarksville, but few were in support of the Vietnam troops. Most were blatantly against the war. Some blamed the government, but many blasted the soldiers who were there doing their job, standing up for people who had no one to stand up for them.

THE SCREEN DOOR SLAPPED CLOSED, alerting the crowd assembled in the living room. All eyes focused on him, whether he liked it or not.

Everyone spoke at once. MC's ears roared, more from stress than noise.

"Didn't anybody ever teach you people not to get between a mama and her only chick?"

So much for a quiet entry. Mom had invited the whole family to welcome him home.

His sweet mama, at a solid five-foot, one-inch tall, reached him before anyone else. For a moment, MC was six, with Mom hugging away his hurts. Now, he had to lean down to hug her, and he could protect her more than she could him.

The aroma of boiled ham and a spread that would put a church potluck to shame enticed him. He'd eaten since landing on US soil, but this? This was what he imagined the banquet in Heaven would be like.

While Mom tried to gather everyone in one place, he turned to see his cousin's hand on his arm.

"Welcome home, cuz!" Will Morgan grabbed him into a hug before MC had a chance to say anything more, patting him on the back.

He winced at sharp pain in his partially healed shoulder, but Will's excitement surprised him the most. As kids, they were inseparable, but as the teen years came along, MC sensed a rivalry on Will's part that he never understood.

"How are you, Will?" His tone was forced, awkward.

"Good. Doing good." Will shook his head, appearing reluctant to look MC in the eye. "The minute I got word you were hurt, it hit me hard."

"Yeah, me too. Literally."

They chuckled, and the atmosphere cleared.

"My number came up." He spoke quietly, his gaze finally capturing MC's. "Dad got me a deferment for law school."

MC swallowed. He understood. How could he make Will understand?

"It's okay, man." He choked the words out.

"I was pretty upset at Dad, but he'd done it before I had a chance to think about it." Will glanced over his shoulder at his Dad on the other side of the room. "I told Dad if anything happened to you, I would go over there, whether he liked it or not."

MC gave Will what he hoped was a smile, not a grimace. "I'm glad you didn't go. If everybody went, there would be a lot more messed up people around. We need guys like you here, taking care of things."

Will nodded and held out his hand, which MC took without hesitation. "Welcome home, MC. I missed you."

Before he could answer, Mom pulled on his good arm. "We need to ask the blessing so everyone can eat. You can visit while you eat."

As if that would happen. He grinned at her, then winked at Will. "Where's Grandpa?" He should have been here.

"Coming in the door right now." Mom pointed to the entry. "And it looks like he brought a friend."

A bundle of reddish-golden fur rushed him, and every bit of anxiety and fear of what would happen next left. For the moment, anyway.

"Rusty." The older red Border Collie licked his face as MC knelt and hugged the dog with his good arm.

"I kinda thought you might like to see this fella." Grandpa Brendan reached down to help MC up, then hugged him fiercely. "I missed you, boy."

"I missed you, too, Grandpa." Warm tears burned MC's cheek, and he feared it would worsen since his grandfather was also smiling through tears.

"Looks like you've had your wing clipped," Grandpa said, gesturing toward his arm.

"Just temporarily. I have physical therapy a couple of times a week, and I go back to the VA hospital in a month for a checkup."

"We'll make sure you get in a little activity." The older man winked.

He and Grandpa. They had an understanding.

Mom shook her head sternly. "Not too much, mind you."

"Yes, ma'am."

She held up a spatula to get everyone's attention. "You'll all get a chance to visit with MC, but let's eat this ham while it's still hot." She gestured to Dad. "Connor?"

"Will you all bow with me as we give thanks?"

Everyone's head bowed, their eyes closed. But not MC. He'd learned if you close your eyes, things changed. Or worse … you might not open them at all.

Chapter Three

Nancy Jean Baker paused her note transcription, rubbing her tired eyes with her fingers. It had been a busy day, even before her lunchtime encounter with Bert ended in disaster. They hadn't planned to meet—she hoped no one thought they had. He'd taken his mother to the bus station for a trip to Huntsville, and she'd been in Clarksville to pick up supplies for the clinic. They'd bumped into one another at the diner, where she went in for a quick bite before heading back to Park Haven.

Bert was way too happy to see her. For her own comfort, anyway. She'd waited until they got to the parking lot between the restaurant and the bus station before she tried to let him down easily that she didn't want to go out with him again. She'd hoped to nip the idea in the bud before he asked her again, but he was too quick for her.

Not a happy camper.

He had the nerve to tell her she should smile more, get out and have more fun.

From the moment she agreed to go out with Bert Conway a few months ago, she'd second-guessed herself. He was nice enough, but he wanted more than she was prepared to give, hence the attempted brush-off.

The clock read 6 p.m. An hour of daylight left. The ache that crawled up her neck and into her head was getting worse. The only help, besides medication, was a change of scenery. She had to go home and get some fresh air. She reached down next to her, smiling gently at her trusty canine. Maybe run with Major. He needed the exercise as much as she did.

It had been a long winter.

Nancy felt the bun on her head. What started the day as a sleek, severe hairdo had relaxed, and she tucked a wayward strand behind her ear and covered the typewriter where she had been typing her notes.

In veterinary school, most of the experienced vets scribbled their notes by hand and passed them on to an assistant to record. She didn't want anyone to go through the agony of deciphering her hieroglyphics, so she developed her personal brand of shorthand.

She paused to straighten the picture hanging next to the clinic's front door. How long before it would be acceptable to take it down? It depicted her predecessor, Dr. Phillips, and a bright-eyed young man shaking his hand.

The first time she attempted to replace it with something educational, the receptionist threw a fit. No way would the folks coming to Doc Phillips' clinic stand for her removing the photo. The young man was not only the old man's ace in the hole in keeping the practice open, but now a decorated soldier. He'd joined the Army and gone to Vietnam, shocking everyone. He could have obtained an exemption.

After a heart attack sidelined the long-standing vet, Doc Phillips contacted some friends at Auburn to get replacement recommendations. Most students didn't want to go to a backwater town like Park Haven, but for Nancy, it was a nice reprieve from the intensity of her education. That, and she refused to move home. She'd have taken any opening anywhere from Alaska to the Everglades if it meant staying away from Decatur.

Rumor mill stated MC Dunne had arrived back this week to recover from his injury. What was it about someone who was considered "perfect" to an entire community that turned her off, completely? Looking more closely, she admitted that, yes, he was good-looking. Maybe not *completely* turned off.

She never mentioned she remembered MC Dunne. A year behind her at Auburn University College of Veterinary Medicine, she'd never met him, but she had noticed the rising star. Popular, didn't get into any trouble, and admired by all, including professors.

The man she saw today in the municipal parking lot was a far cry from the fresh-faced young man in the picture.

Had he ruined his chances at a career in veterinary medicine?

"Mom, I love you. You know that."

MC expected his mom to want him to stay with her, but he hadn't expected tears. Pulling out the green-and-gold covered dinette chair, he sat next to her.

She mopped her face with the handkerchief she kept in her apron pocket. The fact that she still wore aprons to do her housework was cute. Most women deemed them old-fashioned, but not Mom. If it was good enough for her homemaker mother, it was good enough for her.

After a deep breath, she glanced up through damp eyelashes. "I know you do. I think it's just hitting me that I could have lost you." She sniffed loudly. "Remember Ted Simmons?"

MC nodded. Of course, he did. Ted was a year behind him in high school. MC talked the coach into trying him out as point guard senior year.

"He was in Tokyo ..." MC swallowed thickly. "I was gonna see him, but ... I found out after my surgery. He didn't make it." If only MC had known sooner, he could have given Ted a touch from home. There wasn't enough time.

Mom wrung her hanky in her hands. "Myra and Bob are devastated. Then we learned you'd been injured, and your dog—"

"Yeah. I know. It could have gone a lot differently." He had to interrupt. Talking about tragedy might be helpful for some people, but not for him. Not now.

There were days he wished he had died instead of Gunnar, but people didn't understand—they would call him crazy. So, he kept those thoughts to himself.

Dad came in and poured a cup of coffee, gesturing to the pot. "Want a cup?"

MC nodded. "Thanks."

Dad sat the steaming mugs in front of them. MC paused, looking down, putting behind him the fleeting thought that the mugs matched the chair covers, exactly. "I'll stay a few days, but I need to get a place of my own. Figure some things out." He grinned. "Minimize the dog hair in your house."

Mom snorted. "You know I'd take any amount of Rusty's hair."

MC smiled. "You'd just increase the vacuuming." He stared down at the cup between his hands. "I just need some time."

Dad put a hand on Mom's shoulder and squeezed. "I know, son. We'll try to give you some space. Any thoughts about what you're going to do? Are you going to call Rebecca?"

MC shook his head. He'd neglected to tell his parents about the "Dear John" letter he received while he was overseas. "No, I'm not. She made her choice, and it wasn't me." He shrugged. Rebecca. Her shallowness devastated him for a while, then it irritated him. She'd done the right thing to break it off. Some guys were crazy to get back home to their girl only to find they'd changed. Was the girl different, or was the soldier?

"Oh, sweetie." Mom's tears gathered again.

"I'm okay, Mom." He reached over and squeezed her hand, smiling at her.

"As for work ... until this arm heals, I can't do a lot. I'm still on Uncle Sam's dime until the doc releases me."

"Speaking of doctors, what about your doctorate? I figure you could get a little money from the GI Bill." The crease between Dad's eyes made MC scoff.

"Not as much as they used to. I guess they've spent too much on this war. Not much left to take care of the ones who fought it."

The questions. The suggestions. They were just beginning. He may as well get used to well-intended comments.

~

MC WAS TWELVE AGAIN, following Grandpa around the farm, Rusty at his heels, trotting along like a pup. The farm had always been MC's favorite place—a bit of heaven that had been in the family since the early 1900s. Daffodils, or "March flowers," as he called them, dotted the edge of the woods and down the lane.

Grandpa Brendan had built the big white farmhouse for Grandma Evangeline, hoping to fill it with children. That never happened, but once a young Connor Dunne, MC's dad, came into their lives, they never turned back. The tragedy of Brendan's brother James's death changed their lives. Brendan's nephew became his and Evangeline's son, both legally and emotionally.

"What's happening with Uncle Patrick's cabin?" A thought formed in MC's mind. Could he repair it with a bum arm? Could the old cabin be a safe haven for him? Give him some privacy? The nightmares and flashbacks would come. No question about that.

MC wished the place had the power to take him back to a time before Rebecca. Before Vietnam.

A fresh start.

Grandpa chuckled. "Not much. Your Grandma used to get after me to either tear it down or restore it." He shook his head sadly. "I couldn't bear the thought of demolishing it. The cabin and your Great-Uncle Patrick were there for us from the start." A hint of Chicago slipped into his grandfather's accent that hadn't been covered over by his years in Tennessee.

"Do you think it's still livable?"

"Well, it's full of junk, but I've tried to keep the roof intact. Maybe some critters in there, but I think, overall, it would be worth restoring." He shrugged. "Power's still on. I haven't had the time, nor the energy, to take it on, especially since I started working on the chapel."

MC nodded, taking in the small structure. "Grandpa Morgan always laughed about us holding on to it. Said he wouldn't waste good carpentry skills on bad construction."

Why did Grandpa Brendan insist on working on the chapel? MC wasn't going to ask. What good would it do for anybody? Maybe a little of Grandpa Morgan's practicality made its way into his DNA after all.

A run-down chapel. The house of God. MC smirked.

If the deity was supposed to be everywhere, why rely on a broken-down shell of a chapel to meet God—if He even existed?

Grandpa smiled, shaking his head. "Your mama's daddy taught me everything I know about carpentry, but he didn't suffer fools, did he?"

"He did not. I'm glad I got to work with him and with you over the summers during high school. Hey, if you hadn't connected with Grandpa Morgan, Dad might not have met Mom." MC stood, head tilted, thinking. Bad arm or not, would renovating the cabin be worth his time?

"Those were good times." Grandpa's piercing gaze caught MC's. "Are you saying you'd like to take it on?"

"Maybe." He considered his grandfather. At nearly seventy, he could still do a day's work. Would he be willing to help?

"I may be retired, but I think, between you and your bad arm, and me with my 'advanced age,' we could do something with it. Nothing pressing at the chapel. Are you thinking you'd like to live in it?"

Grandpa might be old-school in a lot of ways, but, unlike his late Grandpa Morgan, he had a compassion that trumped the acceptable in polite society. For many people, it was a sign of weakness to admit to combat fatigue or what they were now calling "Vietnam syndrome." One must accept what's happened and move on.

MC hadn't talked to anyone about his experiences in the war, but he imagined Grandpa Brendan would be there for him if he needed him. If anyone in the family understood trauma, it was him. Based on little things that were said and the random sad look crossing Grandpa Brendan's face from time to time, he suspected there were things he never talked about, to anyone.

He took a deep breath. Rusty pushed his soft head under his hand, quietly asking for a scratch, which he received. "I think it would be a good place for Rusty and me."

"I agree." Grandpa put an arm across MC's shoulders. "And after we get that done, you can help me with the chapel."

Chapter Four

MC didn't wait for the renovations to move into the cabin. As he dropped his duffel on the ancient mattress, he thought about the living conditions in the jungles of Vietnam. His buddies there would be jealous.

He would stay here, clean it out, start making repairs, and help on the farm as needed. Having just one good arm limited his activity, but he could still feed and water the stock. One of the cows was about ready to calve.

New life. That's what he needed. As spring progressed quickly, new life popped up all around him.

A knock at the open cabin door turned him around. "Anybody home?"

MC smiled at his grandpa, feeling happier than he had in some time. "Come to greet the new tenant?"

"Yes. I thought you might need a few supplies." He set the box of sundries on the makeshift cabinet. "Not much by way of indoor plumbing, but you know where the outhouse is. I figure you've had worse."

"You know it. That old outhouse is like the Taj Mahal compared to some of the latrines over there." MC chuckled, but it sounded harsh, even to himself.

Grandpa Brendan peered around at the boxes and trunks. "A lot of that stuff probably needs to be pitched." His lips settled in a thin line. Without a word, he was telling MC he was there, and he would listen whenever needed. Mainly it said, "I love you, and I hate what you've gone through."

"I won't throw anything away without asking." He cursed the tears that threatened—no, dared—to fall. "Thanks, Grandpa."

He sniffed loudly and swiped his sleeve across his face.

"Think nothing of it. I've got a pot of chili on the stove as soon as you're ready to eat. Dark is around six."

MC nodded. "I'll check on Betsy before I come up."

"She should be ready calve any time now. It's her first, you know."

"I remember her birth. Do you still have her mama, Gertie?" Talking about normal things relaxed MC. No plans for the future, questions about his health, just farm talk.

"You haven't been gone that long. She had her calf a few weeks ago."

"She's a good one."

"She is." Grandpa Brendan held up his hands, then put them down. "Enough small talk. I've got a few things to do while it's still light. There's a hole in the chicken run, and you know how those coons are."

"Pesky little suckers, aren't they?" MC laughed. It was a family joke that Grandpa Brendan and the raccoons were not friends.

"Indeed." He pointed at MC. "Don't get smart with me, young man."

"Wouldn't dream of it."

Grandpa turned and walked away, chuckling.

Coming here was a good decision. MC could heal in more ways than one.

Why did the phone never ring at a reasonable time?

At 1:30 a.m., the sound woke Nancy from a vivid dream. A relaxing dream. Floating down the river on a raft, no dangers, just sunshine, birdsong, and the lull of water lapping against the banks. Oh, how she wished it were possible to revisit dreams.

She squinted at the clock and groaned before putting on her professional hat. "Dr. Baker." She'd reeled it off enough times that she could almost answer the phone in her sleep.

"Nancy, this is Brendan Dunne. Betsy's having her first calf, and I'm afraid we're having a little trouble. Can you give us a hand?"

She had encountered Mr. Dunne both at church and for animal care. If only she could claim him as her grandfather since she'd never met either of hers.

Would she get to officially meet the elusive but widely touted grandson, MC Dunne?

"I'll be out there in about thirty minutes."

"Thank you, and drive safely. It's not worth you having a wreck coming out here."

She smiled at the phone. "I'll be careful."

"I'll make some coffee—I'm sure we'll need some by the time this is over."

Brendan said his goodbyes and ended the call, and Nancy, in fully awake, vet-on-call mode, pulled on her jeans and coveralls, then donned her rubber boots before checking. She was ready to head out the door.

Once she'd made the mistake of not wearing another set of clothes under her coveralls. She fell into the muck as she delivered a breech colt. Muck in the worst sense of the word. She had to wear it until she got home. On a damp day, she could still smell it in her truck.

That one incident taught her a valuable lesson: don't pin all your hopes on one pair of coveralls and boots.

MC RAKED his hand over his face. They had to call the lady vet. If only he wasn't trying to work with a temporary limitation, he wouldn't have to assist a woman in what should have been *his* job.

It had all been set—Doc Phillips would retire gracefully about the time MC graduated with his doctorate in vet science. He'd already set aside a down payment on the practice and had plans to work toward securing the rest of the financing.

But Vietnam and the U.S. Army changed the trajectory of his life.

He heard the truck pull up. Grandpa hadn't returned from the house. Making coffee, he'd said. Why? If this woman was as good as Grandpa indicated, it shouldn't take more than an hour, and they would all be tucked into their beds for the remainder of the short night.

Who was he kidding? Even the best vets faced a stubborn birth from time to time.

Betsy struggled again—contractions were getting closer and closer together—so MC knelt, rubbing her neck and speaking to her gently.

"Hey, girl. Help is on the way. You'll be okay."

A decidedly feminine voice from behind him said, with a chuckle, "If wishes were ponies, then beggars would ride ..."

MC turned to see a medium-height, slender girl who couldn't weigh much more than a hundred pounds. His evaluation must have shown because she frowned.

"I'm stronger than I look."

What just happened here? His lips twitched, but he refused to give in to a smile.

He stood, hampered a bit by his injured left arm, and held out his right hand. "MC Dunne. You must be the new lady vet."

"I am." She stared him in the eye as she pulled on gloves. "And I have a name—*Doctor* Nancy Jean Baker."

There was that twitch again. Odd. He hadn't smiled in a long time, and now his mouth itched to do it twice in one setting.

"Well, Doctor Nancy Jean Baker, nice to meet you. I hope, between the two of us, well three, counting Grandpa, we can safely deliver this calf."

She nodded and went to work.

Now he remembered her. He hadn't known her name, but she was ahead of him at Auburn, finishing up about the time he went into the Army.

That would make her, what, one? Two years older than him?

The main thing he remembered about her was her glorious dark brown hair. So different from Rebecca's blond curls. Nancy Baker had always pinned it up or captured it in a ponytail. What would it look like down around her shoulders?

Where did that come from?

He also remembered her intense expression. Determination.

Back then, she had one goal—to become an excellent vet. And to stay ahead of every male veterinary student in the school.

He peeked at her again. She'd been at the bus station parking lot. Put Bert Conway in his place. And that put a smile on MC's face.

The three worked in tandem, and after several hours Betsy finally gave birth to a healthy calf. Dr. Nancy Jean Baker wasted no time packing up and heading out. Grandpa could have been the cat that swallowed the canary.

"Didn't I tell you Doc Nancy would get the job done?"

MC shook his head, watching Nancy's truck leave the driveway in the early morning wash of sunrise.

"You did, Grandpa." He smiled at the older man. "How about I finish up here, and you go back to bed for a few hours?

Grandpa gave him a sweeping gesture. "Pshaw. I'm fine. Might take a nap after lunch, but there's nothing like a new birth to start the day right." He clapped MC on the back and whistled as he left the barn.

How was it that the one person standing in the way of MC's lifelong dream turned out to be the most intriguing person he'd ever met?

Chapter Five

Nancy blew out a sigh of relief. She rolled down the window of her 60-model Chevy pickup. Maybe the wind in her face would wake her up. No more sleep for her tonight.

Today.

Sunrise had arrived.

She understood why Mr. Dunne had called. It wasn't an easy birth. The sturdy bull calf decided to back out of his warm, cozy home instead of meeting it head-on like a proper birth.

It never got old, though.

Would she get to stick around long enough to see if Young Master becomes a bull or a steer?

MC Dunne, aside from his obvious injury, knew his stuff. If he'd been in full form, he would have never needed her help. She remembered MC in the hallways of the vet science building. His dark good looks and ready smile back then were in stark contrast to the serious, broken man she worked with during the wee hours. He'd aged five years in two.

What had his experience in Vietnam left him with? There were stories about veterans coming home only to suffer nightmares and waking terrors.

It was almost as bad for the families. Her brother Steven died on the battlefield, and her father returned to the drinking problem he'd had as a young man. She'd heard one never really gets over it. It's always there, lurking.

For Dad, it reared its ugly head. Maybe if Mom had been alive, she could have stopped the violent streak that emerged. Nancy had a childhood empty of more than the occasional swat—mostly from Mom —but while her father was drinking, he struck out at anyone in the way.

And she was always in the way.

Shaking away the memories, she pulled into the lot at the local eatery a half-mile or so from the clinic. Coffee. That's what she needed. It would only take five minutes. Mr. Dunne's coffee had kept her going, but she needed an infusion of the good stuff, and the Park Haven Café had the good stuff. This early, it would be fresh.

The bell on the door jingled, arousing the breakfast crowd, making her wish she'd glanced in the rear-view mirror to see if she had dirt, or worse, on her face. Too late now. Her eyes fell on a waving hand.

Will Morgan. And … Bert.

Great.

Nancy liked Will. She did. He was a good guy. They'd gone out a few times, but there was never a spark. Why couldn't she develop deeper feelings for him? His disappointment as she told him such saddened her, but it looked as though he'd recovered well. Had she led him on?

She'd refused to go out with Bert a second time, and now all she could think of was Will's gentlemanly behavior compared to Bert. She had no confidence in her ability to select men.

Especially after Danny.

According to her tech, Mary Ann, it happens that way sometimes. One party has serious feelings and is bound to be hurt when those feelings aren't reciprocated.

What she'd do without her bubbly friend, Nancy had no idea. She couldn't fathom facing the dating arena on her own. The fact that Mary Ann was her veterinary technician—very married, and very pregnant —made Nancy listen to her. She'd obviously excelled in the art of finding the right mate.

"Hey, girl! What are you doing here this early?" Mavis stood at the register. Did she ever go home? "Are you joining us this morning?"

"Hi, Mavis. No, I just need a large coffee to go."

Mavis pulled a ball-point pen from her well-sprayed hair and wrote down the order. "Got it. Anything else?"

Nancy paused. Her stomach growled, and the overnight animals at the clinic would have to be fed as soon as she got there. "Would it be possible to put a sausage patty on a biscuit? That way I can eat it while I drive."

Mavis laughed. "I'm sure Joe can do that. I'll have him wrap it up for you." She shouted the order to the kitchen behind the register, then searched for something.

"I know we got another package of Styrofoam cups and lids. They're here somewhere." She rifled around, and suddenly straightened, with a smile on her face. "Found 'em!"

"Thanks, Mavis." She sat on the bench next to the door. Takeout orders weren't the norm for the café, but they aimed to please.

"Hey, Nancy." Will paid his bill and stood next to her, Bert Conway in line behind him, studiously avoiding contact with her. "Tough night?"

She chuckled. "Calves, like babies, don't tend to come at convenient times."

His laugh rang out. "I suppose that's true. Anybody I know?"

"Probably. Mr. Dunne's Betsy."

"I am familiar." He smiled. "My cousin MC is staying out there, I think."

"He is." She tilted her head. "Are you cousins on his mom's side?"

"Yeah, the Morgan side. We share a grandfather, but Grandpa Morgan was no Grandpa Brendan."

"You call him Grandpa too?" She chuckled.

"I spent more time out on the farm with Mr. Dunne than I did with Grandpa Morgan. They were close friends, but two more different men never lived. MC had the great honor of being the 'favorite grandson' to both of them." The humor on his face was contagious. It seemed he didn't hold a grudge.

Maybe she'd given up on Will too soon.

Bert interrupted her thoughts. "Nancy, how are you?" So, he'd decided to act like they'd not argued just days before.

Two could play at that game.

His smile broadened, making her feel uncomfortable. Why didn't she like him? Maybe she was paranoid. She'd already established the fact that she had no skill at picking men.

"Hi, Bert," she said, then turned back to Will. Maybe he'd get the message.

"I'm jealous. Both my grandfathers died before I could remember." She crossed her arms and peered back into the kitchen. The smell of sausage spiked her appetite. "Mr. Dunne called once they got stuck. MC's injured arm made performing a breech delivery pretty much impossible." She shrugged. "Otherwise, he could have handled it on his own."

Will nodded, a strange expression crossing his face. "I hope everything heals up the way it should. I would hate for him to have to start over again." He glanced at her. "But then, if he was okay, you'd be leaving, wouldn't you?"

Bert's eyes widened at Will's comment.

She stared at Will. It was way too early in the morning to deal with outdated ideas of what a woman "should" and "should not" do by way of occupation. Several in the area would prefer a male veterinarian. They'd as much as told her so.

Seriously? This, coming from Will? She might have expected it from Bert, but she thought Will was on her side. Maybe for family, though, there was a double standard. Disappointing.

Mavis set her cup and the bag holding her biscuit sandwich on the counter.

Saved by breakfast.

Will was, at least. That thought of giving Will another chance? Nope.

If she spoke, anything she said would be in anger, and she'd end up saying more than she should, so she stood, walked over to the register, paid her bill, and thanked Mavis. Without a backward glance, she pushed the door open, creating quite a jangle with the forcefulness of her exit.

Nancy sat in the truck for a few minutes to get her blood pressure down, then headed to the clinic and sat in the parking lot to finish her biscuit. She knew if she went in, she'd hit the ground running.

Observing the small building that housed the Park Haven Veterinary Clinic, she picked apart the issues she'd vowed to have fixed—eventually. A little paint, some cleaning, and it would be like new.

Doc Phillips had been gracious enough to finance her purchase of the clinic. To be honest, he probably thought she wouldn't be here long.

He, and everybody else in this town, would be surprised. She wasn't planning to go anywhere.

How long had she been here? A year. The clinic still had GREGORY PHILLIPS, DVM, painted on the sign. That would be an easy fix. She'd ask her vet tech, Mary Ann, to handle it. Nancy had learned her assistant was also Park Haven's resident sign painter.

Then again, maybe Nancy didn't fit in here. Someone once told her she might live here a long time and never be "from" here. But during the last twelve months, she'd learned it was an inclusive community. She found a church she liked—it's where she met Mr. Dunne and Will, and Mr. Dunne's son and daughter-in-law, MC's parents. At first, some of the farmers in the area doubted her abilities, but she'd shown them brains, not brawn, got the job done.

The sun was completely up, and traffic increased. She wadded up the paper from her biscuit sandwich and put it in her empty coffee cup before getting out of the pickup.

The day wouldn't start itself.

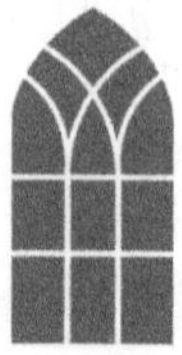

Chapter Six

April

S pending two solid weeks clearing out years of clutter from the cabin wasn't MC's idea of a good time, but the mindless task relaxed him. With the sling, he could only do about half as much fetching and carrying as usual.

Probably just as well. The longer he took, the more he could hide out on the farm, away from people.

But if Mom had anything to do with it …

She and Dad weren't happy he moved to the cabin so quickly. They tried to talk him out of it, wanted him to take a break, and let them take care of him.

Besides, they were busy people. Community, church, and neighborhood. They attended some kind of meeting every day or night of the week.

To be honest, the activity made him a nervous wreck. He hadn't gotten up the nerve to show up at church yet. Grandpa hadn't said a word, just watched as MC took breaks, rambling all over the farm the minute he couldn't work inside the cabin anymore. Sometimes the same claustrophobia he'd experienced waking up in the Medevac helicopter litter pod hit him out of the blue. Confining. Oppressive. Suffocating.

He had to get out in the fresh air.

If the people around him could read his thoughts, they would run as far away from him as possible. It wasn't natural—the things that came to mind at the oddest times. A sound. A flash of light. Sudden movement. Anything could trigger cold sweats and a crushing fear that was impossible to explain.

Those close to him kept asking him what his plans were for the future. They didn't realize he'd spent nearly a year believing he had no future. There was no point, people were dying all around him. He thought he'd be next. Had to be.

Everything was over for MC the night Gunnar was killed, and he was injured. So many soldiers continued dreaming of a family and career "as soon as they got home." As if they were invincible.

They weren't.

The war left MC empty. Hard to make arrangements for a blank future.

To become the veterinarian he intended to be, he would have to go back to Auburn and finish the doctoral program.

He could afford it, and with Rebecca out of the picture, he wasn't getting married any time soon, if at all. Nothing required him to get a job right away.

But he had doubts.

Do I even want to be a vet anymore? Will I recover enough to do the job?

Every decision called for another one.

MC reached the back corner of the bedroom, where he found a metal file box tucked away. Uncle Patrick's? He rubbed the dust and cobwebs from the top of the container, then opened it carefully.

Newspaper clippings, a lone ladies' glove, a boy's flat cap, a Bible. Had Grandpa seen this stuff?

MC held the hat in his hand and smiled. Was this Dad's? He may have been wearing it upon arrival in Tennessee from Illinois as a boy.

As an orphan.

MC sensed a sad smile on his face—smiles were hard to come by these days. The feeling was unfamiliar.

Dad.

Confident, courageous, strong … he'd been a frightened ten-year-old, abandoned and sent to live with Grandpa Brendan and Grandma Evangeline. They lavished the love they had for ten children on the one they were blessed to raise.

No more would come.

Hearing the door open, he saw Grandpa entering the cabin with a paper bag.

"Hungry?" He held up the bag.

"Depends on what you've got in that bag."

"Well, it's not pizza." Grandpa laughed. "How 'bout burgers and fries?"

MC stood and brushed the dust off his hands. "Sounds good." He walked over to the old pump handle in the kitchen and gave it a go. He'd primed the pump the day before, so, though there were no "facilities" in the cabin, he did have running water. He could wash hands and heat water on the stove to clean up.

He liked roughing it. He'd had to in Vietnam, but here? Here, it was optional.

Sometimes he went to Grandpa's and took advantage of the shower he and Grandma had put in the enclosed back porch. Grandma once said it was the only way to keep the outside dirt from coming in.

MC wanted simple, and you couldn't get simpler than a rustic cabin in the woods.

Grandpa pulled the paper-wrapped sandwiches and containers of fries out of the bag and put them on the table. "Thought a milkshake might hit the spot."

"Mmmm. Strawberry." MC took a long swig. "My favorite." The cool, creamy liquid slid down his throat, bringing back memories of happier days. "Will and I used to race to see who could drink our shake the fastest without it hitting us in the head." He held up the disposable cup. "We should have been savoring it, instead."

"Youth is wasted on the young, I always say." Grandpa laughed.

"How's retirement going?" MC studied his grandpa's face. He never would have thought retirement was in the man's vocabulary.

Chewing slowly, Grandpa appeared to be thinking deeply. "It's fine." He took a deep breath. "I sure thought Evangeline would be here to share it with me."

MC nodded and took another bite of his burger. If he spoke, he'd break. Losing Grandma right after he left had been another blow. He still expected to see her hanging clothes on the line or feeding her brood of chickens. He was getting tired of his emotions spilling out all over the place.

"You could always go back to work."

Grandpa chuckled. "Don't think I haven't thought about it. No, I'm content here on the farm." He studied his grandson. "And now you're home."

How long before Grandpa started the "what's next" inquisition?

"I found a box I'm pretty sure belonged to Uncle Patrick, or maybe Grandma." MC wadded up the paper wrapper and tossed it in the bag before getting up and lifting the box onto the table.

He carefully pulled out the hat and glove. "There's more stuff in here, but I thought you might like to have these."

"I'll take the box to the house and look at it later." Grandpa glanced in, and MC noticed a strange look on his face as he closed the lid on the box.

He caressed the lone glove, yellowed with age, and smiled, holding it to his nose for a bit. "I guess it's my imagination, but I can smell Evangeline's perfume." He sniffed again. "I bought many a bottle of Shalimar for your grandmother."

Laying the glove aside, Grandpa picked up the small hat. "Your daddy had this on when he arrived from Illinois."

"I wondered about that."

"You've taken me back fifty years. Uncle Patrick welcomed us with open arms." Grandpa shook his head. "For a bit, I didn't know if your grandma and I were going to make it. We'd wed quick, before we left, to protect her reputation, but ..." His left eyebrow quirked up and a look of delight came across his face. "It took a while for her to realize I didn't just marry her to protect her."

Grandpa had never talked much about hard times, and MC was

surprised to hear about the quick wedding. And to protect her reputation? There had to be more, but Grandpa would share when he was ready.

"You loved her."

"From the moment I laid eyes on her."

Chapter Seven

"Your grandma would be proud," Grandpa said once they pronounced the cabin "done."

All MC could think was "what now?" He'd have to start making some decisions, but he was stuck.

MC took the farm truck to town to pick up supplies. He'd avoided it long enough, but today he had the urge to drive around and explore old haunts. Check out the creek bridge between the farm and town, buzz by the high school, and finally, visit the local grocery store.

After nearly six weeks, it was the first time he'd been out on his own without either Grandpa or Dad.

If one more person asked MC if he planned to take over the animal clinic, he'd explode.

Before Vietnam, he had plans. He'd get home, marry Rebecca, finish school, then take over the practice.

Before, he had hope and a future—Rebecca *had* agreed to wait, and he *had* assured Doc Phillips but … a lot had happened since then.

Only weeks into his first tour of duty, he received Rebecca's letter gently explaining she'd met someone and couldn't wait for someone who might die in a jungle.

It crushed him as much as if a tank pummeled him into the ground. They'd made a commitment to one another, not with rings or solemn ceremonies, but with the panic and reckless abandon of youth and wartime. He'd never thought to have anyone else, ever.

Why did she promise herself to him only to reject him?

Recovering from the injury, losing his K9, and his unit being almost decimated, he'd thought it was all over for him. The nightmares that had been occasional became regular.

Now anger ruled.

Anger at himself, at the world, at God.

How could a loving God put them in harm's way? MC grasped that his comrades weren't perfect, but they didn't deserve this. Gunnar certainly didn't.

Without Gunnar, he made a point not to care. Not to care what happened to him, not to get close to others, and certainly not to share his feelings with his family or the shrinks at the army hospital in Tokyo.

Stoicism only gained him a Purple Heart. He'd just as soon not have it.

Entering the grocery store on the edge of town, a weight settled on MC as he surveyed the shoppers with their metal carts circling the establishment.

Strange and familiar, all at once.

Conrad, the store owner, caught sight of him from his perch at the service desk and approached him with an outstretched hand, which MC took without hesitation.

"Good to see you, young man."

"You, too, Mr. Conrad. Good to be home."

"I would imagine." A shadow crossed his face. "We hear from Jack and Jimmy every once in a while. I hope they'll get to come home soon."

MC's old classmates, twins, were in different branches of service. They figured, since they couldn't serve in the same unit, they might as well explore their options.

"Jack is in the Marines, right?"

Mr. Conrad nodded. "He's with the unit that went into Laos."

"Tough stuff."

"Not sure where Jimmy is."

"Special Ops?" MC had learned the Air Force fought what people were calling a "helicopter war." Jimmy was a pilot.

"Afraid so." Mr. Conrad peered off. A glint of tears sparkled in the older man's eyes. He straightened and smiled, pushing, MC could tell, the emotion down as far as possible. He clapped MC on the shoulder—his good one, fortunately—and said, "It's good to see one of the old gang home. Praying the rest of you will finish well and come home safe." Clearing his throat, Mr. Conrad said, "Thank you for your service."

It was the first time he'd been told such outside of close family members.

 ⁓

"SORRY." Will's neck turned red. His embarrassment amused Nancy.

"We are two professional adults sharing a table during a rush. No need for apologies." But she'd take one.

Will walked in after Nancy placed her order. There wasn't a table to be had at noon on a Friday. If people weren't working downtown, they were shopping. Mavis came over to ask if she minded sharing her table, and of course, she didn't.

She wanted to forgive him for his thoughtless comment that morning. The red on his face indicated that he understood he'd messed up earlier.

During the brief time Nancy dated Will, they found out soon enough that they were destined to be friends—good friends—and nothing more. There were no sparks there, and even as limited as her dating life had been, she realized she wanted more.

If people wanted to think they were "an item," let them think.

At least he hadn't brought up the idea of her leaving to make way for his cousin to acquire the clinic. Not yet, anyway.

Mavis approached with Nancy's sweet iced tea and her order pad. "What can I get you, Will? The usual?"

He closed the menu and handed it to the red-haired waitress. "Sounds good. Could I get a side of crow with that?"

The waitress glanced from one to the other. "I wondered if you'd get around to that."

He turned to Nancy. She could feel her face heating. "I'm sorry, Nancy. It was thoughtless of me to insinuate that you were here temporarily until MC came home."

Nancy took a deep breath and smiled at him, brow arched. "I forgive you." Forgiving Will was easy.

"Thanks. It won't happen again."

Mavis snorted. "It better not, or you'll find yourself waiting for the next table instead of sharing one with a pretty girl." She held up her pad and got back to business. "Roast beef, mashed potatoes, green beans, and cornbread?" She smirked. Will was nothing if not predictable.

"Got any fresh tomatoes yet?"

"Fresh straight from Mexico. How does that sound?" She chuckled at the look on his face.

"No thanks. I'll save room for pie, instead."

"Noted. We've got apple and cherry today." She winked and grabbed the menu on her way to the kitchen.

Nancy broke the awkward silence. "What's happening in the world of the law?" She took a long sip of sweet tea. Magical elixir. Nothing like it.

"Not much. Met with a couple to fill out their will, a few real estate transactions." He shrugged. "This isn't exactly a hotbed of excitement in the law."

Nancy grinned. "I guess not. There's always the county attorney race. That can be exciting."

"Not when it's your dad running." Will took a deep breath and all but rolled his eyes. "I guess I should be glad there's enough business for him to go 'politickin' while I keep the office running."

"If you ever want to do a stint as a vet tech, I may have a temporary opening soon." Nancy swirled her straw in the red-frosted tumbler.

"Mary Ann getting close?"

"Very. I hadn't thought about it, but I've got to get someone to cover for her maternity leave."

Mavis arrived with her BLT and fries. It smelled so good. The cook had certainly perfected the art of frying bacon.

"I guess I should be more worried about the idea of her not coming back." Nancy rolled her shoulders. "But I'm not going to think about that now. I'm going to eat my lunch and enjoy it."

"Even if it does have those tomatoes from Mexico, huh?" Will laughed at her good-natured glare.

Mavis set his full plate in front of him, putting a hand on her hip. "Everything look okay?"

Will gave her a chef's kiss. "Mavis, You've made my day. Will you marry me?"

"I don't cook it, I just serve it." She shook her head. "Besides, I don't believe in robbin' the cradle."

Will shook his head in mock disappointment. Hand to his chest, he said, "Alas, I must go on, though my heart be broken."

"Well, I must go on and get the mayor his lunch, or he'll start bellowin'." She winked, then tucked their tickets under the edges of their plates. "Holler if you need anything."

"Thanks, Mavis." Nancy smiled as the older woman sauntered through the tables. "That woman has a calling."

"She does, at that."

They ate in silence for a few minutes.

"I know who could fill in for Mary Ann." Will's face lit up like he'd solved the issue of world peace. "MC."

Nancy twisted her lips, hesitating. Yes, he would be amazing. She'd watched him at the barn while she helped deliver the calf, and observed his experience and technique. He was almost certified, wasn't he?

But then there's the arm. In knowledge, she had no doubts about his suitability, but what about the physical aspect? Would he be able to do the job?

How did she feel about being in close quarters with someone she should consider a rival—a fly in the ointment, so to speak?

Was that the real reason for her hesitation?

∽

MC LEFT THE STORE, driving into town to take care of his banking business. He still had an account at the Community Bank of Park Haven. He'd gone so long without having cash on him, and now he had to write checks on everything. That had to stop.

Parking down the street, he walked briskly up the sidewalk, past the café. He glanced in, figuring he'd see some familiar faces.

Sure enough, there she was, in the window.

Dr. Nancy Jean Baker.

He had to smile. She'd called him on the "lady vet" thing—she had a name, and she expected people to use it.

She had spunk, he'd have to give her that.

He saw her dining companion and stilled.

Will. Were they an item? He didn't have a clue, but then he didn't know much of what went on around here. He did hear her refuse to go out with Bert, which made her rise in his estimation.

Stood to reason she would be attracted to Will. He had prospects, after all. If he had any budding feelings for her—which he told himself, he didn't—he tamped them down at the idea of coming between Will and anyone he might love.

His excitement upon discovering her there slowly dissipated. He wasn't sure why. They'd delivered a calf together. Not exactly what you'd call "showing a girl a good time."

He shoved his hands in his pockets and continued to the bank, head down.

Any thought of feelings for Nancy had to be quashed.

Chapter Eight

MC was almost back to his truck. He recognized the decidedly feminine voice calling his name.

Nancy. She'd left Will pretty fast. Maybe she had to get back to the clinic.

He turned and acknowledged her waving hand as she rushed toward him.

"Dr. Baker."

"Hi MC. Call me Nancy. Please."

His lips twitched. "All right. Nancy. What can I do for you?"

She narrowed her eyes, chewing her bottom lip nervously. Indecision. She wanted to say something but hadn't quite thought it through.

"I have a proposition for you."

His laugh sputtered out, surprising both of them. First time in a while he'd laughed without forcing it. He pulled it together and focused on her reddening face.

"Do you, now?"

"Get over yourself." She shook her head and glared. "I wondered what your plans were for the next, oh, six to eight weeks?"

He closed his eyes for a second, determined not to explode the way he wanted to. Hadn't he just thought, if anyone else asks his plans, he'd fly apart in a million pieces?

Nancy didn't deserve that, so he took a deep breath and shook his head. "I have no idea."

She flinched. Hadn't expected that response, had she?

"I … understand."

No, she didn't.

But she continued, anyway.

"I'm not sure what you can and can't do with your injury, but I have a temporary opening for a vet tech. Mary Ann is going on maternity leave, and she's pretty irreplaceable."

"Mary Ann's having a baby?" He smiled and glanced off for a second. Little Mary Ann. He remembered her.

Sweet girl.

He remembered determining to pay attention as she got old enough to ask out. As soon as he got to Auburn, he met Rebecca and never thought about Mary Ann again. His loss.

"That's great. She'll make a great mom." He looked down with a frown. "But, I'm not sure I can help you."

Nancy's eyebrows rose. Had she forgotten that he was, at least temporarily, limited by the shoulder injury? Did she expect him to jump at the opportunity? Should he?

"Okay. I mean … if you'd like to think about it?"

Her eyes were almost sapphire-blue. Beautiful. Those "limpid pools of azure" authors described in paperback romance novels at the supermarket check-out stand?

She had those, and yes, he could easily get lost in them.

"I'll think about it." As soon as he said it, he regretted it.

That's all he needed, to have to make a decision. He sat in his truck, still parked, willing his heart rate to slow.

A passing truck backfired, making his heart stop, and his vision cloud. It only lasted a few seconds. What it if lasted longer than that, and what if it happened when he was with somebody? Would he hurt them? For sure, he'd scare a civilian if he reacted the way his first instinct played out—hit the ground and go for cover.

But it passed.

Before starting the truck, he pulled his arm out of the sling and stretched it, then put it back. The last thing he needed was a chewing-out from the VA physical therapist. Therapy helped. They'd started weight-bearing exercises, hoping to encourage more flexibility. His ankle was coming along faster than his shoulder.

Just before pulling into the driveway, he spied Grandpa kneeling next to something on the side of the road.

No.

Please, God, no.

He braked as quickly as he could without skidding off the road.

"Grandpa?"

If a man could age ten years in a morning, Grandpa had done so.

"I'm sorry, son."

"Is he gone?"

"Not yet. He's suffering, though."

"Did you see who hit him?" If he caught them, he'd …

"I heard brakes squealing going around the curve, but didn't think much about it until I didn't see Rusty lying on the back porch."

MC nodded, a lump in his throat as big as a baseball. "I need to get him to Nan—to Dr. Baker."

Grandpa nodded. "I don't think he'll make it." He stood and put an arm around his grandson. "Fifteen is a good long life for a pup."

MC was ten when Rusty came into his life, and fifteen when he assisted Doc. Phillips in sewing up a bad cut on his dog's foot. After that, he thought of nothing but becoming a veterinarian.

The lump was still there, and tears threatened. If he could hold on to the anger coursing through him at the thought of a motorist hitting a dog—a pet—and simply driving away, he could make it to the clinic. Otherwise, he'd fall apart.

∾

"Oh, goodness, MC, what's happened?"

From the back room, Nancy's attention was caught when she heard the door thrust open and Mary Ann call his name.

Mary Ann struggled up from the rolling office chair, meeting him halfway as he walked in the front door of the clinic, struggling under the weight of his burden, sling cast aside.

"It's Rusty."

She directed him to the first examination room, clean and ready for the next patient, almost running into Nancy as she helped settle the patient. "I'm in the way here."

As Nancy used one hand to examine his injuries, she rubbed his head with the other, murmuring comforting words to the dog, and by association, to the owner.

Stethoscope back around her neck, she glanced up at MC. "It sounds like he's got some broken ribs and a fractured right hind leg."

The expression on MC's face undid her.

"You mean … he's got a chance?"

"I think so. His age isn't in his favor, but he's an otherwise healthy dog, and I'm not seeing or hearing signs of internal bleeding or a collapsed lung."

Nancy handed him the stethoscope so he could listen for himself. He gazed up at her, hope in his eyes. In his right mind, MC would have discerned the dog's condition. Panicked? Not so much.

MC hugged the dog's head, Rusty responding with a tired tail wag.

"If he's still wagging that tail, it's another good sign he's got some fight left in him," she said.

"What do you need from me?" MC pulled on his training. "I want to help if I can."

This man loved his dog. No wonder they'd made him a K9 handler.

"I'm going to need to sedate him to get the ribs back in place and set his leg." She rubbed gently along the injured leg, Rusty's yelp indicating his pain.

MC nodded, and took the stance of one ready to hold him down if need be. The muscles in both arms were flexed, and she could see the pointed end of a tattoo on his right arm underneath his T-shirt. She wondered.

She didn't think Rusty would fight the needle, but dogs were unpredictable. The most gentle, domesticated animal is still an animal.

The needle slid gently into the dog's left leg, and the nervous wagging slowed to a stop.

"I don't like sedating a dog of his age, but I gave him a small dose. I'll just have to work quickly."

MC hadn't said anything in a few minutes, but then, her attention was on her patient. The silence between them was comfortable. Maybe MC was the answer to her prayer for help. It was ultimately up to him. If he didn't take the job, she would have to start beating the bushes.

While she worked on Rusty's ribs, she watched, unobtrusively, as MC probed the fractured leg. She hadn't asked him to, but his help would give her more time to concentrate on the more dangerous injury. His strong, gentle hands manipulated the bone back in place before they put a cast on it.

She checked the leg. The bones lined up perfectly. "Good job. Thank goodness it was a closed fracture."

MC nodded. "No worry about contaminating the wound."

Her lips twitched. Yes, she'd ask him again tomorrow, when he came back to pick up Rusty.

Chapter Nine

"MC? Wake up, son."

The images were seared into his brain. Didn't matter if he slept or laid awake, MC still pictured bodies. Machine guns still roared in his ears. He still wished for safety. Security. A soft hand to ease the pain.

He opened his eyes to see the sun coming in the window above his bed.

"Grandpa?"

"You musta been having a humdinger of a dream." The old man was concerned. MC could tell. "You were thrashing out so much I was afraid you'd mess up your shoulder again."

MC flexed his arm, attempting some of the movements PT would have him do later that day.

"Better than last night." Better, but not good. He wouldn't tell Grandpa that, nor would he tell him about the dream. Not like it was the first.

MC sat up and slung his legs out of the bed, putting his head in both hands, then raking them down his face, feeling the stubble of a few days' growth. The sights, sounds, and smells of the dream he'd just had were still there, waiting for him to close his eyes.

"I brought you some coffee." Grandpa handed him the red plaid thermos that had been in the family for years.

The mind was a funny thing, bringing fragments of random memories at odd times. He had an image, a sensation, of Grandma warning him to be careful of it—it had a glass liner, after all. Having gone through the Great Depression, everything had to last as long as possible, whether it be a piece of furniture, a scrap of fabric, or a Thermos bottle. They didn't want to break it.

"Thanks." He took a swig. Every sip woke him a bit more. It pulled him farther and farther away from the dream that threatened to pull him down and keep him.

"You okay?"

MC nodded. "Nice thing about dreams is most of the time you don't remember a thing," he lied, glancing up quickly. He had a hard time looking Grandpa in the eye.

His grandfather studied him carefully, not saying anything for a moment. Then, he startled, as if remembering why he was there.

"Oh. Nancy called."

"Rusty?" A feeling of intense foreboding—probably a remnant of the dream—came over him. "He's gone, isn't he?"

Grandpa waved his hands and shook his head. "No, son, he's not gone. She said he wagged his tail like he was glad to see her this morning."

If he were alone, MC would have cried.

NANCY REACHED down to rub Rusty's head. She probably should have put him back in his crate until MC came, but he was no trouble. He hobbled along behind her as she went about her morning duties When he got tired, he stopped. Major took the interloper in stride, accustomed to being around other animals.

She knelt in front of him and dug her fingers into the cottony-soft fur around the old dog's ears, almost nose-to-nose with him. "You, Rusty, are a sweetheart."

Tail thumping.

"Yes, you are. I'll bet your daddy never calls you that, does he?"

Rusty's tail continued to wag as Nancy chuckled. She couldn't imagine Mr. He-Man MC Dunne calling his dog "sweetheart."

She considered the aging Border Collie. There was some gray mixed in with the burnished red on his nose, but other than that, he had the demeanor and energy of a much younger dog. Not a pup, but certainly not a geriatric canine.

"You know, Rusty, I always envied girls with hair the color of yours."

"Maybe you should take him with you to the hairdressers. I'm sure she could mix you up a match."

Nancy had to laugh at Rusty's tilted head. Mary Ann came in quietly and overheard her conversation with her patient.

"Hair this dark isn't meant to be dyed red. Way too much trouble." Nancy considered her assistant. "How are you this morning?"

"If I said fine, I'd be lying." Mary Ann shrugged. "But I know it's temporary, so I can deal with it."

"Try to stay off your feet as much as possible, okay?" Nancy worried about her. Glancing down at the young woman's ankles, she noted a bit more puffiness than last week. Her delivery was getting closer.

"I will." Mary Ann scanned the appointment schedule. "Looks like a light day, so that's in my favor." She sighed, bending her knees to put her purse in the bottom desk drawer. "My balance is so off I don't dare bend straight over."

"I can't imagine."

"Me, neither." She grimaced. "Then there are the false labor pains."

False labor? How many times were real labor pains mistaken for false labor?

"You're sure?"

"I'm sure. Now, let's get the day started, shall we?" Mary Ann turned quickly toward her desk, running into the file cabinet on her way. "Clumsy." She glanced up at Nancy, then away.

The "ding" from the front door sounded, taking Nancy's attention from Mary Ann.

"Hey, MC, come to visit the patient?" Nancy smiled. Had she

developed a sixth sense or something? She thought of him, and he came.

MC wasn't well. The dark circles under his red-rimmed eyes indicated a sleepless night, and the pain accompanying it.

Maybe it was her. Looking for things that weren't there.

"Yeah." He knelt to get on Rusty's level and hugged the dog. "He seems to be getting around pretty well."

"He's a good patient."

MC quirked an eyebrow. "I see he's not in the kennel."

Nancy's cheeks heated. Maybe he didn't notice.

"Age has its privileges."

"How are you, MC?" Mary Ann smiled from her chair.

"I'm getting along. I hear you're about to get some time off?" He grinned at the vet tech, and Nancy experienced an unexpected rush of something unfamiliar. Jealousy? Ridiculous.

"'Fraid so." She patted her belly. "I understand human babies are like animal babies—they pick the time and place, not the mama."

"That's what I hear. Never plan to experience it, myself." MC chuckled, then glanced at Nancy. "Got a minute?"

"Sure." A rush of excitement shivered through her, and she immediately tamped it down. She showed him back to her office—the one that would have been his, had he been here at the time Doc Phillips retired. Rusty followed along, slowly.

MC sat in the chair across from her, at the desk. "I've been thinking about your offer, and seeing Mary Ann, I understand why you want to get something nailed down."

Nancy's eyes widened. "You think so too?"

"Yeah, and I haven't seen her in five years. It won't be long."

She laced her fingers together on the desk and sat up straight. "So, you've thought about it." She wrinkled her nose. "Is it a yea or a nay?"

He sat, for a moment, his gaze unable to meet hers, then took a deep breath, looking her in the eye. "I'm going to have to say no."

Chapter Ten

Not what he'd planned to say.

He'd decided on the way. He would accept the offer and try his best to do the job. Before he could say it, his head started pounding, and his chest tightened.

To be completely honest, he was scared. Of what, he couldn't say. Could be any number of things.

It was just that the dream was so real.

Nancy sat in stunned silence. "Are you sure? We can make accommodations for …"

Accommodations. He scoffed, inwardly. She'd bruised his ego. It would be a blow to his manhood.

He didn't need her pity.

He wasn't worth her trouble.

"I know you could, but after yesterday …" and last night, he couldn't help but think, "Still a lot of pain, a lot of healing to do." In more ways than one. He worked his shoulder a little to emphasize the physical and minimize the mental.

"I—I understand." Now she had trouble meeting his eyes.

He cleared his throat, uncomfortable at lying, but knowing he would be more uncomfortable if something happened and he lashed out. He'd awakened more than once in the hospital, pounding on his pillow, seeing the enemy in his mind's eye. He remembered the time he laid out a male nurse—a big, strapping guy. What if it happened with Nancy? He couldn't ensure her safety around him.

"I've got physical therapy in Clarksville twice a week and appointments at the VA hospital, so that wouldn't work with the clinic schedule."

"I could work with that, schedule the bulk of office visits on those days, and I would not expect you to go out on large animal calls."

He stiffened, heart racing. "I appreciate that, but I'm afraid I'm still going to have to decline."

Nancy's gaze didn't leave him, and he couldn't call her bluff.

After a few uncomfortable moments, she faltered and glanced down at her hands, and cleared her throat. "You have to get back on the saddle eventually."

It was none of her business. The curse word he almost used died on his lips.

The words, gentle though they were, punched him in the gut. It was a "tell me something I don't already know" moment on the one hand, and on the other? His good hand curled in a fist.

What was the point?

He rose, and Rusty stood up shakily, in solidarity. "I think I'll be the judge of when I'm ready." Even he could hear the icicles in his tone.

She nodded. "I didn't mean to …"

He didn't want to hear it. The smart thing would have been to walk away. Leave. Instead, he gave in to the emotion. His anger spiked, and he spoke, low, intense, and cold. He walked toward her, emphasizing his height and power. "Everybody wants to know what I'm going to do next. They seem to know what is best for me. Put on a sling, and a man becomes an invalid, a second-class citizen, waiting to be told what to do. I'm not that man."

As he stepped closer, Nancy stood her ground and stared him in the eye, stretching herself to her full height. She didn't back down. "You misunderstood me—"

Rusty rubbed up against MC's leg, reminding him why he was there. He interrupted before she could say anything more. "Is he okay to go home with me?"

Nancy hesitated, her eyes never leaving his. As she spoke, there was an edge in her voice. "Sure. Let me get his paperwork."

MC nodded, unable to speak, the adrenaline of the angry scene ebbing. It was a good thing he couldn't say anything. If he did, he'd say something he would regret.

He'd done enough of that already.

~

MC LEFT WITHOUT ANOTHER WORD. The set of his jaw and the clenched fist made Nancy unreasonably angry. She wanted to scream and throw something, but instead settled for slamming the file cabinet drawer after filing Rusty's folder. She hadn't been this angry since the last time her father hit her.

The event confirmed her decision to get out of the place she'd called home.

She turned to see Mary Ann at her elbow. The girl walked quietly for her size.

"Need something?" Nancy was not in the mood to talk, but she could tell Mary Ann had something to say. Her face paled. Not her usually rosy, ready-for-anything self.

Mary Ann closed her eyes tightly and held up her finger in a "wait" gesture.

"Mary Ann?" Nancy observed the pain and discomfort on her face. She could deliver babies for cows, cats, dogs, and horses—you name it, she could do it—but deliver Mary Ann and Bobby's first child? Please, God, no.

"What's happening?" Nancy detected a flicker of panic, more than concern.

Her assistant waved off her concern. "I'm fine. It's passed."

Tilting her head and twisting her lips, Nancy waited and raised her eyebrows, encouraging Mary Ann to expound.

"You've not met the MC I remember."

Nancy took a deep breath and let out a heavy sigh, irritated at the heat crawling up her neck and onto her face. "Maybe you should come out and say what you want to say."

"It's not my place, especially while I'm putting you in a bind ..."

"You are not putting me in a bind." She frowned, her anger beginning to dissipate in the face of Mary Ann's obvious unease.

"Anyway, it's none of my business, but I think something happened over there—probably more than one thing—and it's got him spooked. I've never known him to fly off the handle, or to leave without speaking." Mary Ann shook her head. "It's not like him."

"How well did you know him, before?"

Her grin, never far from the surface, came out gently. "Not particularly well, but I grew up with a major crush on him."

"Oh?" Nancy arched a brow and waited patiently, arms crossed, tension easing. This could get interesting.

Mary Ann scoffed. "Oh, he was four or five years older than me. I was in junior high, so he didn't give me the time of day— long before I met Bobby—but he was sweet, you know? He was practically engaged before he left for 'Nam." Mary Ann shrugged. "Active in church, always there any time anyone needed help. I halfway expected him to become a preacher, not a vet."

Only one thought came to Nancy's mind. She wasn't proud of it.

Oh, how the mighty have fallen ...

Chapter Eleven

A cool snap, what the farm folks called "Dogwood Winter," put spring off for a few days, the nights not quite freezing, but MC felt it in his bones. He needed to stock up on some wood to burn in the pot-bellied stove in the corner. Especially with Rusty in recovery mode.

He could only carry about half what he could have with both arms, but he hadn't been down so long that all of his muscles were weak.

MC had a lot of time to think. Too bad praying wouldn't do any good. Seemed like in the last few years anything he considered prayer came from the "help me" category.

And had He? Had God helped him?

MC had done his best. Lived the best he could. Tried to stay on the straight and narrow. The times he faltered, he owned up to it and asked for forgiveness.

What more could God want from him?

MC peered down at Rusty, but for a split second, he'd swear it was Gunnar, and the gently rolling hills of the farm were swampland and jungle. He shook his head as if that would shake away the horror of the hallucinations, more like "waking nightmares." They came over him at odd times.

An episode never lasted long.

What if he found himself in that world inside his mind, and he couldn't get out? Did that happen? Would he hurt Grandpa or anyone else around?

No way could he work with Nancy until he figured this out. If he ever did.

"This might speed up the process." Grandpa Brendan came toward him with the wheelbarrow.

"Only got one good arm."

"But I've got two." Grandpa put a hand on MC's good shoulder. "You load it up, and I'll push. How's that for teamwork?"

Teamwork. MC hadn't considered it might be prudent to accept help. His concentration had been on wading through the healing process on his own for the most part. Oh, he accepted the use of the cabin, and he hadn't refused a few bowls of chili.

His silence after Grandpa's question led to a closer inspection by the older man. Grandpa's eyes narrowed. "Everything okay?"

An unintended snort ripped from MC.

Grandpa twisted his lips. "Wrong question. Let me try this. You makin' it okay?"

"I guess it depends on your understanding of okay." MC walked to the wood pile and stacked what he held. "If you're asking if my arm is healing, then I'd have to say yes. Otherwise?" MC shrugged and returned to loading, unable to say anything more.

"The Lord allows the old Devil to put roadblocks in our way sometimes. He did say we'd have suffering in this world."

MC ran a hand through his lengthening hair. He had hoped the scruffy look would keep people away.

"You know what collateral damage is?" He fixed Grandpa with a look.

"Sure." Grandpa tilted his head, curiosity on his face. "On the news, Huntley and Brinkley call it secondary, accidental damage."

MC's stomach twisted. He'd been on the front lines stepping over "collateral damage."

"Collateral damage is death. Plain and simple. Did you know 'friendly fire' victims are considered collateral damage?" He threw another log in the wheel barrel. "You know, when our own people get shot by one of our own."

Grandpa nodded. "I see."

How to explain it … and should he? No point in weighing down his grandfather, heaping his burdens on someone he loves.

MC made himself smile. "I know you do." Lying. That's what he was doing now.

Wasn't that going to push God even farther away? If He existed.

"I'll be fine. Just—Rusty's injury made me think of Gunnar."

"Your scout dog?"

He nodded. "The Army considered Gunnar 'collateral damage.'"

The injured collie limped toward them. "Boy, you need to stay down." MC stretched out his bad arm so he could cradle Rusty's head in both hands. Staring into the canine's eyes, MC shook his head.

"I guess we're all collateral damage in some way, aren't we, Rusty?"

Guilt settled on Nancy like a cloak. She'd overstepped her bounds with MC. It wouldn't surprise her if he never spoke to her again.

The idea put a damper on any enthusiasm she'd been able to work up throughout the day.

It had been the longest day she could remember. She tried to keep Mary Ann from overdoing it, so that meant doing more of her everyday tasks.

Their last scheduled patient left the clinic. Sweet relief.

After writing up her notes and filing them in her office, she wandered out to the examining room area where she'd left Mary Ann sorting supplies.

"Mary Ann, I think …"

Nancy stopped suddenly as the pregnant woman standing on a step stool begin to sway, then buckle.

Rushing to Mary Ann's side, Nancy's heart constricted in fear. What happened? Did she pass out? Nancy should have sent her home as soon as she spotted signs of premature labor.

"I'm fine." Mary Ann sighed, then winced as she tried to get up.

"Ever tried to save a beached whale?" She struggled to get her feet under her.

Nancy grasped her hand, anchoring herself for leverage, then stopped. "Are you sure you need to get up? Maybe I should call an ambulance? Or Bobby?"

"I fell off a stool, not off a cliff." Mary Ann twisted her lips. "My center of gravity ain't what it used to be."

Between the two women, they got Mary Ann off the floor and into a chair.

"Are you sure you're okay?"

Mary Ann took a deep breath and sagged. "I'm fine. I'm just tired of being so awkward." Her voice sounded close to tears.

"Go home."

"I just want to …"

"No, we're done for the day, and you need to go home and get those feet up." Nancy tilted her head to look at Mary Ann's ankles. "Look at those. You've been having pains all day, and now you've ended up on the floor." She pressed her lips in a thin line and paused.

"Okay."

"Furthermore—" Nancy stopped. "Did you say 'okay?'"

Mary Ann held up both hands and chuckled. "You've convinced me."

"Good." Nancy frowned, worried. "Do you need me to drive you home?"

"I'm fine. If anything happens, I'll pull over and flag down traffic."

Nancy shook her head, her heart squeezing at the thought. "You are not making me feel better."

"Not my job, Dr. Baker." Mary Ann winked. "I'll call Bobby and tell him I'm on my way home. Knowing him, he'll laugh and wish he could have seen my latest trick."

"If he laughs, I'll beat him up." Nancy gave a strong nod of her head.

"Not necessary. I think I can take him." She arched a brow. "These days, I'm in a higher weight class."

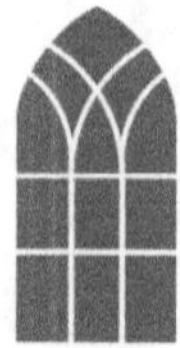

Chapter Twelve

MC was beat. Exhausted. Not only had he struggled with carrying wood in for a fire, but he couldn't get Nancy off his mind.

The only way he would sleep would be to take painkillers, and he didn't want to. It would be so easy to fall into that trap. He'd tried it. Fortunately, while he was still in the Tokyo hospital, the doctor recognized the signs of dependency and cut him off. He received treatment long enough to get over the budding addiction.

The VA doc in Tennessee, on the other hand, shuffled patients in and out like cattle, barely glancing at his records. He came home with an amber bottle of pills that he kept hidden in the back of the cabinet.

He pulled it out and held the bottle in his hand, then set it down on the cabinet in the kitchen area of the cabin. He'd wait.

A knock at the door interrupted his internal debate. Grandpa Brendan.

"Come in."

"Saw your light."

"Yeah." MC wasn't in the mood to talk, but he wouldn't disrespect his grandfather by telling him that. "Lot on my mind."

Grandpa narrowed his eyes, then glanced at Rusty. "You didn't come by the house, so I assume everything's still okay with Rusty. Anything I can help with?"

If Grandpa comprehended all the things going through MC's mind at any given moment, he'd run from him. But no, if ever there was an example of unconditional love, it was his grandpa. He'd love him through it.

"Nope. I'm good."

"You know you can talk to me. I've always been a pretty good listener." Grandpa chuckled. "Had to be. You're Grandma talked a blue streak."

MC could see the compassion shining through the lighthearted words. "I was just thinking about Uncle Patrick."

"The Preacher." Grandpa looked like he was far away for a minute. "He was my sounding board. Always had a joke, an old saying, or a sermon to go with any problem a body might have. And all of that with an Irish lilt."

MC remembered falling asleep to those tales in the very chairs they sat in today.

But back to the present. He couldn't stay in the past, as much as he'd prefer to. "I have a good feeling about Rusty," MC said, finally. "Nancy's a good vet." His face heated. No way he would tell him how he'd treated her earlier that day.

"I agree." Nothing else. What was Grandpa's opinion on the whole idea of a woman being expected to give up a job to a man?

"She's asked me about filling in for Mary Ann while she's on maternity leave."

The older man nodded, his expression blank. "Right down your alley, I'd say."

What would Grandpa say if he realized he'd already burned that bridge?

"Might give me time to figure out whether or not I want to go back to vet school."

He wasn't sure where that came from. His head screamed at him to stay away, but his heart? His spirit? He craved normal. He wanted a life.

"It might, at that." Grandpa pinned him with a look. "Can you do the job?"

"I could do the work—whether or not my shoulder would hold me back, I don't know."

"How is it tonight?"

"The pain has grown from a whimper to a shriek." MC winced. "On the other hand, I carried Rusty in and help set his leg last night."

"You're paying for it now."

He shrugged. Maybe he just had to get used to being in pain. "I'll live."

~

LONG AFTER TAKING four aspirin and raiding Grandpa's freezer of all the ice he had, MC lay in bed tossing and turning.

Sleep would come.

Maybe.

It didn't come most nights.

MC jumped at a loud *bang* coming from outside his tent.

He reached over, feeling the ground in the pitch dark.

Fur. He recognized the feel of that coat.

"Hey, Gun. Where'd you come from? Somebody out there?"

On high alert, soldiers were scrambling around him. His eyes got used to the absence of light. On the New Moon, or in dense cloud cover, it took longer to see the black, white, and gray images. No color at night unless a mortar exploded. Then everything stood out in sharp relief.

The *rat-tat-tat* of machine guns came from … where? They were all around him.

He grabbed Gunnar's leash, and instinct kicked in for both. The occasional flash of light hurt his eyes, but it was just enough to enable him to take cover.

Wait. A body on the ground. Jerry?

The next flash revealed more bodies. Donnie. Frankie. Sal. So many.

Confusion set in. They were killed months ago. Weren't they? Was he victim to some sort of cruel trick by the Viet Cong to rattle opposing troops? Had he been captured, or tortured? He knew what they did to POWs. Mind games. Was he a prisoner of war?

No. He'd seen Donnie die right next to him.

Another shell hit, and MC could see a glimpse of the landscape around him.

The bodies. They were sinking into the swamp.

Confused, he knelt and put his arm around his partner, Gunnar. His coat was different.

The next flash of light came. He glanced down. Gunnar wasn't next to him. Rusty was. Gunnar lay across the way, not moving. A hot piece of metal seared his shoulder and MC went down. In and out of consciousness, something tugged on his backpack. The machine-gun fire was fading, farther away, MC watched as Rusty dragged him away from danger.

Just like Gunnar tried to do.

How did Rusty get to Vietnam?

Suddenly, the small space shrank. He was in the pod of a Medevac helicopter. Someone—he couldn't tell who in his current nebulous state—hovered over him, trying to staunch the bleeding.

Friend or foe?

Chopper blades revved up, and MC drew back to hit the cloudy figure messing with him. He would fight anybody that came along. Kill if he needed to.

As his vision cleared, brilliant blue eyes stared at him in horror. Was it that bad? In the flashing lights of the landing pad, he recognized her.

It couldn't be. His mind *must* be playing tricks on him.

Rebecca? No, Nancy.

Nancy, in Vietnam?

"You'll be okay." She touched her soft, cool fingers to his cheek and smiled at him as he drifted back into the blessing of unconsciousness.

Chapter Thirteen

Nancy could hear a sound coming from far off. Annoying, it got closer with each passing moment. She opened her eyes as little as possible and glanced at the clock.

Nine in the morning?

What happened to her? She hadn't slept this late since high school.

She found the culprit: The light blue princess phone on her bedside table. Not only did it ring, but it also shook the nightstand so much that her lip balm fell to the floor.

Pulling her hand from under the covers, she reached out, pulling the receiver to her ear.

"Hello?" She cleared her throat.

"Dr. Baker?"

What day is it? Saturday?

"Mary Ann?"

"That's my name, don't wear it out." The familiar giggle sounded tired and a little loopy, but happy.

She could hear other activities in the background.

Mary Ann?

"He's here!"

"What?" She sat us straight in the bed, the previous afternoon's events flashing in front of her eyes. "Are you okay?"

"Even better. I'm a mommy."

Nancy could hear her cooing at the newborn.

Her voice softened so much it almost brought tears to Nancy's eyes. "Did the fall start your labor?"

"The doctor said between my blood pressure dropping and my ungainly sense of balance, it's a wonder it hadn't happened before then." She paused, whispering something to someone near her. "I'm fine. I have a bruised ego and a little scrape on one ankle, but other than that, if it sped things up, I'd highly recommend taking a swan dive before labor."

Laughter erupted from Nancy's mouth. "Oh, what time can I come?"

"This afternoon. I can't wait for you to see him." She could hear the new mama sigh on the other end of the line. "He's perfect."

"He'd have to be." Nancy's biological clock chimed, and she tamped it down. She certainly didn't have time for that. "I'll see you after lunch."

"Thanks, Dr. Baker."

Nancy closed her eyes and shook her head. She'd never had many girlfriends. Driven to do her best and solve her problems before anyone else had to, she'd not made the time. She realized something just then. Mary Ann was her best friend, and she still called her "Dr. Baker."

"Mary Ann?"

"Yes?"

"Call me Nancy?"

"I will do my best."

Nancy hung up the phone and sat there for a few minutes. It boggled the mind to think about the miracle of birth. Oh, she dealt with it frequently in the animal world, but humans? It came across as more of a miracle to her.

"Thank you, God, for seeing Mary Ann through the birth of her little one." A thought came to her mid-prayer, causing her to look upward for good measure. "And please, please send me a person to fill in for her."

As much as she anticipated seeing Mary Ann's new baby, she

would admit only to herself that this couldn't have come at a worse time.

She'd run out of options. She had to find someone. Now.

THE FRESH AIR was a welcome change. After waking up in a cold sweat from the reality of the nightmares that plagued him, he'd gone outside and walked an hour, then slept an hour. Repeated three times.

The coffee long gone, MC and Will started on the cooler of Cokes sitting in the bass boat between them.

"Thanks for dragging me out here." MC stared at his line, not wanting to meet Will's eyes.

"Thought it was about time we had a day off."

MC cocked his head and grinned. "A day off from what?" This. This was what normal felt like, even if it was fleeting.

"Life, man. Life." Will opened the cooler to reveal enough food for a week. "Need a sandwich?"

MC turned and snickered. "You were prepared for anything, weren't you?"

Will shrugged. "We gotta eat." He opened the basket and pulled out a couple of wrapped sandwiches. "I called Mom last night and sweet-talked her into making us some food. Tuna or pimento cheese?"

MC considered. "Your mom does make the best pimento cheese I've ever eaten." He grinned. "I'll go with the cheese."

"I hoped you'd say that. Mom said she fixed it for you, anyway."

"Tell Aunt Janet, I appreciate it." He took a large bite of the sweetened cheese mixture. In the South, there were two schools of thought on sugar in pimento cheese, just as there were two schools of thought on sugar in cornbread.

"I'll do it. She said to invite you to supper if you're available."

"I'll check my social calendar." MC laughed. It hadn't happened much. He found he liked it. "Oh, look. There's an opening."

They clinked their bottles in salute, then settled back down to the serious job of fishing in a lake that had a questionable number of fish.

They might not catch anything, but MC would have to admit he was glad to be with just Will, for a change.

Will broke the silence.

"Nancy said she came over to help with a calf."

MC had wanted to bring up Nancy but didn't know how, exactly, to do that. "She did. Good vet, seems like." He glanced at his cousin, who nodded.

"She is." He cut a glance at MC, then studied his sandwich carefully. "Pretty girl."

MC wouldn't go there. "I remember her from vet school."

Will's head whipped up in surprise. "No kidding?"

"She probably doesn't remember me. She was a couple of years ahead of me."

Quiet again. "Nancy said she'd approached you about working for her, but you turned her down."

MC could feel his heart beating faster. Will trod on delicate territory. He didn't want to explain himself. Not now.

"Bad timing."

Will nodded, eyes trained on his line. "We went out a few times."

"So, you're dating?" What MC wouldn't give to get out of this conversation at this moment. He'd rather not bring up Bert and the scene he'd witnessed the day he got home.

Will laughed, his countenance clear. "No, afraid not."

"I ..." If he continued, Will would deduce his interest. Taking a deep breath, he veered off of mentioning Bert and went with the more recent. "I spotted you two eating together at the café."

"Yeah, no tables available, so she agreed to let me sit with her." He grinned. "I consider her a friend, that's all. I don't think she's dating anyone now."

The temperature must have risen. MC's collar tightened, all of the sudden.

Good to know Will's heart wasn't broken when Nancy decided to move on. Conversely, the idea that she was, after all, available, ramped up his anxiety for some reason.

"I'm sure she'll find someone soon. What about the community college?"

Will gave a loud guffaw. "To find a boyfriend, or a vet tech?"

MC gave his cousin a mock glare. "The latter, you idiot."

"Got you though, didn't I?" Will reeled in his line and turned to face MC. "You interested?"

Interested? Good question. After tearing her apart with words the day before, she probably wouldn't get within a hundred yards of him. She would be better off that way. He had to get his emotions under control, not just for her safety—but for the security of everyone.

"She's keeping the clinic going, isn't she?" Let Will think what he would. His interest lay in the clinic.

"Do you plan to take it over, eventually?" A concerned look crossed Will's face.

"Not sure." MC reeled in a nice-sized crappie.

Will whistled. "Not bad."

"Yeah. A few more, and we'll have supper."

"Sounds good. Mom said she'd cook it if we'd clean it." Will cast his line and settled in. After a few moments of silence, he spoke again. "I guess it would be right and proper for her to step aside when—"

"More like if ..."

Will shrugged. "Okay, when and *if* you decide to finish up at Auburn."

"Is that how you feel? That she should step aside?"

Beyond his mother, grandmothers, and cousins, MC hadn't given much thought to "women's rights." Most of the ladies in his life were homemakers. They kept the home fires burning while the men made the living and maintained order in the world.

Why, then, did it rub him the wrong way to think of Nancy handing over the practice she'd built back up after Doc Phillips retired?

Chapter Fourteen

"I can't."

The phone in Nancy's hand shook. Was this what a nervous breakdown felt like? Her heart threatened to beat out of her chest.

As soon as her oldest brother spoke, her mind went right back to the day she left home.

The day she'd finally had enough.

"Nancy, he's asking for you." He paused. "Are you going to refuse a dying man's wish?"

She closed her eyes. Before Mama died, she'd been "Daddy's girl." The only girl after two rough-and-tumble boys. He called her "the apple of my eye."

Besides the occasional swat, had she even been spanked before Mama died? She didn't think so. The violence didn't start until Steven died in Vietnam.

The drinking increased. The yelling. And eventually … the abuse. Hitting her any time he experienced a twinge of anger.

She last spoke to her father during her freshman year in college. Finally, she had a place to live outside their house. He gave her a black eye that day, but she stood up to him.

She went back to school with a made-up story about waking up in the middle of the night and running into the door.

They bought it.

Why would she tell them her dad hit her? She didn't want anyone to think her own flesh and blood would be "like that."

"Richard, I just … can't." The tears formed. If they started, would they stop?

She could hear her brother sigh into the phone.

"Nancy, it couldn't have been as bad as—"

The tears stopped. "Yes, Richard, it could. I have the scars to prove it."

She imagined his eye-roll, which is what he always did any time the subject came up. To him, she was being *dramatic*.

"Well, he can't hurt you now." He paused. The line remained silent for several moments before he spoke. "You can stay with us."

Richard kept talking, trying to convince her to come to Dad. Did she have to get graphic in the details of the horror she experienced while Richard enjoyed life at college?

He hadn't been there.

And it wasn't just Dad. Before Steven died his buddy, Danny—no. She vowed never to tell. Dad may have hit her, but he never tried anything like *that*. That would have been grounds for killing him.

Unless it was all her fault.

But God.

She had received forgiveness for her sins. Did she have to forgive Dad for his? Or Danny? But he couldn't hurt her anymore. He was killed during the Tet Offensive. He wouldn't benefit from her forgiveness. Would she?

She could, theoretically, forgive. But forget? Nope. Impossible.

"I'll come." She scrunched her eyes tightly. Was she making the biggest mistake of her life?

NANCY RESCHEDULED her patients who had appointments over the next few days and posted on the clinic door the number of the veterinarian in Clarksville. He'd agreed to be on call for emergencies. Doc Phillips, bored out of his mind, recovering at home, agreed to be available for phone consultations. Between her promising to visit her dying father and Mary Ann on maternity leave, there was no way she could carry on, anyway.

Mr. Dunne agreed to pick up her dogs from the fenced-in backyard and take care of them for her. Major and Rusty became friends after the accident, but Biddie, fond of barking at anything that moved, wasn't allowed at the clinic unless she was sick.

Maybe by the time she got back, she would have someone to fill the technician position.

MC's face crossed her thoughts. Maybe he would change his mind.

No. He was adamant.

She only threw one change of clothes into a bag. No reason to pack more, because she wasn't staying more than one night.

Was her father really dying? She'd thought of him as nothing but a liar since she turned eighteen.

He said he loved her. Lie.

He'd never do it again. Lie.

The "if you hadn't … I wouldn't have," made her feel guilty, like if she could have done something better, or right, his reaction would have changed.

All a lie.

Nancy supposed everyone had a secret, some kind of shame they hid from the world.

She wanted to trust God with her secrets. If only she could bring herself to let go of them.

Sometimes those secrets—those horrible events—were all she had to hang on to. She had to be strong to endure that. Strength in herself reinforced the idea that she didn't need anyone else.

But the constant striving to be better, stronger, and more self-reliant took its toll. How much more could she take?

Placing her toothbrush in her bag, she sank to the edge of her bed, arguing with herself.

Could she, or could she not, do this?

She prayed she could remain calm. That she could find some good out of all that happened. That he would know what he'd done and be repentant.

At the last minute, she placed her Bible in the bag with her clothes. There weren't any Bibles in her brother's house or her dad's that she could remember. Did Mom have one?

She called Richard's number and spoke to her sister-in-law. "Hey, Linda, I'm getting ready to leave."

"Good. I'm glad you're coming. I wish …"

"Yeah, that it was under different circumstances." She sighed. "Looking forward to seeing y'all, though."

"Same here. The kids are excited."

The one bright spot.

Linda continued. "I wish you weren't driving down here alone."

The drive from Park Haven to Huntsville, Alabama, only took four hours, but she wasn't getting an early start.

"I'll be fine. I've been on my own for a while, now."

She hung up the phone and closed her eyes for a few seconds.

Oh, Mama. How I wish you were here.

Chapter Fifteen

"Looks like physical therapy has been helping."

The Veteran's Administration doctor in Nashville nodded his head as he examined MC's left shoulder. He took a moment to peruse MC's chart, then took his glasses off and peered at the patient.

"You're pushing yourself. Good. I can tell your muscles are staying toned." The doctor paused. "A lot of guys are talking about having nightmares. You experienced any lately?"

MC shook his head. He just wanted to get out of there.

Walking through this building was like walking through another nightmare. Men—veterans of all ages, in wheelchairs, missing limbs, shuffling around in robes, or dragging IV stands. Some were just sitting, staring at nothing, probably drugged out of their minds.

He figured those were the ones who talked about it. Wouldn't it be worse to get it in the open? Talking about it made him think about it more. Dream about it more. Didn't it? He could get over this hump. He wouldn't tolerate weakness in the head.

"I'm good."

"Glad to hear it." The doctor shut the folder and—maybe it was his imagination—appeared relieved that MC didn't want to talk.

"See you in three months, then we'll talk about getting you reinstated."

MC wanted to scream, "NO!" but managed to internalize the shudder working its way through his body. The idea of returning to active duty made him feel sick.

He'd given them two years of his life. How much more could he give?

Not talking, MC climbed into Dad's pickup and pondered the doctor's final statement.

The sling could go away unless his pain increased or he injured it in some way. If he thought he needed the support, he could use it. His lifting limit had been raised, thank goodness. He was tired of carrying wood one stick at a time.

Once they reached the outskirts of Nashville. Dad broke the silence. "What'd the doc say?" Not much had been said while trying to navigate downtown traffic.

MC appreciated Dad taking off work to bring him to the VA. Appreciated the encouragement and the space his family gave him.

"He was impressed with my progress." MC stopped there.

Dad glanced at him while stopping at a light. "Well? That's a good thing, isn't it?"

Was it?

"He wants me back here in three months, then he'll evaluate my fitness for duty."

The loud sigh that came from his father mirrored the one he'd expelled as soon as he left the doctor's office.

"Yeah." MC glanced over at Dad and glimpsed moisture in his front-facing eyes.

"Did you talk about the dreams?"

How—Grandpa.

"I asked Grandpa not to say anything," he growled. MC couldn't stay mad, but it rankled.

"He was worried about you."

MC took a deep breath and let it out slowly. No need to say something he'd regret, later.

"I didn't talk to anyone about that."

Dad nodded. "I get it." He caught MC's gaze. "I do."

What could he say? Dad did a stint right after World War II, but never saw combat. How could he get it?

MC may as well say what's on his mind. "You don't go from combat duty to being soft in the head."

"Nobody thinks that."

He scoffed. "Yeah? Let some of the home folks observe me having a flashback. It ain't pretty."

He hadn't intended to say that. The worry in Dad's eyes almost did MC in.

"I'll be okay, Dad." He stared out the window at the disappearing hills and flat landscape. "If it's not better next time, I'll say something."

Maybe.

Probably not.

～

"What's this?"

MC got out of Dad's truck and was greeted by not one dog, but three. Maybe Grandpa picked up another stray?

"Hey, boys." Grandpa came from the barn and waved a hand. "Dr. Nancy had to go to 'Bama for a family emergency, and I offered to take care of Major and Biddy."

"What happened?" MC's brows drew together.

"She said her brother called. Their father is at the point of death and has been asking for her." Grandpa shook his head. "She's never told us anything about her family."

Dad asked the question on MC's mind. "Where's she headed?"

"Huntsville."

MC frowned. "Not too far. Did she go by herself?"

Grandpa chuckled. "Who would go with her? Mary Ann?"

"I see your point."

Dad gave him a half-smile and patted MC's back. "She'll be fine. She's a big girl." He peeked at his watch. "Me, I need to check on the crew at the Adams' place. Let 'em know I'm never far away." He winked and jogged to the driver's side.

Grandpa called out, "Bye, son. Tell Marjorie thanks for the banana bread."

"Will do."

The two men passed some silent message between the two of them. They were as close as MC was to his dad, so it wasn't surprising.

"Can I interest you in a slice?" Grandpa tilted his head, waiting for a response. Probably to more than his question.

"Since I know the baker well, I'd love one."

"And maybe you can fill me in on what the doctor said."

"Maybe."

Grandpa, tall and rangy like Dad, put an arm across MC's shoulders as they made their way to the farmhouse. "I'll ply you with coffee and bread. How's that for incentive?"

MC chuckled. "You ever thought about going into the blackmail business?"

Grandpa stumbled a bit.

"Grandpa?" MC stopped. Grandpa's face blanched, making it almost the color of the house — pale and white.

"I'm okay. Blood sugar must have dipped." He regained his color. "Your mama sent me exactly what I needed, didn't she?"

Blood sugar? Diabetes didn't run in the family. Didn't track.

MC paused at the foot of the porch steps as Grandpa, sagging slightly, made his way into the house. Following him in, MC continued to look for more signs of ill health. Was it just him, or did Grandpa look a little more stooped than he'd realized?

Chapter Sixteen

Nancy hated hospitals. Even on happy occasions, like visiting Mary Ann and her new baby—she still hated going in there.

Hospitals were, in her experience, where people went to die.

Nurses in white dresses and starched caps scurried around, taking care of all the business the doctors didn't deign to attempt.

With her interest in science and the medical field, her high school chemistry teacher tried to talk her into nursing school.

That's what girls did. They became nurses or schoolteachers.

White dress, starched cap, white hose, and rubber-soled shoes versus whatever she wanted to wear?

People versus animals?

It hadn't been a hard call. Going to veterinary school had been on her radar since she read the James Herriot books in junior high. She didn't regret a single moment.

She paused at the door to her dad's room. Richard stopped her with a hand on her arm.

Did he regret shaming her into coming?

"He looks pretty bad. You haven't seen him in a long time."

She nodded, unable to speak.

Giving him a wobbly smile, she cleared her throat of the emotion gathering there. "I'm trying hard to remember the good times."

"Childhood. Those were good times."

Nancy never broke eye contact, causing her brother to falter. "After Steven died, and you were away at college, he was on his best behavior whenever you came around. You didn't believe me." The old feelings of betrayal rose inside her, and she twisted her lips in disgust. She gazed into his eyes, tears gathering. "I've never been able to figure out what I did wrong."

Richard couldn't face her, but at her last comment, his head snapped up. "You did nothing wrong. I was aware something wasn't right, but I didn't want to face Dad. After you left, I gave him grief for being so hard on you. I wish I'd been there." He shoved his hands in his pockets and scanned around him, everywhere but at Nancy. "I'm sorry for being a coward, Nancy."

She nodded. If she spoke, she would burst into tears, and she didn't know if she could stop once she started. Why hadn't he told her this before?

Nancy pushed the heavy door open, and there was her father, a shrunken shell of a man. She hesitated. He didn't look like the same man who'd yelled, screamed, and hit her all those times.

John Baker, the man she'd come to hate, the man who ruined her life in so many ways, turned his head to see who was at the door. As their eyes met, all she could see was fear. Did he think her capable of exacting revenge for so many wrongs?

He didn't know her at all, did he?

She walked up to the bed and sat in a chair next to it, not touching him.

The moments stretched. They eyed one another warily, waiting. For what? Nancy didn't know.

Richard came and stood behind her, hand on her shoulder. "I got her here, Dad."

He nodded and finally spoke, the worried expression on his face replaced with the old superior, controlling attitude. "Took long enough for you to come."

"I almost didn't."

"You know, a girl should show respect for her elders. That's what I was always taught." A spasm of coughing stopped her father's speech.

"I tried to, Daddy." The squeeze on her shoulder let her know her brother supported her. Better late than never.

"You made me afraid of you. I told Richard and Steven what happened, but they accused me of being a 'dramatic teenage girl.'" Her tears dried up as her anger grew.

"Well, you were pretty dramatic." Her father's eyes avoided both hers and her brother's.

Richard knelt next to Nancy, next to the hospital bed. "Why'd you do it, Dad? I didn't want to believe it, but it makes sense."

A flash of fear once again crossed her father's features. He'd lost the hard, uncompromising expression she'd come to know all too well. Instead, he shrunk before their eyes. He was at their mercy.

He couldn't hold their gaze. Was he trying to gather up some courage? If so, the only courage he found was negative. "I did what any other man would have done with an insolent daughter. Why, my sister ..."

"Aunt Jean?" She'd always wondered why Aunt Jean very seldom attended any family functions, save funerals. Had she suffered at the hands of her father, Nancy's grandfather? Nancy had never met him, and her father seldom mentioned him. Maybe he'd been afraid of his father like she'd been afraid of him. Did Dad hurt her?

So many wasted years. Could she have counted on her aunt for support all this time? Maybe they could have helped each other.

Or had Nancy truly been wrong in running from her father? Maybe if she'd stayed. If she'd been a better daughter, not so stubborn as he always said ...

As she sat there, doubting herself, she observed a shift in his expression. His frustration and embarrassment—his natural defense mechanism—were turning into a sorrow too deep for words.

AFTER THE ALTERCATION with her dad, Nancy left the hospital and went to his house. Her mind raced in many directions. Dad. Aunt Jean. Patterns of abuse. What to do with all of Dad's stuff.

She should reach out to her aunt. Aunt Jean represented the last link to her extended family, and now that she understood why she'd stayed away, the time had come to contact her.

Richard offered to go to the house with her, but Nancy wanted this first time to be alone. Wanted to see if something, somewhere, could give some explanation for her dad's attitude toward her.

She needed to know if she was to blame for his abuse.

Her childhood home smelled like cigarette smoke and illness. He never quit smoking, even as the death sentence of cancer became a foregone conclusion.

Not surprising.

Walking through the empty house, she paused at the door to her old room.

She leaned her forehead on the cool wood. So many memories. Her haven. After hitting her, Dad never came in there to apologize, check for any injuries, or anything. He simply waited until he was sober and tried to act as if nothing happened.

Turning the knob slowly, stale air rushed out.

Nothing had changed. Nothing. The clothes she'd left behind were still strewn across the bed. The last *Teen* magazine she ever owned, lay open to an article about teen heartthrob, Fabian.

Somehow, after that, she never considered herself a "teen" again.

It hurt to see her past untouched as if no one cared if she came or went. She turned and walked out, closing the door behind her. She'd think about this another time.

Focus.

Phone numbers. There should be an address book in the hall on the phone table if he hadn't moved it.

Yes, the address book was there. Most of the names, addresses, and phone numbers were written in Mom's neat script. A few with her handwriting, and some later entries in her dad's heavy hand.

She found the address—Jean Bell. Aunt Jean. She hoped her number was still the same. Taking a chance, she dialed and listened as the line rang twice, then answered by a familiar voice.

"Aunt Jean?" Nancy had recognized her voice as soon as she said "Hello."

"Nancy?"

"Yes, it's me." Silence. "I—I wanted to let you know that my dad's not doing well."

Aunt Jean finally replied. "I'm sorry, Nancy." Then gave a long pause.

"I don't —"

"Do you—"

Both women chuckled at their over-talking.

Nancy spoke first. "We're at cross-purposes, aren't we? I wanted to let you know, in case you needed to say anything to him."

Please, let her come. Nancy was pleading silently, hopeful that she could reconnect with a woman with so many of the same issues as she.

"I have nothing to say to him." Was there a sniff before she continued? "Do *you* need me?"

Her aunt's voice was low, not angry and belligerent like her father's.

How to answer a question like that?

"Only if you feel you can come."

"Hang on a minute."

Nancy could hear other muffled voices as if Aunt Jean held her hand over the receiver.

"Nancy … I don't know how much you know."

"I know enough to know you and I have a lot in common." The tears returned, and she involuntarily sniffed loudly into the phone. "Sorry."

"Your dad and I had a lot in common at one time, too, but then, after—"

"When Mom died?"

Pause.

"Then, and Steven. That's when he gave in to his demons completely." Silence. "Nancy, I wanted to bring you home with me."

Nancy closed her eyes and pressed her fist at the hurt welling up in her chest. She could have had her Aunt Jean as a mother figure. She had toughed it out, but there were so many nights of crying herself to sleep, scared to leave her room.

And then, when Danny …

"It might help us both to talk about it." Nancy tried to be gentle and calm, but even she could hear the entreaty in her voice.

"After all these years?" A loud sigh came over the phone. "I doubt it. Thankfully, you never met your grandfather."

No, she hadn't. She'd wished for a grandfather, something more along the lines of Brendan Dunne.

But that wasn't the issue.

"So, can you come? I'm staying at Richard's house." She took a deep breath and widened her eyes, trying to control her tears and her voice. "Aunt Jean, I don't know how long he's got."

"I'll come. For you and Richard. Not for John."

Chapter Seventeen

May

The last few days had been rough. MC thought he was making progress. That the dreams were becoming less intense.

Until last night.

All in his head. The dreams got longer and more vivid each time they invaded his sleep, and sometimes his waking hours.

A good night's sleep. That's what he craved.

He found broken glass shards on the floor across the room from where he'd thrown a tumbler. A mark on the opposite wall revealed the place it hit.

He couldn't go on like this. It not only scared him, worrying about hurting others, but it also made him angry. Rip-roaring, chaotic, outrageous anger. He had to *do* something.

The chapel. Grandpa had been working on it, trying to keep it intact for the generations to come.

MC didn't think his generation needed to bring any kids into this crazy world. It would be wrong on so many levels.

But, because he loved Grandpa and he didn't want it said the last generation of Dunnes let it go to wrack and ruin, he'd work on it and take over as many of the farm chores as he could.

Grandpa worried him. The little stumble earlier, catching him staring off into space at odd times. It wasn't like him.

He'd always had the youngest grandparents. Dad, a ten-year-old Connor, had been adopted by Grandpa and Grandma as a young couple in their mid-twenties—Grandpa was only fifteen years older than MC's dad.

It couldn't last forever. Someday he would lose Grandpa.

When he went outside to clear his head, everything was dripping, but then the sun broke through the clouds left over from last night's thunderstorm.

Thank goodness. The bucket on the step measured four inches of precipitation since yesterday.

Rusty barked and pulled MC back to the present. He'd stopped in the middle of the lane to the barn and stared at the chapel. Rhythmic hammering echoed. Grandpa. He could use some help.

MC smiled down at the trusty dog. "I'm okay, buddy." He scratched him behind the ears. "Let's go check on Grandpa."

MC made the turn onto the seldom-traveled drive to the chapel. He'd avoided it. Right now, he didn't know where he stood with God, and where God stood with him.

He waffled between feeling responsible for so much and being angry at a God who could let such atrocities happen. He could "talk the talk," but could he still "walk the walk"?

As MC drew closer, he observed Grandpa on a ladder, nailing a shingle back on the roof. "Need some help?"

"I thought I heard Rusty bark a while ago." He climbed down the ladder and laughed as Rusty re-acquainted himself with Nancy's dogs, Major and Biddy. "Looks like he's glad to see them."

The three dogs frolicked, causing the elderly Rusty to look as young as the two-year-old terrier mix, Biddie. It took a few minutes, but the overly serious shepherd-mix Major joined in.

MC's lips tugged in a natural smile. He didn't even have to force it.

That was a first in a long time.

He peered up at the chapel front. The door needed painting and some repairs, as did everything else.

"You think you can get this place shored up to last a few more years?"

Grandpa's gaze surveyed the building, precious in his eyes, MC could tell.

"I think it will be around for a few more generations."

Probably not, but MC would keep that to himself. He'd stopped trying to plan for the future.

"Roof leaking?"

"Yeah, that wind that came along with last night's storm did a number on the shingles. I found water all over the inside." Worry was etched on Grandpa's face. "That's the last thing we need."

MC nodded. Every carpenter's worst fear—water damage. He'd learned that working summer breaks with his Grandpa Morgan.

"How's the arm?" Grandpa nodded toward his sling-free left arm. "I see you're trying it out."

"So far, so good." MC stretched it out, grimacing a little. He was relieved it wasn't too bad.

"It's good enough to steady me on a ladder."

Grandpa lowered his brows a moment, then nodded and said, "I'll get some shingles out of the barn and meet you back here in ten."

MC nodded. His movements were free without the sling, but he didn't want to overdo it. Mom would have a fit if she knew he was even considering climbing a ladder, but the last thing he wanted was for Grandpa to be up on a ladder with nobody within earshot. Talk about a recipe for disaster.

He walked inside and surveyed the water on the floor and around the stained-glass window behind the platform. Grandpa wasn't kidding. MC could see daylight peeking in from above. No wonder.

The sun shining though the ancient window almost blinded him in contrast to the darkness inside. He rubbed a hand along the frame, wincing once he touched the moisture.

He knelt at the bottom sill, looking closer at the damage. It wasn't just moisture from this storm. The frame was coming apart.

"Looks bad, doesn't it?" Grandpa dropped the bundle of asphalt shingles at the doorway and joined him at the window. "Been a long time coming."

MC nodded. "A stiff wind could destroy the window."

Why did he care? To him, the window only brought back memories of the horrors of the tiny chapel they'd holed up in during that last mission. Beyond that, it symbolized faith in a God he doubted.

"It needs to come out." Grandpa shook his head. He was far away for a moment, as he had more and more often, lately. "For sure we don't want to lose it. It's been in the family for nearly a century. Uncle Patrick and Father brought it to America with them. I'm surprised my father let him have it. Your grandma and I helped build the chapel, and we helped Uncle Patrick install it."

MC recalled the story. Uncle Patrick wanted a piece of Ireland, the place of his birth, to stand as a symbol of his roots, and his faith.

What would happen at the end of the Dunne family line? Grandpa never spoke of his Chicago family nor the reason he came to Tennessee. Said he liked to focus on the future, not the past.

MC agreed, to an extent. Why, then, was Grandpa determined to restore the chapel and now the window?

"Nancy, would you get the door, please?"

The doorbell rang as Linda and Richard were wrangling their three-year-old Jason into the highchair so they could get dinner on the table.

"I got it." Nancy grinned at the picture she hoped she'd never forget of her brother doing all he could to assist his wife. She never remembered her dad helping Mom do anything.

When she opened the door, her face froze for a second. "Aunt Jean."

The older woman nodded, tears welling in her eyes. "Oh, Nancy, sweetheart." They embraced, and Aunt Jean squeezed Nancy tightly as if making up for the years she'd missed.

They were both in tears by the time they stepped away and faced one another.

Nancy glanced toward the dining room nervously. "We're about to sit down to supper."

Aunt Jean appeared unsure. "I should have called first instead of hightailing it down here. I can—"

Richard came in as she spoke. "Aunt Jean, I'm glad you're here." He gave her a quick hug. "We've got plenty for supper. Linda's cooked enough for an army regiment." His chuckle had a note of sadness in it.

"I don't want to be any trouble …"

"No trouble at all." Richard retrieved a chair from the hallway and carried it into the dining room. "Honey, Aunt Jean is here."

"Oh!" As Linda came through the kitchen door, she smiled in her surprise. "Welcome."

Jason strained, attempting to escape the high chair. Richard shook his head. "He's not used to eating in the dining room."

The laugh cleared some of the tension in the room.

Aunt Jean walked over to the preschooler and sat down next to him. "Sweetie, I'm your Great-aunt Jean. What's your name?"

He acted surprised at someone addressing him directly with so many people in the room. "Jason."

She held out her hand. "Nice to meet you, Jason." He took it, grinning as she shook it firmly as if he were an adult.

Richard called the others to the table as Linda set an extra place. "Ryan, Lisa, supper."

The ten-year-old Ryan and five-year-old Lisa came tearing through the dining room, heading for the kitchen. They stopped short when they saw an unexpected person in the room.

"Whoa, there." Richard caught his daughter as she attached herself to his legs, suddenly shy. "We're eating in the dining room tonight."

"Because Aunt Nancy is here?" Lisa peered around from her perch in her daddy's arms. She whispered loudly, "Who's that?"

"That's *my* Aunt Jean."

"Is she mine too?" Lisa frowned, confused.

"I'm your *Great*-aunt Jean, but you can call me Aunt Jean."

"This whirlwind is Lisa, and the tornado that preceded her is Ryan, our oldest." Linda stood behind her chair and surveyed the table. "I think that's everything." She sat, indicating that everyone could sit.

Ryan's eyes widened. "How come we're eating in here, instead of the kitchen? You always say Jason spills too much stuff to eat where respectable folks eat." His confusion lightened the atmosphere. "Does that mean we're respectable, now?"

The adults laughed, which pleased the boy. The tension, the fear of the unknown, lessened.

A feeling of relief overcame Nancy as she glanced around the table. Family.

Linda grinned at her son. "I guess you could say we're taking this one day at a time."

Chapter Eighteen

"Sir, you can't have it both ways."

The nurse attending to John Baker stood patiently, but her exasperated expression spoke volumes. Nancy understood her feelings and thanked the Lord she wasn't the one having to take his cigarettes away from him.

"Are you Mr. Baker's daughter?"

The fight had begun before Nancy came into the room, and she hoped the nurse didn't expect him to listen to her any more than anyone else.

Nancy considered the scene. A stern nurse with hands on her hips, and her dad, a hint of moisture in his eyes.

"I am." Nancy walked to the side of the bed, just out of reach of his hand. She hadn't touched him. "Dad, you know you can't smoke. There's oxygen in the room."

"A dying man should be able to enjoy a smoke if it's what feels good," he grumbled.

"Unless you want to blow the hospital up, I think you're going to have to follow the rules."

Nancy turned toward the nurse. "Is there anywhere we can take him where he *can* smoke?"

With a pitying glance at the patient, she shook her head. "I'm afraid not. He's on oxygen twenty-four-seven. If he's off of it even for a few minutes, his levels drop dangerously low. Add a cigarette to that?"

"A quick, painless death?" Dad glanced up, hopeful.

"No. It might be quick, but it certainly wouldn't be painless, and you'd be endangering everyone around you." The nurse straightened the blanket. "You're going to have to get used to the idea that you're now a non-smoker."

Nancy was grateful to no longer be around second-hand smoke. But Dad? He'd always bragged he'd smoked since the age of ten.

A lot of good that got him. Cancer had now spread from his lungs to his liver, stomach, and bones.

Dad said nothing. The nurse's words must have hit home.

Taking a spot in the chair next to the hospital bed, Nancy sat, waiting for an opening, or at least until she could think of something to say.

All those times she'd thought of snappy comebacks and stinging retorts. Now she had him as a captive audience, and she couldn't come up with a thing.

Had God saved her from having more to regret?

Her dad fidgeted nervously. An addict without his "fix."

"Nancy," he plucked at his sheet.

"Yes?"

"I know we didn't leave things right between us."

She sighed, then swallowed hard. "There's still time if there's anything you'd like to tell me."

Maybe this would give him the opening he needed.

She regarded him, fully, for the first time since she'd been in town. Yesterday, the first day she'd seen him in nearly ten years, his appearance shocked her. Her fear of him still haunted her, and then, she couldn't do more than glance at him from time to time.

Now, she stared him in the eye, only to have him falter.

Was he ... embarrassed? That surprised her.

"I wish we'd had more time with your mother." The tears she thought she'd seen in his eyes earlier quietly fell, triggering hers. She had no sympathy for him. She still grieved her mother at such odd times.

"Me too." She reached onto the bedside table for a tissue. "She would know what to say."

"I'm glad she didn't have to grieve Steve."

All Nancy could do was nod. Mom would have handled his death much better than her husband.

"There's something I've wanted to say to you for a long time. Just too embarrassed to say it out loud. Nothing like being told you're dying to make a man humble."

Nancy remained silent. She'd already, in her heart, forgiven him. Meeting Jesus had led to that. But the human nature part of her that never quite went away? That part wanted to hear him say the words.

"I've not been this sober since before your mama died." He shook his head. "I'm so sorry, Nance."

"For what?" He wasn't getting off that easy.

"For the way I treated you." She wasn't moved by the entreaty in his eyes. "I don't want to shuffle off this mortal coil knowing I'd done you wrong. I'd like to make things right if I can."

He was trying to make peace with the people around him— cigarette-swiping nurses notwithstanding. She wanted desperately to hang on to the anger toward him and her jealousy toward every picture-perfect family she'd ever known. She deserved more, didn't she?

Could she, at this point, *truly* forgive him?

SEVERAL TIMES THROUGHOUT THE MORNING, MC thought working alongside Grandpa was the best medicine.

They'd found more damage to the roof than they thought. Dad brought some extra bundles of shingles and a few sheets of plywood left over from past construction jobs. The roof might not match, but it would be sound.

MC sat on the roof, looking over what they'd accomplished. Mostly demo, but they'd laid the tar paper and begun to patch with shingles.

The stained-glass window washed the interior in the colors of the rainbow, so why not add the same decorative style to the roof?

A low chuckle started from deep within MC. Grandpa headed up the ladder, his head appearing close by. "Something funny?"

Grandpa smiled up at him, probably relieved to find MC in his right mind. He didn't want Grandpa to have to experience his hallucinations and waking nightmares.

"Just thinking about our 'roof of many colors.'"

"I think Jacob of old would approve, don't you?" Grandpa grinned back. The fine lines MC noticed the other day appeared less up here in the sunshine and fresh air.

"I do. I figure if the window can have different colors, why not the roof?"

He wanted to tell Grandpa about the window in Vietnam, but something still held him back. The more time he spent on the chapel, the less he compared it to the destruction of the deserted chapel in the jungle.

Grandpa sat next to him, looking at the roof and beyond. "See that rise over there?" He pointed to the hill where the woods started that led out of the valley and toward town.

MC nodded. He'd had it pointed out more than once. Usually, he would internally balk at hearing the story again, but this time? He had all the time in the world.

"Your Grandma and I drove here from Harrisburg, Illinois. She was sound asleep when we arrived. Not that she could have seen much in the middle of the night." Grandpa grinned, lost in a fog of memory. "We drove all night. After she told me what she thought about the hasty wedding and running off—that I'd ruined her reputation—she finally went to sleep."

This part of the story was new to him. Had she and Grandpa …? No, they had no other children. It wasn't that. So many questions, and yet MC worried if he asked them, the door would close, and he wouldn't learn more.

"That little cabin you're sleeping in? Uncle Patrick and I put her to bed in the bedroom, and we bunked in the next room."

He shook his head. "It was tough. She couldn't imagine anybody not revering their father as she did, hers. Oh, he'd made her angry, but she'd grown up in a home full of love and honor, and she returned it."

"You've never talked about your family."

"I know. That was probably a mistake on my part. Her father agreed with me that it was the only thing we could do. The only way I could keep her safe."

The word "safe" struck MC. He glanced over at Grandpa, sure his mouth hung open in surprise.

Chuckling, Grandpa handed MC the tin-plated, stainless steel canteen and picked up his hammer.

"You're not stopping there, are you?"

Finally, MC had someone besides himself on his mind. It had been a long time. He needed this more than Grandpa realized. They were familiar with the story of how they adopted Dad at age ten. Dad remembered his biological mother, but not his father. He was the son of Grandpa's brother, James, who'd died, but Grandpa never once, to MC's memory, mentioned his parents. Uncle Patrick represented the only part of that generation MC had known.

Grandpa peered at him. "Our branch of the family ends with you." He stared away. "I guess that's why I'm determined to get this chapel back in shape."

"You've never talked about your parents."

"No, I haven't." Grandpa's eyes sank. "There are some things I need to share with your dad. I'm just not sure how."

Grandpa needed an unbiased confidante. Could MC count on Grandpa to be the same for him, or would he be horrified at the things he could tell him?

Chapter Nineteen

Nancy woke to the sound of the phone ringing in the hallway. Richard answered, then nothing. Muffled remarks, "Um-hmm," and "Thank you for calling." The phone receiver gently clicked.

In her drowsy state, she was aware something had happened, but she didn't want to wake up and learn what it was.

Knock-knock.

"Nancy? Are you awake?"

She struggled to sit up and wipe the sleep from her eyes. "I'm up."

"Can I come in?"

Looking around, she grabbed her robe from the corner post of the bed. "Sure."

She sat in bed, pulling the covers over her legs. It was springtime, but still chilly in the mornings.

"It's Dad, isn't it?" The dread in her voice matched Richard's face.

He nodded. "About ten minutes ago."

The knot in her stomach grew with every second. She closed her eyes and dipped her head, her face obscured by the curtain of hair still rumpled from the night's sleep.

"How …"

"The nurse said he passed peacefully."

Why? Why did he get to have peace and not her? Her feelings were all over the place. On the one hand, she grieved for a younger Nancy who lost her beloved daddy. On the other? Relief. Her abuser couldn't hurt her anymore.

Somewhere in the middle lay regret. He'd asked her, just the day before, for forgiveness.

She'd not answered him. Instead, she turned and walked away, vowing to herself to pray about it. Think about it some more. She'd thought, *He's waited this long to apologize, so he can wait a little longer for me to accept his apology and forgive him.*

And now?

Now there would be no forgiveness. She'd squandered the last chance she had to have a relationship with him.

Her heart lurched. Did he have a relationship with Christ? With the God who saves, forgives, and throws our sins as far as the east is from the west?

Her heavenly Father had to be disappointed in her. How could He, a perfect parent, accept such from her?

He would forgive, but the hard part would be forgiving herself.

Cock-a-doodle doo.

The rooster crowed in the barnyard. MC remembered hating that as a kid. He'd craved the obnoxious sound in Vietnam and now tried to count his blessings that he was hearing it again.

Grandpa had been particularly forthcoming the day before. Not that he'd ever been secretive—he simply didn't mention life before coming to Tennessee.

Grandma often told stories of her growing up as the daughter of a judge in southern Illinois, so he had that part of the family tree pretty much memorized. Problem was, Dad was adopted, having belonged to Grandpa Brenden's brother, so his maternal roots went back somewhere in Chicago, to an unknown woman named "Nora."

When he stopped to think about it, MC realized Grandpa and Uncle Patrick talked as little as possible about their former life in Chicago.

They were estranged from their Illinois family. Tension formed any time their stories and memories brought them to the Dunne family in Chicago, so Dad, and later, MC, tried not to ask too many questions.

Maybe today Grandpa would share a little more. Had working on the chapel brought back all the memories?

MC dragged himself out of the cocoon of blankets and quilts and stretched. His left shoulder caught. He'd have to watch it, or he'd undo all the progress he'd made in physical therapy.

Through the kitchen window, he could see the farmhouse, a mist beginning to burn off in the early morning sunshine. The wisp of smoke from the chimney told him Grandpa had stoked up the stove in the kitchen. He had an electric range, but on cool mornings Grandpa liked to cook on the wood stove, "to keep his hand in," as he put it.

MC pulled on jeans and a T-shirt, then a flannel shirt, and hunted around for his work boots. He found them under the edge of the sofa where he'd pulled them off the night before.

Hoping Grandpa already had coffee made, he knocked at his door, glad to hear a robust, "Come in."

"Need a shot of caffeine?" Grandpa waved him into a chair and set a cup of steaming brew in front of him.

"Yours is better than mine any day."

"I doubt that, but I know a bird in the hand …"

"Exactly. Saw your smoke."

Grandpa laughed. "I'm stirring up some eggs. Want some?"

"I wouldn't turn them down."

"You're up awfully early." Grandpa fried up some chopped onions, then poured the eggs into the hot cast-iron skillet. The sizzle of butter with onion and eggs made a delicious sound and an even more delectable aroma.

MC sat in the chair, stretching his left shoulder. The therapist told him to do it multiple times a day. "Barney the rooster didn't get the sleep-in note." He chuckled. "I slept hard."

"A good day's work will do that to you," Grandpa said, watching the eggs carefully. "Probably get the roof done today."

"You think?" MC twisted his lips.

Grandpa nodded. "I took a closer look at the damage on the window side."

After a blessing over the food, they didn't speak as they tucked in.

Grandpa's voice broke into his deep thoughts. "There's some damage to the stained glass."

MC couldn't put his finger on the reason why they couldn't lose the window. True, it had traveled from Ireland to Chicago and then on to Tennessee, and Uncle Patrick and Grandpa installed it in this chapel about fifty years ago, making it a symbol of this part of the Dunne family.

"Can it be fixed?"

"Probably. I'm hoping someone will know of a craftsman around Nashville who is knowledgeable about antique stained glass."

"I'm sure there will be."

A comfortable silence enveloped them as they finished their breakfast. As they cleared the table and put dishes in the sink, Grandpa spoke again. "Nancy called last night."

The slight jolt to his system at the mention of her name was strange.

"How is she?"

"Her father passed, early morning." Grandpa frowned. "She never mentioned more than a brother and his kids. Sad. Never talked about her father." Grandpa shook himself out of melancholy. "Anyway, she wanted to make sure I could keep Major and Biddy for a few days more."

"And, of course, you told her yes."

"I did, and I told her we would check on the clinic."

So, Grandpa volunteered not only himself but MC as well?

MC remained silent and just nodded.

Chapter Twenty

J ohn Baker had requested cremation, and that his ashes be spread on the Mississippi River.

No visitation, no funeral, just a closing door.

The small family had lost so many. Was it healthy to simply treat a person as if they never existed? Nancy was torn. She viewed cremation and spreading the ashes as if the person had never been.

While there were many times she wished she could forget her father, she remembered some good times. While she and her brothers were young, Dad was always in the middle of everything. He adored his wife and kids. Looking back, it was clear he adored his wife, and since the kids were a part of her, he loved them, as well.

Entering the house where she grew up, the finality of her father's death loomed. She'd just been there the night before, but her breath caught as soon as she walked through the front door. This time it wasn't so much the smell of stale cigarette smoke and illness as much as the knowledge that no one lived here anymore.

No one.

Richard put his hand on her shoulder. "We don't have to do this today."

Her brother had bent over backward to comfort her, to assure her that no one blamed her for leaving.

Aunt Jean promised to come to the house later, after Nancy and Richard had a chance to absorb the enormity of the last few days.

Nancy shook her head. "No. I want to at least get a start on going through things. I know there are things of Mom's and things from our grandparents we'll want to keep."

"I'll check out the garage."

The small smile he sent her way made her regret the lost time between them. She longed to know this brother who had always, to her, been larger than life. He and Linda opened their home to a virtual stranger, and the kids accepted her immediately as one of their own.

Never again would she shun someone she loved.

There, she'd thought it. She'd loved her dad. At one time, he was her world, but at the time she needed him the most, he failed her. Were those grounds to write him off?

What would Jesus say?

She drew a shaky breath. He'd say to have mercy. Show compassion. Love her father anyway.

Even in the Old Testament, the prophet Micah said, *He has shown you, O man, what is good; And what does the Lord require of you but to do justly, to love mercy, and to walk humbly with your God?*

Showing mercy and walking humbly was impossible, and unfair, once pride told her that she deserved more.

Nancy opened the top dresser drawer. Mom and Dad had divided up the dresser—the right-hand side, Mom's, and the left, Dad's.

Mom's side was much like her own room—unchanged from the day she left it. Untouched. Nancy fingered a silky half-slip and smiled through tears. Mom always wore a slip. It had nothing to do with anything showing through, but everything to do with the niceties her mama had taught her. A lady *always* wore a slip.

Now, young women were leaving off undergarments right and left. Nancy never had the nerve to do so, but she'd known several girls in college and graduate school who took to the "hippie" lifestyle easily.

Nancy had neither the time nor the desire for such selfish frivolity. If Mom wouldn't approve of an action, she hesitated to do it.

Opening the top drawer on the left—Dad's—she found a jumble of undershirts and socks. There were so few clothes, she could see straight to the items at the bottom of the drawer.

Letters, papers of all kinds, notes, and even pictures she'd drawn as a child.

She pulled out a picture of a house on a hill, with five figures standing next to it. She'd depicted Dad (the tallest, of course), Mom, Richard, Steven, and herself, easily identified by the stick figure's long brown hair.

Next to the yellow crayon sun, she'd scrawled, "I LOVE YOU."

It had been carefully folded and kept in the bottom of his most private drawer.

Digging a little farther, into the back of the drawer, she found a letter addressed to her. It had been addressed to her apartment at Auburn and never mailed. With shaking hands, she pulled the paper out of the unsealed envelope.

She sat on the edge of the bed before her legs buckled beneath her. The words on the page swam before her, tears obscuring the almost hen-scratch writing.

My darling girl, Nancy ...

MC CHECKED to his left and right, feeling as if he were breaking in, even with a key. Nancy had locked the animal clinic up tight. When Grandpa picked up Major and Biddy, Nancy had given him a key to the back door of the clinic, just in case. She'd told Grandpa no animals were being kenneled, but with the drugs kept on hand, she would feel better if they checked.

He could smell the remnants of animals, cleaning products, and medicine. The left side of his mouth lifted in a half-smile—he was home. The last few summers—before Vietnam, anyway—he'd spent here instead of working for his Grandpa Morgan in construction.

Doc Phillips had the heart of a teacher, and MC learned as much from him as he had in many of his classes in veterinary school.

MC wandered around the clinic, checking the supply cabinet, the lock on the medicine cabinet, and the live mousetraps. Nancy said she wanted to catch the one that kept getting into the kibble.

The trap underneath the animal crates had a resident.

"Well, little fella, looks like it's your lucky day. If you'd been at my house, I'd be prying you out of a spring-loaded trap, but Doc Nancy has decided to let you live to fight another day."

He picked up the trap, mouse in tow, and headed out the back door to the fence row behind the clinic to "set it free." As much as he loved animals, he questioned the logic of letting one go only to have it come back in at the first opportunity.

But this wasn't his call.

Deed done, he placed the trap back where it had been, armed. He thoroughly checked the doors and windows to make sure they were locked.

In the office, he decided to try out the "boss's chair." Tilting it back, his eyes were drawn to some awards and framed diplomas on the wall beside him. Looking at the dates, he sat forward.

Since Nancy's class was a year ahead of him, he'd assumed her older than he.

She wasn't. That stern, earnest young woman he remembered from Auburn? Her many 4H trophies and a little math showed her graduating from high school at sixteen and finishing her bachelor of science in veterinary medicine degree in three years. Her DVM was the only education that she didn't condense. She wasn't older, just seriously smart.

Another reason to stay out of her way and forget completing his doctoral degree. No way could he compete with that.

Chapter
Twenty-One

My darling girl, Nancy,

We never considered having another child when your brothers were already in school. I thought a miracle had occurred.

There you were, all blue eyes and a head full of dark hair, looking up at me as if I hung the moon. I wanted to be that for you.

While you were growing up, it scared me to be responsible for the beautiful woman I knew you would become. After Richard and Steven, you were a breath of fresh air. Your mama and I were glad to spend time with you after the boys went off to school.

When your mama got sick, I couldn't function. She still kept me on an even keel, from her sickbed. But she died, and I fell apart.

I wasn't there for you like she would have been if our roles had been reversed. I wish it could have been me to die instead of her. I mean that.

You never knew my drinking days before that. As a young man, I pushed my limits a few too many times, and your mama told me she wouldn't marry me unless I stopped drinking.

That was all it took, then.

But she went and left me. I crashed and burned. I couldn't do as good a job raising you as your mama, so I pushed you away.

When Steve died, something inside me broke. It was too much. I couldn't think, couldn't make decisions, and all my anger came pouring out on the one closest to me—you.

If I don't get an opportunity to tell you before you find this, I'm asking, no, I'm begging you to forgive a weak man. There's no excuse for hitting you. No excuse for yelling at you, cursing you. My addled brain thought if I pushed you away, it would bring your mother back, if only to protect you. Crazy, I know, but when you're under the influence, your mind does tricky things. I became my worst nightmare, my own father. When he lost my mother, he took it out on Jean. Go to her. She won't talk to me, but she would talk to you.

I'm sorry I'm not man enough to deliver this in person. So many times, I almost said something, but there was a devil deep inside of me that pulled me back in and offered me a drink, a pill, or a woman to help me forget.

I'm proud of you, Nancy. You've accomplished more than your mama and I could have ever dreamed. Maybe pushing you away made you push yourself harder. It's my hope, anyway.

I've never been a religious man, but I did read the Bible your mama kept in her bedside table.

She had some verses marked, and I read through them. I like to think Jesus himself gave me just enough time to get to know him and to realize what I had done to you. I'm sorry if I didn't get to talk to you before going Home. I've wanted to see you but didn't know how to ask.

Be happy, Nancy. If me being out of your life helps, I'm glad. Just know I plan to see you again, someday, and when that happens, I hope it will be a reunion unlike any other with you, me, your mom, and your brothers.

God is good. I'm not, but He is.

Never forget that.

I've always loved you,
Dad

With shaking hands, Nancy gently folded the letter and put it back in the envelope, and then into her pocket. She would read it again, later.

The drawer contained letters to Richard, and Aunt Jean, as well. She wouldn't read those, but she'd deliver them.

Footsteps in the hallway warned Nancy she was no longer alone. She grabbed a tissue and tried to fix the damage done by her tears.

"Nance?"

"In here." She sniffed loudly and sent her brother a sad smile.

"You okay?" Worry lines etched his brow.

She nodded. "I found …" She couldn't say any more, so handed him the envelope addressed to him.

～

MC HAD OVERDONE IT.

The doctor told him to take it slow. Take the sling off only a few hours at a time. Protect his arm.

He lost feeling in his left hand and dropped the hammer after climbing down the ladder. He was in trouble. The pins and needles, along with the pain, stretched down his arm to his fingertips. Was it numb, or was it hurting? Maybe both.

Why shouldn't he hurt? He'd survived, hadn't he? Pain is fleeting, and he didn't deserve to feel well. Not yet. Not until he'd paid for the lives of the men they'd lost that day. But he could never repay that debt.

The hot water flowing over his head and down his back didn't help. He leaned on his right arm, head to the tiled wall, letting the pulse of the spray pound his left shoulder. Could he wash away the images that invaded his thoughts?

Grandpa watched him carefully all day. He tried to keep a conversation going, but eventually, MC gave nothing but monosyllabic answers. Numbness overtook his body. He barely registered pain when he hit his thumb with his hammer.

Before, fresh air and hard work helped. Why not now?

Because he wanted to punish himself for every tragedy that happened on his watch.

He should have gone straight to bed. Would have, if he'd thought sleep would come. The last few nights had been bad. Insomnia, indecision, pain. Tonight, his body screamed in pain.

His amber bottle of pills sat on the top shelf of the cupboard. If he took one—even a half—he could get a good night's sleep.

A whole one would be even better.

He trod on dangerous territory. It was too easy. Anything that easy had to be bad, right?

MC pulled a glass from the dish drainer and filled it with water. Just a drink of water. Stay hydrated.

After half the glass, he peered out the kitchen window toward the farmhouse. He told Grandpa he didn't feel up to supper. He'd fix himself a sandwich and go to bed.

He could see Grandpa moving around, preparing his supper. Probably leftovers. MC didn't have an appetite. Everything tasted like dust these days. He'd lost weight but told Grandpa, Mom, and Dad that the work he did on the farm made him lean.

There. In his hand. He shook it, hearing the pills rattle inside the plastic container. It held the secret of sleep. Of peace. How long could it possibly last? All night? Into tomorrow?

Something about going to the clinic the night before pulled him down. MC wasn't jealous of Nancy having the job he'd always wanted. It was more because it was another part of his life that had to be decided, and he was tired of making decisions.

Decisions to do with the rest of his life, however long. Over there, life was short. So much death all around. People's fates changed on a dime.

Here? At home? Life felt very long.

But then, there was the distinct possibility he would have to go back.

Have to go back to Hell on Earth.

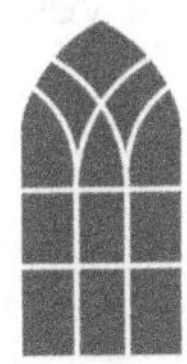

Chapter
Twenty-Two

What was going on? Grandpa? MC's bed shook. Who …? He hadn't slept well enough lately to be that difficult to wake.

Just let me sleep, will ya?

Then the sounds filtered through.

Sirens.

Road noises.

Helicopter? No, machines.

Wait. Where was he?

Back in Vietnam. Had being home been a dream? A hallucination? His arm hurt, but not the searing, burning pain that ripped through him, like before. No, he was numb all over.

He tried to reach down to touch Gunnar, always at his side. Nothing.

Opening his eyes took effort.

MC was on a gurney somewhere in the hospital. His shoulder raged at him. His head came in a close second.

Had the last weeks been a dream? He was in Tokyo, in the hospital. But no, this was no military hospital. As his vision cleared, he perceived the worried, tear-stained face of his mom. Park Haven General Hospital.

He tried to speak, but couldn't for the tube stuck down his throat.

"Don't try to talk." Dad was there, standing next to Mom.

Why …? Had there been an accident? Was Grandpa okay?

Nurses and ER doctors were in and out, checking his vitals, and writing things down.

"Mr. Dunne?" The nurse spoke to him, right in his face. "Can you hear me?"

He couldn't talk, so he nodded slightly.

"Your vitals are improving, so we're going to take the tube out, okay?"

He nodded again.

"It will be a little uncomfortable, but you'll be able to talk."

She didn't lie. After they removed the tube, his throat and esophagus were sore, as if they had been scraped all the way to his lungs.

"You breathing okay?" The same nurse spoke. She was familiar, but what were the odds in his hometown?

He croaked out a "yes," and she patted him on the arm.

"You're fortunate—you slept through the stomach pump. I have a few questions for you …" She glanced at her clipboard. "In the last few weeks, have you wished you were dead?"

Wait. Stomach pump? Dead? His eyes widened in horror, and he searched for his parents. For Grandpa. Is that what they thought?

"I've been miserable, but not that miserable."

"Have you thought that you or your family would be better off if you were dead?"

What? "No."

She nodded, then stared him down. "Have you ever tried to kill yourself?"

"I think if I had wanted to, Vietnam could have accomplished it for me." He tried to smile, but he couldn't.

"Is that a yes or a no?"

"No."

Where were Mom and Dad?

Now that he could move somewhat, he turned his head to see them. "What happened?"

The ER doctor on call breezed in before he got an answer. Dr.

Crandall pinned him with a look. "Young man, you are very fortunate. Did you know that?"

"What exactly happened?"

He studied the chart. "Your grandfather found an open bottle of pain meds on your kitchen cabinet. He couldn't rouse you, so he called the ambulance, having no idea how many you'd taken."

MC raked his hand over his face. Bits of memory settled in place. "I took one before I went to bed."

"That wouldn't have done it. Do you know how many pills you had in the bottle?"

MC nodded. "Sixteen, after the one I took."

Grandpa cleared his throat. "We only counted thirteen."

How could he have done that? MC remembered how dangerous even one could be.

"Did you get up at some point, forgetting you'd taken a pill, and take another?" Mom tried her best to put a good spin on it.

His mind raced with the possibility he'd accidentally taken more pills than he realized. He'd been dog-tired.

"Had to be." He peered at Mom, Dad, and Grandpa. "It wasn't intentional." He shook his head, trying to wrap his mind around what happened. "I don't remember anything after my shower."

Mom's tears ran down her cheeks as she came and took him in her arms. "You scared me to death."

"I know, Mom." He squeezed her back.

If he'd ever thought about ending it, seeing the distress on the faces of his loved ones made it less appealing.

"I'd like to admit you, keep you under observation for a couple of days. This drug can cause cardiac issues."

The doctor didn't look as convinced of the accidental nature of the overdose as his family, and he didn't blame him. If he could remember anything about the night before, he'd feel better about it too.

THE DRIVE back to Park Haven gave Nancy time to ponder and question.

Of one thing she was confident—God loved her with perfect love. Her assignment? Love God, love herself, and love others, forgiving like Him.

But what was real love, and how could love look anything like what her father had for her? He said he loved her, and he apologized, but she didn't trust it. With his track record, she wouldn't put it past him to attempt to find a way to ease his soul into the next world.

Would anyone blame her for walking away from Dad after he begged her forgiveness?

The letter she found shed some light on his state of mind, but she still reverted to that frightened sixteen-year-old who hadn't been able to count on him to protect her.

The Bible was full of stories of sin, repentance, and forgiveness. Who was she, forgiven of her own sins, to pass judgment on Dad?

Did God rate one sin over another?

No.

Were sins of commission worse than sins of omission? Were his drinking and abuse more severe than her sins of attitude and pride?

No.

It didn't seem right. She was "the good one."

A knot in the pit of her stomach grew until she was queasy, but Nancy realized she hadn't eaten since the night before.

That wasn't the only reason.

The combination of guilt and anger didn't help.

Before she realized it, she was pulling into the drive of her little house. She needed to call Mr. Dunne. He'd promised to take care of Major and Biddy and to check in at the clinic. She hoped he'd been able to convince MC to do that—she wanted to encourage him to come to work for her.

After the fifth ring, no answer. Maybe she would just drive over to get the dogs and catch him in person.

Nearing Brendan Dunne's farmhouse, she was unable to stop herself from glancing at the cabin nestled in the trees. MC's truck, but not Mr. Dunne's.

As she walked toward the cabin, gravel crunched. Mr. Dunne's pickup truck materialized.

She turned back toward the house, smiling at him as he pulled himself from the truck.

Shadows were lengthening, and while the days were getting longer, it still got dark by 6:30 p.m.

As she neared, she took note of the pinched expression on the old man's face.

"Hello, there, Nancy. I suppose you want those pups of yours." He smiled at her, but it didn't quite meet his eyes. "Sorry to hear about your father."

She swallowed. "Thank you. It happened faster than we thought." She sensed something wrong.

"Is everything okay?"

Mr. Dunne's eyes flitted toward the cabin, and something deep inside her quivered. Why, she didn't know. Sympathy for her fellow man?

No, she understood sympathy, and it didn't feel like this. This was fear. Something bad had happened to someone she had feelings for.

Feelings?

"MC is in the hospital." Mr. Dunne paused, ducked his head then glanced back up at her. "He had a little trouble with his pain medication."

"Oh, no." Her body went cold all over. Overdose. "Is he going to be okay?"

He nodded. "He will. They're keeping him a few days to make sure."

Past experiences flooded her mind. She had a roommate in college who almost died of a drug overdose. They had to ascertain whether this was an accident or a suicide attempt.

Chapter Twenty-Three

Two weeks after pulling into the Dunne farmyard and learning MC had been hospitalized, Nancy was back. This time, to help inoculate some calves.

She zipped up her coveralls and pulled her bag from behind the seat, then hesitated. Was it crazy to be drawn to a man even more messed up than she?

But the job had to be done.

About the time she got to the barn door, a soft mewing caught her attention. Kittens. Her lips lifted in a smile.

She peered around the doorway quietly, so as not to spook the mama cat and scatter the darlings, but instead of startling the animals, there MC sat on an old milking stool, one kitten climbing up his sling, another toddling around his feet, and the third held gently in his hands.

If only she had a camera. The tiny kittens made him look even bigger than he was. She'd never seen this side of MC.

Gently, she waved to catch his attention. His first glance up, his eyes lit. She'd noticed when he smiled, his eyes brightened. Maybe that was why she tried so hard to help him find the smile.

After a few seconds of silent communication, his eyes shuttered as he glanced down, releasing one kitten, and pulling the other off his sling. Nancy wanted to chuckle at the sight of him working so hard to disentangle the needle-sharp claws from the cloth.

"You're early." MC rose and walked toward the stall where the three calves stood, already angry to be manhandled once today, not to mention being separated from their bawling mamas.

Nancy followed him. "And hello to you too."

His lips twitched.

She heard the calves she'd come to see bawling right back to their mamas, expecting a rescue. When MC gestured for her to bypass them, he took her to the far stall where the most recent calf and his mother resided

"Is this our calf?" As soon as she said it, Nancy felt the flush of heat crawl across her chest, up her neck, and onto her face.

MC grinned, nodding. "This one is a handful. I keep telling him he'll end up as veal if he's not careful."

"Ouch." The mahogany-colored calf would be judged a rare specimen, with slightly curly hair, a sturdy stance, and a bellow that sounded like a calf twice his size. She didn't realize it when she released a deep, satisfied sigh.

He grinned, relaxed, leaning on the gate. "I know. He's something, isn't he?"

"His mama may have carried him, but I kind of feel like we can take a little pride in this fella too." She slid around the other side of the stall gate, holding her hand out in an open gesture.

"I guess we can take some of the credit."

Betsy, the calf's mother, bellowed in the next stall.

She leaned over the wall and spoke to the belligerent mama. "Oh, we're not hurting him." The calf came up and sniffed her fingers, not noticing she scratched his head with her other hand. "There you go, little fella."

"The patience of Job."

Nancy laughed. "Have you read Job?"

"It's been a while."

"Job's buddies and his wife tried to tell him to repent of whatever he'd done and get it over with, and he let 'em have it." She raised her eyebrows. "He might have been patient with God, but not his friends."

"Touché."

"I don't have to tell you—that's one of the main tenets of veterinary science. Waiting and hoping the animal miraculously cooperates."

"Very true." MC stood, watching her.

She was self-conscious, knowing he observed her every move. Looking up, she hoped her face wasn't as flushed as she suspected. "Let's get back to today's patients." She slipped back out of the stall and toward the three older calves, avoiding his eyes. "Do you have the syringes loaded?"

"Here they are." He handed the first one to her, standing close, she assumed, to intervene if the calf suddenly bolted. It wasn't that he made her nervous—more likely aware.

That was the word. Aware. Aware of him every time he came near.

After a minor tussle, the shots were given successfully. The last calf jerked away, and Nancy lost her balance, ending up on the hay in the stall, laughing.

"You okay?"

"Never better. Animals know how to squash your dignity, don't they?"

MC reached down with his good hand to help her up. She didn't argue, simply placing her small hand in his. She realized this was a time to accept help—no need to prove she was capable.

As soon as she got on her feet, he dropped her hand as if it burned. Did it?

Nancy stared too long before she averted her eyes. Looking over at the kittens, she smiled. The young felines were growing braver every minute. Even now, they ventured beyond the hay bales.

"I wish I needed a barn cat." She broke the silence.

"I do too." He chuckled. "Now we have three more animals to feed."

"At least they'll work for their supper. Eventually."

She twisted her lips and finally turned toward him. She needed his full attention.

"Yes?" MC cocked his head in question.

"Keep that thought." She pointed at him gently. "I'm still in need of an assistant at the clinic." He opened his lips to speak, but she shook her head and raised her hands. "I know, I know. You said no. I'm of the belief that a person can change their mind." She wrinkled her nose. "Mary Ann is considering making her maternity leave permanent."

She placed her hand on his arm as it rested on the gate. How could she reach this stubborn man?

Once she realized her touch was bordering on intimacy, she dropped her hand, trying to ignore the tingle.

With a boyish grin, he reached for her.

"Um ..." What was he doing?

He pulled a piece of hay out of her ponytail. "Thought you might not want your next stop to think you'd been rolling in the hay." With a twinkle in his eye, he quirked a brow.

Thank goodness he didn't wink. She would have been a goner. As it was, he'd pulled her up from the barn floor with one strong hand as if she weighed nothing. He could easily have pulled her to himself then, and she wasn't sure she would have objected.

Nancy's face flushed. She must be crimson. The heat of the barn made her want to unzip that coverall and feel a breeze.

"Thank you." She shook her head, sending him a mock glare.

"Nancy, I appreciate the offer, and I'm sorry you'll be in a bind without Mary Ann, but I ... I can't."

Was that defeat in his eyes? She could wait. It was early days yet. How could she convince him he would be okay, eventually? That she wanted to be a friend to him?

"Did you check the community college?"

She sighed. "I did, and they sent a couple of candidates down. What are they teaching kids these days?"

He scoffed. "You make it sound like we're ancient."

"I know. I guess ... I guess I feel like our generation has seen more." Dad's face flashed before her. Steven. Mom. Danny ... She'd seen too much, too young.

Nancy closed her eyes for a moment to gather her thoughts. It would be so easy to park there and relive every stinking event.

As she opened her eyes, she noticed MC staring at her intently. "I know what you mean." He looked away, then back at her. "I still see it."

Her heart broke. Yes, in his eyes, she recognized defeat, but also desperation and utter, utter sadness. What had he seen? What horrors had he experienced?

He cleared his throat and held out her bag, signaling the end of the conversation. "Thanks for your help."

"Is there anything I can say to make you change your mind?"

"It would take a miracle." His face softened into a slight—oh, so slight—smile. "And I don't know that God's in the miracle business anymore."

Chapter
Twenty-Four

For as many Sundays as he'd been back, either Mom or Grandpa had invited MC to go to church with them.

No way could he risk a flashback in a public place like that, and after his hospitalization, he could practically hear the thoughts in the heads of these people whom he grew up with.

"Look at him … they say he tried to *kill* himself with pills."

"Stay away from MC, honey. He isn't right in the head."

"Bless his heart. I wonder if he'll ever get back to normal."

There were a million scenarios, and they all ended up with the community shunning him.

At least his family tried to understand.

Grandpa told him Nancy had a young man from the high school helping out at the clinic.

Good. He'd been confident she'd be able to find someone, even if he didn't have the "extensive life experience" that they both did.

He shook his head to get her out of it. Funny how every thought circled back to Nancy. He went entire days without thoughts of Rebecca and the future he'd once imagined.

Rather than inflict himself on anyone, MC walked the property. His nighttime treks to cure insomnia hadn't worked. So maybe, since after the hospital stay, he'd come close to re-injuring his shoulder, he'd take it easy. Staying off roofs was mentioned. He could only hope fresh air in daylight hours would wear him out enough that he would sleep better.

Sleepless nights wore on him.

He walked down to the creek and then followed it for a half-mile or so. His ankle twinged from time to time, especially on uneven ground. That fateful night he went down, shot, he sprained it, but the doctors considered the injury so minor compared to the shoulder that it hadn't been treated properly. It took a long time for a bad sprain to heal.

Plant life budded and bloomed all over the place. He caught a mama rabbit and her babies outside their hole. Mama didn't waste any time corralling the young ones. The recent spring storms had filled the creek, and it rushed merrily toward the river it fed into.

All things were new.

Except him.

What would it be like to bring Nancy down here? He paused at a place he'd often picnicked with his grandparents. The low limbs of the willow tree framed the spot, drawing him in. This time of year, Grandma would watch for the perfect timing for their first picnic of the year.

He missed her.

But Nancy …

He thought by hiding out on the farm and not having contact with the outside world, he would put her out of his thoughts.

If anything, it made it worse.

"I'm lonely."

There. He'd said it out loud. Maybe just to himself and to God, but he'd said it. He didn't expect God to do anything about it. He wasn't even sure what he believed anymore. He'd prayed while in Vietnam. Oh, how he'd prayed. Cried out to God for protection for himself and his comrades, and look what happened.

He was sick of the "our timing is not God's timing" phrase, which he thought was an excuse for Him not answering prayer.

Yes, no, or wait. He'd been taught that God's answers were one of those three. Wait didn't seem like such a good idea, especially not in battle. With bullets and bayonets flying around the swamps and jungles—with his name on them.

MC shook his head. Nancy. She needed someone stable. Someone with prospects. Will assured him that he and Nancy didn't have feelings for one another, but MC couldn't imagine those feelings wouldn't grow, given time.

Would he be able to sit by and watch Will court Nancy?

It would drive him crazier than he already was.

Crazy enough to head to Auburn and finish his veterinary degree?

MONDAY AFTERNOON FOUND Nancy covered up in paperwork, forms, and reports beginning to overtake the top of the desk. Today she would teach Brent how to file, at least.

Brent had been a life-saver. Farm-raised, he was used to large animals, and he'd grown up with dogs and cats. He talked to her about the possibility of going to pre-vet school after he graduated from high school in May.

At least Nancy would have him for the summer.

She still tried to take care of the office work, as indicated by the current state of her desk, but he'd proven himself adept at making appointments and acting as a go-between between the animal owner and herself when things got busy.

The next round of in-clinic appointments began at 3:30, and it was almost that time. A snuffle at her knee caught her attention. She scratched Major's head. "Are you ready to go home and see Biddie?" He laid his chin on her knee, his solemn brown eyes looking up at her.

Why did they make her think of another pair of solemn brown eyes?

Stop it, Nancy. You don't have time for this.

She'd seen Mr. Dunne, as well as MC's parents, Connor and Marjorie, at church every Sunday—but never MC.

Maybe he'd given up on God. She wanted so badly to tell him not to. Give God time. Be patient. God was still in the "miracle business" he'd referred to.

But had she exhibited patience as bad things happened to her? Or, more recently, with her father? Had she gone to her family expecting a miracle?

The lump just below her throat, in her chest, overwhelmed her at times. She'd waited too long. She didn't give her father the peace that anyone, even the worst of parents, deserved.

But he asked. He confessed what he'd done, and the regret had been palpable. Maybe that was her miracle.

"Anybody home?" Brent's voice triggered the bounce in Major's step, and he rushed to the door to greet the young man, tail wagging.

The cheery greeting snapped her out of her reverie and back to the present. "Back here. Hi, Brent. How are you?"

He paused outside the office door and stashed his pile of books, tightly clasped together by an old leather belt, on the shelf above where winter coats and jackets would have been a month ago. "I'm good. Spent all day Saturday working calves. Wish there was a way to dehorn them before they got too big." He shook his head.

Nancy agreed. Dehorning cattle, even though farmers considered it necessary, was the least-humane practice she had to perform.

"Maybe someday they'll come up with a way to lessen the pain, at least." She pushed her chair back and put on her white coat. "Who knows? Maybe you'll be the one to develop a new method."

The thoughtful look on his face made her smile. Vet school, and the veterinary profession, would be lucky to have him. She had a feeling he could be the change the farming community needed.

In the meantime, she had a date with a twelve-year-old house cat who needed her shots. And from Nancy's experience the last time she countered Miss Kitty, she fully expected hissing, spitting, and scratching from the moment she walked through the examining room door.

Chapter
Twenty-Five

After a week back in a sling, MC got permission to leave it off with the understanding he couldn't push it to the extent he had before. If numbness returned, he put the sling back on and rested.

Rest. He hadn't had a good night's rest in over a month, except in the hospital. Not a good example.

The last few days of rain stopped the nighttime ramblings and had him pacing the floor of the cabin. He could spend the day working in the chapel with Grandpa, but at night, he didn't want to disturb his grandfather's sleep.

The sunshine warmed his face.

He paused to pick up a few limbs that had fallen off the ancient maple tree between the cabin and the farmhouse, then made his way to the chapel. The sun hit it just right. The small steeple was weathered, but the wind and storm hadn't hurt it.

But the window didn't look right to him. A sick feeling in the pit of his stomach told him they were going to have to get that window fixed sooner, rather than later.

"Morning, son." Grandpa raised a hand and walked toward him. "Sleep well?"

"Yeah," he lied. No reason to worry him.

Grandpa's pace matched his as they walked to the chapel. His keen gaze told MC he knew better than to believe what his grandson said, but Grandpa didn't say anything. "Looks like we need to get that window seen about. Think we can get it out today?"

"I don't see why not." MC took out his pocket knife and dug around the sill plate of the aging window. "Looks like the only part broken is in this corner. I think it finally gave in to gravity and weather."

Grandpa nodded. "We'll do Uncle Patrick proud."

MC carefully removed the thin wooden beads that held the window in place. They'd placed masking tape on both sides of the glass to hold it together as much as possible.

Carefully—oh, so carefully—they tilted the window and carried it over to the makeshift table created out of a panel of plywood and sawhorses.

Finally, they got the window in a horizontal position and took their hands off the window, both breathing a sigh of relief.

"I don't care if I never do that again." Grandpa mopped the perspiration from his brow.

"Me, neither, so let's make sure it's done right this time." MC sat on the pew next to the glasswork of art, staring at its beauty even in its less-than-perfect state. The comparison with the Vietnamese chapel's window was beginning to fade; the family connection to this one was drawing him in.

Grandpa adjusted his bifocals to study the pieces of glass. "There are a few cracks that we can have replaced."

"And the one piece that came most of the way out." MC nodded. "Where does it go from here?"

Grandpa pushed his hands in his pockets, eyes still on the window. "There's a restoration place in Nashville. They do work for a lot of churches." He glanced up at MC. "You up for a road trip?"

MC nodded. He didn't want to. Didn't want to leave the farm. He figured only Grandpa could talk him into it.

"Good. I made us an appointment for tomorrow." Grandpa grinned and winked at MC.

"Nothing like waiting 'til the last minute to tell me."

"Didn't want you to have time to talk yourself out of it."

MC shook his head. Grandpa had him right where he wanted him.

~

THE DRIVE to Nashville with Grandpa had been uneventful. On their way back home, they stopped at a diner along the road and had the typical greasy-spoon blue plate-special of meat, three sides, cornbread, and dessert.

The pies in the case were tempting.

The waitress was no Mavis, but she kept the drinks topped off and the cornbread coming. It was nice, for once, to be in a place where nobody stared at him as if he might explode any minute.

MC took his arm out of the sling and stretched it while they waited for the slices of coconut cream and cherry pie they'd ordered.

"Two weeks is a lot quicker than I thought they could do." Grandpa poured creamer into his coffee, glancing at the counter to gauge the moment their dessert would arrive.

"I've got my VA doc appointment in a couple of weeks," MC grunted. "It was supposed to be in July, but my little stint in the hospital had them changing it from another three months to six weeks, instead."

Grandpa nodded. "Can't hurt. And, it'll save us a trip. Kill two birds with one stone."

The pie arrived, and for the first time in a while, MC's mouth watered. The "mile-high meringue" on the coconut pie was impressive.

"That pie's too pretty to eat." Grandpa chuckled. "But this looks pretty tasty too."

Calm, and comforting—spending time with Grandpa was the best medicine. He'd decided if the love of God resembled anything like the love of his grandpa, he needed to think about it more seriously.

Chapter
Twenty-Six

Nancy had been so busy the last few weeks, even with Brent's help, that she'd neglected the business side of the clinic. She made the mistake, with no time to get to the bank during open hours, of hanging on to cash in the little safe in her office. Fortunately, nobody thought about a veterinary clinic as a possible place to break into for a quick infusion of cash. Drugs, maybe. Cash? No.

She was leaving the bank when she turned at the sound of her name.

Bert.

Since their first, and thankfully, last date, she'd been cordial, but sometimes, even at church, she was aware of him watching her, biding his time. Maybe waiting until she appeared lonely.

So far, she'd been able to put him off without outright refusal. Well, except for the altercation in the parking lot of the bus station.

Maybe she'd overreacted. Men acted like that. Didn't they?

She closed her eyes and smiled. Maybe she could feign being in a hurry?

"Hi Bert, how are you?"

"Never better, never better." He paused, looking at the people milling around. "Can I have a word with you?"

She checked her watch.

"It'll just take a minute." He gestured toward his office, labeled "Assistant Branch Manager."

She stood next to the desk in the cramped room.

"Have a seat." He claimed his desk chair and gestured to the set of chairs across from him. Was he making a concerted effort to be respectful?

"I really don't …"

He stood. "Sorry, I know you have animals to treat."

Why did he make it sound like the value of her profession reached just a hair above a hobby?

He smiled at her, puffing out his chest a little. The wide blue-and-orange tie jiggled a bit as the buttons across his chest tightened. Almost as tall as MC, he was soft, whereas she imagined MC was made of lean muscle. She couldn't help making the comparison. "I wondered if you'd be interested in going out to dinner?"

"Um …"

"Before you say no, I've got tickets to the play at the high school a week from Friday." Bert shrugged. "Not exactly Broadway, but I like to support our kids."

"And the arts."

"Of course." His smile came across as genuine enough. "I hope you didn't misunderstand my intentions last time we went out."

She was pretty sure she hadn't "misread his intentions," but was he asking for forgiveness? And if he was, could she extend it to him?

"And I was rude when I saw you in Clarksville. I'd just had an argument with my mother, and was taking it out on all of womankind. I'm sorry if you took it wrong." Bert was piling it on.

Was this an apology or a way to explain away bad behavior? On the other hand, we're called to forgive because we were forgiven. She had to forgive her dad after he was dead. It was too late to restore that relationship. Never again would she have that hanging over her.

"How about it? A night celebrating 'the arts' and a good meal, maybe?"

First thought? Could this be an opportunity to live out her faith? Maybe he was seeking to do the right thing.

Second thought—MC. What would it be like to attend a local

function with him? As his date? Her assistant, Brent, had a supporting role in the high school production, making it reason enough to attend. She'd love to hear what MC's laugh sounded like.

Random.

"What do you say?"

How long had she sat there, her brain whirling between theological questions of forgiveness and daydreaming about a man who wasn't in the least interested in her and basically told her so? Looking at her watch, she'd only been in la-la-land for less than a minute.

She took a deep breath and pasted on a smile. Why not? She planned to go anyway.

He couldn't be as bad as that niggling feeling she had told her. He'd risen in the ranks of the local bank. One couldn't get more conservative than that.

Maybe she should ask Mary Ann what she thought.

No, she was at home, enamored of her new baby boy. Nancy secretly hoped Mary Ann would come back soon, but she couldn't blame her one bit for wanting to stay home with him. Some days Nancy longed for a home and family of her own. She hadn't had the best example in her parents. But her brother? He had done well.

"I'd like that." There, she'd said it. The impulse to roll her eyes at his smug look of triumph had to be squashed. She'd give him one more chance.

"How about I pick you up at six for a quick dinner, then we can head to the auditorium?"

"Sounds nice." She peeked at her watch again. "I've really got to go. My next appointment is in ten minutes."

"Thanks, Nancy. See you next Friday." His smile made her pause, but surely, she imagined it.

Could she trust him?

❧

Sleep.

It was vital to health and sanity, and yet, closing his eyes scared MC to death.

The last deep sleep? His accidental overdose. Not exactly the kind of sleep he needed.

Grandpa drove to Nashville for the combination VA doctor appointment and to retrieve the window. There, in the warm sunlight coming in the back window of the pickup truck, he'd slept. Why? Because he was safe. Maybe he should start sleeping during the day.

He dreaded the appointment. How he would like to skip it and go right to the window artisan. But unfortunately, if he didn't keep up his appointments, the government wouldn't pay for treatment.

Treatment—a generous description.

Some people compared the care they received at the VA to a veterinarian—he resented that.

"You don't have to go in with me." MC hated to drag Grandpa in and out of the large building. "Just drop me off, and I'll find you afterward."

Grandpa nodded. "I can do that." He grinned at MC. "Brought my Sunday School book with me to study, just in case."

Of course, he did.

Leaving Grandpa comfortably ensconced in the pickup with his quarterly and Bible, MC entered the building.

So many people.

This time he tried not to look around at his fellow patients. Tracing his way through the halls that seemed too narrow for a hospital, he soon found his doctor's office.

He picked up a year-old copy of *Newsweek* and was halfway through an article on the moon landing when his name was called.

"I understand you had a little health scare a few weeks ago." The doctor, same as last time, glanced from the chart to MC, a question in his eyes. "Have you had any other … er, episodes?"

Oh, brother. Here we go again.

"It wasn't attempted suicide."

The doctor nodded.

"I took a pill, then woke up not realizing it hadn't been long enough to take another." He glared at the doctor. "That's all."

The doctor scribbled in his folder, nodding. He had the authority to send him to Middle Tennessee Mental Hospital.

"You understand you'll have to pass a psych eval to get back into active duty?"

Ah, so this was the "Suck it up, buttercup" speech.

"I'm handling it." If he'd had any thought of telling the doctor about the craziness he'd been going through, he killed it then and there.

"If you want to continue receiving veterans' benefits, you'll have to." The doctor pulled out a note from the pages on the clipboard. "Looks like your stateside commanding officer wants you to contact him at Fort Campbell ASAP."

Bile rose.

The doctor sat on the stool across from his chair. "Look, I see a lot of guys in the same shape as you, having trouble getting integrated back into civilian life." He shrugged. "Thing is, you've got to prove you're ready either to go back or to stay and be a productive citizen. According to your family doctor, you're not ready for either one right now."

He couldn't get out of there fast enough.

MC came out of the building with his sling in his hand, not on his arm. He enjoyed the freedom of not wearing it. Within a few seconds, he spotted Grandpa's truck. His grandpa could buy a new one but couldn't give up his rusty 1962 International Harvester Light-Line.

MC'd never understood why, with a myriad of colors available, his grandparents chose "Coral Pine." To him, it was pink. Grandpa always said he let Grandma pick the color that time. At least it was easy to find in a parking lot.

"How'd it go?"

How to answer? He frowned. "I'm not sure."

"You're either okay or you're not."

"The arm is better." MC scoffed. "He told me I'd have to pass a psych evaluation to go back to active duty."

Grandpa pulled out of the parking lot, heading south toward the stained-glass repair shop. "Doesn't sound like they care much about your mental state if the evaluation is the only thing they go by."

MC hadn't considered it would be this hard. He thought once he got home, the fight would be over, and everything would go back to life pre-Vietnam. For two years it was all about survival. Keep himself and his dog alive, and defeat the enemy.

Now? His enemy was time. It stole his sleep. Invaded his dreams.

Sometimes it robbed him of everything he held dear. His reason for going to Vietnam was to keep the home fires burning. Life would be good—*after*.

Instead, he got home and things weren't the same. A part of him understood that. Maybe it wasn't that *things* were different, but *him*.

Chapter Twenty-Seven

Nancy came home to an empty refrigerator and a couple of dogs wanting her attention. There'd been too much going on to rectify either.

Rummaging through the cabinets in the small cottage, she found a can of tomato soup and some milk that passed the "smell test."

"Cream of tomato it is."

She stirred it together on a slow burner, and as soon as it started bubbling, her phone rang. Great.

Turning off the burner, she picked up the baby-blue phone with the extra-long cord and brought it a few steps into the kitchen. Maybe it would be a quick call, and she could get right back to it.

"Hello?" She held the phone to her ear with her shoulder and commenced stirring.

"Nancy, it's Richard."

"How are you?" Why did she have a feeling she wouldn't like this conversation?

"I know you're busy with your tech out of commission, but we've had someone ask about buying the house."

Whoa. She couldn't say anything but instead turned off the burner and sank into a kitchen chair.

"I told them we hadn't got Dad's things out yet, and that I'd have to talk to my sister—hence the call."

She could imagine his smirky expression.

"I understand." She closed her eyes. It had to be done. It was the job of the younger generation to attend to the belongings of the older, and now it was their turn. "How long do you think it will take?"

"I'm hoping a weekend will get it—it's all the time I have available."

She picked up her pink notebook/planner from the counter where she'd dropped her things on her way in the door.

"I'll have to see if my standby is available. If he is, I can come this weekend. How would that be? Do you think Saturday and Sunday will be enough time?"

Her brother scoffed. "It has to be, doesn't it?"

"I'm sorry it's all on you."

"Hey, don't be. I can start pulling the perishables—food and medicine—and save the grunt work for you."

"Cute." She had to grin, though, at what she noticed, even over the phone—fondness. Warmth. "If there are any of the housewares you and Linda want, you're more than welcome to it."

"I'll tell her. She's had her eye on a quilt, I know."

"I'm sure there will be enough stuff to go around, and then some." She paused, a mist clouding her vision. "It's happening, isn't it?"

"Yeah." Did she imagine the sound of a sniff on the other end of the line? "But hey, we gotta do it, and if we can sell the house, we're that much ahead. Dad had a few debts we'll have to pay off."

She sighed. Of course, he did. "I'll make that call. If I can get an answer tonight, I'll let you know. Tomorrow at the latest. Will that work?"

"Sounds good. Thanks, sis."

"Love you."

"Love you too."

She hung up the phone, her heart strangely lifted. That may have been the first time they had expressed love for one another. It was a God-thing that she was comfortable being the instigator.

~

So far, the three emergency on-call vets within a fifty-mile radius—including Doc Phillips—were unavailable on short notice. Nancy hadn't given up, but she doubted the success of her mission. She needed to be there with her brother. The sooner they took care of their dad's things, the sooner they could look to the future instead of constantly glancing back at the past as if a specter followed them around.

Only one more name came to mind. MC Dunne. He'd said no to every request and offer, but would he—could he— do this for her? She could call, but something told her this request needed a personal touch.

Driving up the gravel road to the farmhouse and cabin, she parked. Rusty met her at the door of her truck.

"Hey, boy, looks like you're healing up nicely." She squatted on the ground to love on him, and wished she'd thought to bring one of the dogs with her. "Sorry I didn't bring one of your buddies."

"Nancy." MC's voice stopped her, and she straightened, slightly irritated at the leap in her chest upon hearing his voice.

Not fair. His gravelly voice shouldn't affect her like that.

"Hi." She stood there, her hand still resting on Rusty's head.

She avoided looking him in the eyes. MC's eyes were so, so dark. Mysterious. They might draw her in. "Looks like Rusty is healing up nicely." She got up the nerve to glance up at him, feeling the heat on her face. Some girls didn't blush. She didn't just blush, she turned a brilliant red. There was a gentle smile on his face.

"He's doing well. No infection. The cast came off without any problem." He shrugged, a little sheepish. "I probably should have brought him back to you for that."

Her lips twitched. "Anyone else, I would say, yes, you should have. I think you know your dog, and you know how to care for him."

"Rusty and I have been together for a long time." MC leaned forward to caress Rusty's silky head, putting his eyes even with hers.

"He's special."

"You have no idea." The look on his face was impassive. No emotion. If he felt anything, he'd gotten very good at hiding it. Much better than her. He stood and held out his hand to help her up. Her mind went immediately back to their last encounter. In the barn.

"I've come to ask for help again."

MC straightened, stuffed his hands in his pockets, and glanced away. As he turned, she could see the black curls on his neck, brushing his collar, begging to be touched. But she didn't.

"Nancy, I ..."

"Look, I wouldn't ask, except my brother needs my help. We gotta go through my dad's things. I told him I could only come for the weekend, but every emergency vet I usually call is unavailable this weekend. It's two days." She searched his eyes, hoping he could see, without her saying it, that she was begging this time.

He stretched his neck, as if to pop it, took a deep breath, and leaned up against her truck, arms crossed this time. Staring in the distance, Nancy wondered about his thoughts. What was he looking at, if anything?

"You might not get any calls at all. Sometimes we have a quiet weekend."

"Do you think anybody would trust me to take care of their animals, even in an emergency?" He shot her a look that pinned her to her spot.

"What do you mean?" So, he'd had a little trouble readjusting. Just about everybody that came back from Vietnam had trouble getting back to "real life."

"You know what people are saying."

She closed her eyes and took a deep breath. "Honestly, MC, I've been so busy the last few weeks, I don't know what anybody is saying." Her frustration must be showing. "I just know you are my last hope at being able to get away to take care of my dead father's property."

He nodded, head down as if his shoes were the most interesting things in the world.

"So? Can you be on call for a couple of days? I can leave a message with the service that you are not a licensed vet, but I've seen you at work. You are highly qualified to take care of most emergency cases." She stared at him. Earlier, she didn't want him to look at her. Now? Now she needed to see his face. Gauge what he was thinking.

Chapter Twenty-Eight

Saturday morning dawned bright and clear. The budding trees and spring flowers blooming gave Nancy hope it would be a good day. That there wouldn't be any triggers that laid her out completely.

They'd accomplished a lot the evening before.

Clothing to the homeless shelter? Check.

Dinner eaten and the kitchen packed up for the Salvation Army? Check.

Magazines boxed up to take to the dump? Check.

Books, many of them hers, packed and loaded in her truck? Check. Her little house wouldn't know what hit it.

Richard had called it "done" around ten p.m. the night before. They'd all put in a full day's work at their jobs, then came to the house and put in the equivalent of another.

They saved the attic until that morning, thank goodness. It was dark enough in the daytime, with the gable windows lighting it somewhat. At night, it gave her the heebie-jeebies.

They each picked up as many empty boxes as they could carry up the creaky stairs. When they got to the top, they all stood for a moment, looking at the unreasonable amount of stuff that had accumulated over the years.

"Did Dad get rid of *anything*?" Nancy started picking through the nearest pile. There were at least ten lamps, some of which were broken. An old chair in bad shape. A rocking horse and a cradle were pushed into the corner. Christmas decorations—most of which Nancy hadn't seen since Mom died—were everywhere. Boxes, trunks, and a clothes rod filled with moth-eaten clothing rounded out the items they needed to go through.

"Something tells me it would be easier to light a match than to go through all this stuff." Richard's shoulders sagged in defeat, and they hadn't even begun.

Nancy and Linda regarded one another with a nod, squaring their shoulders.

Linda pinned her husband with a look, and said, "We can do this."

He threw his hands up, accidentally hitting a bare light bulb that burned out who knows how long ago. "I'll go look for some spare bulbs. We need all the light we can get."

"They're in the box next to the back door. I had a feeling we might need some, so I didn't get rid of them." Linda pulled out a large black trash bag and handed Nancy one too. "Shall we start with the low-hanging fruit—trash?"

"Yes, ma'am." Nancy eyed the clothes, most of them ruined by now. "Let's start there. There may be some things to salvage."

"I highly doubt it, but if we get rid of that stuff, it'll give us more room to sort other things."

After replacing the burned-out light bulbs, Richard scrounged through some boxes in a corner of the attic. "Hey, I found some of my trophies."

Linda glanced at Nancy and shook her head. "Great. I have a feeling they'll be going to our house."

"I heard that." He walked over with a particularly large one. "This one, mainly."

Nancy read the inscription and laughed. "First Place, Morgan County Spelling Bee."

"Hey, not bad for a fifth-grader. I beat out the eighth-graders."

Linda laughed. "I don't see any sports trophies."

"No, I was an egghead, and proud of it."

"Runs in the family, I'm afraid." Nancy smiled, still digging through a box she'd come across with her childhood memories. "Steve was the jock. Mom graduated top of her class, and Dad had a scholarship to a college in Missouri but didn't go."

"Yeah, back then, if you wanted to get married right out of high school, you didn't go to college." Richard gave her a sad smile. "I wonder if things would have been different if he'd taken that scholarship?"

Nancy paused and peered at her brother, who so resembled their dad. "If that had happened, we probably wouldn't be here."

He nodded. "Still, would he have been happier? Would he have treated you better?"

Her heart hurt for the guilt Richard carried. He was at home in the good days. The days before Mom's sickness changed the dynamics of their family, and they had a sober Dad.

"What's this?" Linda pulled out a small trunk from under the eaves. On top, the gold letters read "Adeline."

"No idea." Nancy walked over to her sister-in-law. "Let's pull it over by the window where there's more light."

Richard dragged it into place and tried to open it. "It's locked." He stared from one woman to another. "Do you want me to break it?"

Nancy thought a moment, and she jumped up. "I think I know where the key is."

She ran down to her room and pulled out the drawer in the jewelry box that had been Mom's. After she died, Nancy asked Dad if she could have it, and he was glad to get it out of his sight. There, nestled in the bottom in yellowed tissue paper, lay a gold key.

Once upstairs, the key slipped in and turned easily in the lock, but the lid stuck.

Richard tried to pry it open but couldn't get a good grip on it. "Now, I need a screwdriver."

Nancy made her second trip down the stairs, this time returning more slowly, but with the tool Richard requested. "Here you go."

She bent over, looking over his shoulder, and clapped at the slight "pop," and the trunk opened.

"Oh." Nancy pulled a small stool over to the trunk and carefully pulled things out. It had been packed ever-so-carefully, undoubtedly by Mom. She'd never seen the wedding album or the scrapbook of memories from their parents' courtship. The siblings gaped in wonder. "These are amazing."

"I remember the albums, but that doesn't explain the name on the trunk." He reached farther down into the container, finally pulling a box out, also bearing the name "Adeline."

Both hesitated. Nancy spoke first. "Do you want to open it?"

Richard shook his head. "No, go ahead."

She carefully lifted the lid off the yellowed box, to find crocheted and knitted blankets, bonnets, and booties. Opening a tiny velvet jewelry pouch revealed a gold baby ring and necklace, still as shiny as new, she imagined.

"These things were never used." Nancy glanced up at her brother, tears in her eyes.

Putting the items back in the order they came out, she placed the box carefully back into the trunk and closed the lid.

"We need to call Aunt Jean."

Chapter
Twenty-Nine

Tears trickled down Aunt Jean's face as she fingered the delicate items from the box marked, "Adeline."

"We were all so excited." Jean smiled through her tears. "Adeline would have been the oldest grandchild, instead of you, Richard."

"What happened?" Nancy passed her aunt a tissue.

The older woman sighed, sadness etched on her face. "You know, we didn't talk about things like this in the forties." She shook her head. "My, have times changed. Maybe if John had been willing to talk about it after he got back from Europe …"

Looking down at her hands, she absently fingered the delicate white bonnet. "Your mom found out she was pregnant about six months after she and John were married." She smiled. "Lucy and John were so excited. They had big plans. I begged Mother to teach me how to crochet so I could make the bonnet and booties. I started as soon as we learned she was going to have a baby."

Aunt Jean put her hand on Nancy's resting on the table. "Your mom had a rough pregnancy. Had to be on bed rest for the last few months. As far as the doctor could tell, back then, everything was fine with the baby, so he advised her to rest and wait for delivery." She closed her eyes. "Then, we got the phone call from John about Adeline's birth, and I couldn't wait to see her." Jean sighed. "I didn't know anything was wrong, but afterward, Mother said she could tell something wasn't right as soon as she laid eyes on the precious child. She was pale and lethargic, with a blue cast to her skin. She didn't seem to want to eat. So, so sad."

Nancy was stunned. She might have had a big sister. "How long …"

"She lived three weeks. Just long enough for us to fall completely in love with her. Mother said she was too good for this world—that the Lord wanted her back with Him."

Just imagining the pain her parents had gone through made Nancy hurt in her heart.

"After the funeral, your daddy shut himself off. He wanted to dull the pain, so he started drinking. He'd started drinking to excess in Germany before they married. His unit liberated one of the Nazi concentration camps. I can't even imagine what he saw, or the things he had to do. He never talked about it, and we didn't ask."

Jean shook her head sadly. "But this time? This time he wanted to obliterate his senses. He wanted to forget there'd ever been a baby, and he forbade us to talk about her. Even your mom."

"But how did she survive it, not able to share it—especially with her husband?" Linda shook her head in disbelief. She reached for Richard's hand, and he squeezed it. "I can't even imagine."

"Nobody could. Several people, including our pastor, tried to talk to him, tried to tell him Lucy needed him more than ever." Aunt Jean swallowed. "We started noticing bruises on Lucy's arms. I caught her trying to cover them up one day, and I asked her. She admitted to being tired. So, so, tired, and she didn't know how much longer she could take it. It wasn't long until she found out she was pregnant with you, Richard."

"Was that why you didn't want to see Dad before he died?" Richard gave her a sympathetic look.

She nodded, grabbing another tissue. "Partly. I hated him for hurting her. For doing to her what our daddy had done to Mother and the rest of us. It wasn't all about his experience in the war."

So, their dad followed the pattern. Her father hit her. His father hit him. Did no one give him an example of how to be a man? A real man?

"Lucy finally told him she was pregnant again, and that she would leave him if he didn't stop drinking and if he ever raised a hand to her or their child again."

They went through some boxes of things that had belonged to their dad's family—pictures of people they didn't recognize, old linens, and documents. After that, Aunt Jean left, promising that they wouldn't wait so long to get together, now that they'd reconnected.

Nancy, Richard, and Linda sat around the table, stunned.

"She left him, eventually, when she died." Nancy was trying so hard to understand what made a person violent with another. "He stopped drinking for her. She was gone, so he started again."

"Right after Mom died, he talked about being angry with her." Richard stared off into nothing, thinking. "I thought he was crazy, talking about being angry at someone who died."

"Some family tree we've got here, isn't it, brother?" Nancy's words had an edge to them. She completely understood being angry at someone who'd died—she would probably always be angry with her father. But how to stop the cycle?

Linda stood up, packing the little things back into the trunk, then the wedding pictures and other photographs. They were all pictures of happy times, or in the case of Baby Adeline, horrifically sad times.

"What if …" Richard glanced at Linda and started to speak, then stopped.

"Sometimes you have to depend on the offshoots of the family tree to get things right." Linda went to her husband, still seated at the table, and hugged him tightly. "You're not your father, nor are you your grandfather."

Nancy studied her family. They were all hurting because of one man. Linda nailed it. Being abusive was a choice made by the abuser.

At that moment, Nancy made a conscious decision—she would not be a victim.

Chapter Thirty

MC raked his hand over his face as he left the Soldier Support Office. He'd done it. He'd come, alone, to see his Commanding Officer, only to find out he wasn't there. After waiting an hour, he decided to go home and called instead.

"Lieutenant Dunne?"

MC straightened at his name. "Major Jackson." He turned, walked to his CO, and saluted.

"At ease, Lieutenant."

MC eased back into military formation—feet apart, right foot in place, and hands clasped behind his body. His shoulder injury made it harder than he thought it would.

Major Jackson chuckled. "I mean truly at ease, soldier."

MC cracked a smile. He'd met the major a few times. Always a stand-up guy, but then he also had the power to send him right back to Vietnam.

"How are you, Lieutenant Dunne?"

"Good, sir."

"Glad to hear it."

"Yes, sir."

The major's eyes narrowed, focused on MC's face. "I'd say you're due a haircut, but my son's hair is twice as long as yours, and I've been told by my wife to mind my own business." He took off his hat and rubbed his hand across his bald head. "I guess I should be proud my son still has hair to grow."

MC tried to relax. Something about encountering a neatly pressed uniform after sharing the horrors of war made it incongruous.

"I apologize for not calling sooner, sir."

Major Jackson waved him off. "Don't think anything of it. I know you're still healing. I get the reports from the VA doc. He seems to think you're much improved, but still a little wobbly." He clasped his hands behind his back. "Does that sound like an accurate assessment?"

"Yes, sir." MC stared down at the toes of his boots, his mind doing somersaults, wondering what the major had to say. "I understand you want to talk to me about what comes next?"

"I do." The major nodded across the drive at the base commissary. "Would you like a cup of coffee?"

"Sir, I've been drinking coffee for an hour."

He burst out laughing. "I suppose you have. Well, if not that, how about a Coke?"

"Thank you, sir."

They walked over and grabbed a table at the back.

Once settled with drinks, the major continued. "As you can see, you have options. If you want to re-up for another tour in Vietnam, we can make that happen." Major Jackson quirked an eyebrow at him. "But I don't think that's what you want, is it?"

"No, sir. May I be frank, sir?"

"By all means." The major leaned back in the booth and took a sip of his coffee.

"I had almost finished my second tour, sir. If I were to go back, well, I don't think I would come out alive."

Major Jackson straightened. "There are state-side assignments, as well, if you think you might be interested. I understand you were almost finished with your veterinary degree before you were drafted."

"Yes, sir."

"You could have gotten an exemption for being in school."

MC took a deep breath. He peered down at his hands, wrapped around the sweating glass of Coke, then back up at the Major. "I'm not one to shirk my duty. My country called, and I answered to the best of my ability."

"I understand. I think the Purple Heart and the Silver Star both tell us a lot about the quality of your service."

"Thank you, sir, but all I did was survive."

"That's where you are wrong."

"Sir?"

"I read in your file that you were shot saving three men in your unit. To me, that spells bravery. It's why you were awarded the Silver Star. It is presented to anyone who—" he looked down at the file in his hand and read aloud, "—is cited for gallantry in action against an enemy of the United States." "

MC didn't know. In the craziness of being pulled off the battlefield, losing Gunnar, and passing out cold, he didn't know he saved lives that night. It was all a blur.

"Your unit captured a high-ranking Viet Cong leader a week later, and it was because you saved those particular lives." The major cleared his throat. "Now, I understand you lost your partner on that run."

Gunnar. "Yes." What could he say? "He died saving my life."

The major leaned forward, drawing MC into his gaze. "I don't want that to go to waste."

"Sir?"

"We have a position opening up for a dog handler trainer at Fort Benning, Georgia."

Could he, maybe, repay the debt he owed to Gunnar?

MC HAD a phone installed after he'd lived in the cabin for a few weeks. He'd thought he could get away with using Grandpa's phone and stay under the radar that way. Being the emergency contact for Dr. Nancy Jean Baker, he was glad he had it.

But then, all weekend, he worried it would ring.

He had a lot to think about that night. Major Jackson gave him options. And, he had more options than staying in the U.S. Army.

Fort Benning was about fifty miles from Auburn, where he could finish his DVM. Could he work and finish his credentials?

Maybe he should forget the Army and go to Auburn, all in. But then, he loved the military K9 program. The project had proven invaluable.

There were so many things he'd like to see changed. First and foremost, what happens to the K9 after it's injured or retired or its handler goes home? He'd never been able to get a straight answer about what would happen after the war ended. He could be the change the program needed.

Maybe being a veterinarian wasn't in his future. Nancy was doing a good job. If he went back to the Army, would he grow to resent her for taking his spot? Why did he care?

Nancy.

MC leaned back into the soft chair, feet on the ottoman, thinking about her. What did he have to offer? A messed-up head that could as easily turn to drugs as to God. He scoffed. Probably more likely to turn to drugs, these days.

At what point did he start leaving God out of his life? He hadn't completely abandoned his faith in Vietnam, although he had started going his own way and expected God to catch up. Back then, he had an amazing girlfriend and thought he could singlehandedly win the war on behalf of Uncle Sam.

There were things he and Rebecca did—things God, their parents, and his religious background wouldn't approve of, so, he let that part of his life slide. Kept up the appearance of being a Christian. Mom and Dad weren't around, so who would know?

It didn't take long after he arrived in Vietnam for the doubts and insecurity to creep in. He read his Bible and had more questions than answers. Job? This guy spent chapter after chapter asking God why this was happening to him.

MC could relate.

It started a few months into his first tour—and about the time he received Rebecca's letter.

The ringing phone pulled him out of his head.

So much for nobody needing emergency vet help this weekend.

Chapter Thirty-One

"Do you need help loading him up?" MC hoped his first emergency call would be his last.

"He doesn't weigh much. I can do it."

Mavis had called in a panic. The usually calm, cool, and collected waitress was beside herself about her beloved poodle, Jingles. The little dog was all she had since her husband died in Korea.

"Meet me at the clinic."

"On my way." Mavis hung up without a goodbye.

MC grabbed the leather bag and rushed to the truck, waving at Grandpa on the porch. "Emergency at the clinic. Be back later."

Grandpa saluted and smiled. It probably tickled the old man to see MC so intent on something.

He arrived at the clinic quickly, unlocking the door as she drove up. Holding the door open while she carried Jingles into the examining room, MC shook his head. "Jingles, what have you gotten yourself into?"

He had to grin. This kind of emergency he could handle.

The round beef roast bone encircled Jingles' lower jaw, creating panic in the little canine. Anyone nervous about dogs needed to steer clear of this one.

"I don't know where he found it. I haven't cooked a beef roast in ages." Mavis was in tears. "I found him like this after work, running in circles like a crazy thing. I like to have never got him still enough to see what was wrong. I tried pulling it off, but it's stuck on there good."

"You wouldn't have been able to hold on to him and get it off at the same time, so you were right to call." He glanced up at her as he checked his vitals. "I'm sure you'd rather have Doctor Baker."

"Nonsense. I've seen you take care of this community's animals since you were a kid. I trust you."

Relief flooded through him. He had Mavis's confidence, but what about other people?

"I'm going to have to sedate him, because if I don't, one of two things could happen. He could jerk his head and end up with a dislocated jaw, or I could end up with a dog bite." He smiled at Mavis, and she calmed down. "It sounds worse than it is."

She took a deep breath. "Do it."

He nodded, then went to the cabinet to find the sedative and syringe to give Jingles the injection. In a few minutes, the struggling dog relaxed, and MC worked on getting the bone off his lower jaw.

"We'll try to work it off, first, maybe with some lubricant. If that doesn't work, we'll use the bone saw."

Mavis's eyes grew round. "Isn't that dangerous? What if you cut him?"

"A bone saw is a flexible wire with handles on both ends. Don't worry, Jingles won't be in any danger. Some people try to get these off with a hacksaw, but we can do better than that." He grinned at her. "He'll get a good nap and wake up without an obstacle in his mouth."

She nodded, stroking the sleeping dog. "You'll be okay, Jingles. Doctor Dunne will take care of you."

Doctor Dunne. Wow. Nobody had ever called him that before, and he liked it—even if it wasn't entirely accurate.

"Just MC, no doctor yet."

"You will be. I have faith in you."

MC wished he had as much faith in himself as Mavis did.

He pulled out a tube of petroleum jelly and daubed some around the bone where it was stuck behind his canine teeth. Wriggling it back and forth, it didn't budge.

"Would you be up for some assisting?"

"Sure. What do you need?"

"See how I'm pulling on the skin around his jaw and teeth? Try to hold it back, and maybe I can pull it off."

Mavis did as MC asked. After several tries, they both straightened. "Nobody ever said it would be easy, did they? I guess this is the dog equivalent of a kid sticking a penny up his nose." MC considered his patient.

"Will you have to cut it off?"

"I'm afraid so." He searched the cabinet where Doc Phillips kept the bone saw, and, sure enough, Nancy hadn't moved it. Thank goodness. The anesthetic wouldn't last much longer, and he didn't want to waste time hunting equipment.

He threaded the twisted wire through the bone, then attached the other handle to the "eye" at the end of the wire. Pulling back and forth, quickly, powder from the bone flew out, and after a few minutes, it was through. The other side had to be cut, as well, to get the bone off his jaw, but it took less time than the first. In no time, Jingles was free.

"Thank you, Jesus." Mavis glanced heavenward. "MC, you were a lifesaver. I sure wouldn't have wanted him to have to deal with that until Dr. Baker got back. Bless her heart, she needed the time to get her daddy's affairs in order."

"She should be back on Monday."

MC examined the dog's mouth for lacerations, but only found a few scratches on his lower gums. He rubbed some disinfectant on the wounds. "He'll be fine once he sleeps off the sedative."

"Thank you so much. When I saw you were the emergency vet, I was relieved. I didn't want to go to someone I didn't know." She chuckled as she picked up the limp poodle. "'Course, I didn't know Dr. Baker at first, either, but she fit in real well from the beginning."

Of course, she did. He sighed inwardly.

"I'm sure. She's a good vet."

"What are your plans to finish up your vet training?" She gave him a sideways glance, arching a brow in question.

"I'm not sure. There are a few things I'm considering."

"Well, you trust God to lead you, and He will. He sure won't lead you wrong." She adjusted the dead weight of the dog. "Listen, next time you're in the diner, coffee and pie are on me, you hear?"

MC smiled at her. He had dreaded a patient calling with an emergency. If he had to perform a slight miracle, it was a relief that he could do it for Mavis.

"Thank you, Mavis. I appreciate it." He glanced down, then back up at her. "As for the future, I'll try to keep that in mind."

She shook her head, a sheen of tears in her eyes. "If my arms weren't full of dog, I'd give you a hug."

Chapter
Thirty-Two

Nancy's brain whirred as she drove back to Park Haven. Could she call it home, yet? Maybe. Too many variables, not the least of them a variable named MC Dunne.

She still wasn't 100 percent sure what the MC stood for. The fleeting thought made her wriggle in her seat. Thinking about him was not productive at this point. It was nice of him to agree to watch over things while she was gone, but she couldn't count on him.

Could anybody?

At one time in her life, she would have tried to change him, but now? Older and wiser Nancy knew better. He'd been in a relationship that ended. Did she want to be the one to pick up the pieces? She had vowed not to be a victim, and with his issues, both personal and combat-related, it could happen so easily. Being attracted could easily turn into feeling sorry for him, and that could turn into a lifetime of regret.

She'd seen that play out in her parents' life. This trip explained even more. The trunk they'd found labeled "Adeline" rode in the bench seat beside her, with some other items that belonged to her mother. Recipe books, a few dishes, and her jewelry box.

There were a few things in the bottom of the trunk underneath the baby items that they hadn't disturbed. Richard packed the items, closed and locked the lid, then placed it next to the jewelry box.

She'd get to it. Now, she wanted to get back to some semblance of normal. Work, church, and being part of a community. After the last few weeks, she'd never neglect her family as she had before. But, now, she needed to get back to her little house and her bed.

Nancy wondered if there'd been any emergencies for MC to handle. There she went, thinking of him again, but this time in the line of duty.

Passing the clinic, she saw MC's truck. Oh, no. Something had happened. She pulled into the parking lot next to the single vehicle and went to the back door, finding it unlocked.

Pushing it open quietly, she peered in. She could hear rustling in the area of the examining room, so she went there.

She found MC intent on cleaning instruments in the way they'd been taught at Auburn, handling the instruments as if he'd never been away. As if he were already a vet in earnest. If he didn't finish school, the veterinary community would be missing out.

"Hey." She smiled as he jerked his head up, startled.

"I didn't hear you come in."

"Sorry. You were deep in thought." She watched as he put the saw away, and her eyes widened. "The bone saw?"

He chuckled, more relaxed than she had seen him. "Don't worry. I didn't have to perform an amputation."

"That's a relief." Pieces of beef bone still lay in the tray, and she laughed. "Who was it this time?"

"Jingles."

"That's a new one for him. How do you get the idea across that dogs and cooked bones don't mix well?"

He shook his head. "Purely accidental. Mavis said she hadn't cooked a beef roast in months."

She nodded. "Amazing what a dog can find, isn't it?"

"It is." He put the cleaning solution back in place and took off the lab coat he wore—not one of hers. He'd found the one with "Dr. Phillips" embroidered on it.

"Nice coat." She smiled at him.

He pulled at it, looking at the name on the coat. "Maybe it helped."

"I'm sure it did. Doc Phillips is a good man."

She watched as MC stared at the cursive embroidery for a moment. Did he imagine it with "Dr. Dunne" displayed, instead?

"I'm finished up here. I put everything in the report." He handed her the folder and shrugged into his army-green jacket. "Nothing else came up."

She opened the folder, looking at his precise, almost engineer-like printing. Very thorough. "Great. Sometimes it does, and mostly it doesn't. I had Brent on tap to feed the kenneled animals, but no way he could have handled this."

He nodded. She could tell he wanted to say something, but instead, he took a deep breath and grabbed his keys from the peg where his jacket had hung.

"Thank you, MC. I really appreciate it." She tried to get him to return her gaze, but he would look, then shift his eyes. Look, shift.

After a moment, he focused on her. His eyes were troubled, but clear.

He smiled. Actually smiled at her. Victory.

"Glad I could help. Mavis has promised me a piece of pie and coffee on her, so I think I came out ahead."

She smiled back, feeling fluttery things in her chest and stomach that worried her, a bit—not physically, but emotionally.

MC GOT HOME LATE—EXHAUSTED, amped up, and adrenaline still pumping. Was it from treating Jingles? Maybe God, or something in the universe, trying to tell him he needed to go back to school and finish his degree?

Or was it the encounter with Nancy?

He scrubbed a hand over his face. He had to stop thinking about her. She deserved more than he could give.

His thoughts went around in circles. He jerked himself up out of his chair and put on the jacket he'd just taken off. Walking at night hadn't exactly cured his insomnia, but it made him feel better and stronger. He'd take what he could get.

The moon was full, and in the clearing, he could see as well as if it were daylight. He stopped as he got to the chapel and the small cemetery next to it. The small steeple gleamed white in the moonlight.

"Okay, God. I'm here. I want to know if You're real, or if I've been fooling myself all this time. Grandpa believes in You. I used to believe in You. It seems Nancy believes, as well. I just want some peace. Not even complete peace—any little bit would help."

He walked up to the steps of the chapel and sat, gazing at the moon and stars above. Wide awake, he had nowhere to go, nobody to see. He could sit here all night if he wanted to.

I have told you these things, so that in me you may have peace.

The sentence, the verse, came out of nowhere. No, it came from within. From childhood, he'd been taught to "hide His words in his heart," meaning scripture, and they'd memorized verses from the Beginner's class forward. He'd kept it up until he got to Asia.

Peace. Could he give up the idea of being a vet if it meant he could explore a relationship with Nancy? Would he, and everyone around him, including Nancy, be better off if he were gone? It didn't take long for Rebecca to realize that a relationship with a soldier is fraught with uncertainty. She gave up before they had a chance to put right the things they'd done wrong.

Prayer forgotten, he took the burden right back on his shoulders, pondering the questions that plagued him.

He could go anywhere in the world and get a job. He had some skills he didn't have before the Army. The training position at Fort Benning intrigued him. Major Jackson said if he took this, he would automatically get a promotion, which would put him in a position to make changes in the K9 program.

Five hundred miles. Park Haven to Fort Benning. The people he loved would be close enough to see occasionally, and far enough that he would minimize the chances of running into Nancy.

Another option, Start over somewhere else.

But he couldn't leave behind the issues he carried with him, and that was why he had to forget Nancy. Kill even the bud of an idea of her.

Letting out a breath, he got up and started walking again.

Why did his thoughts always come back to Nancy?

Chapter Thirty-Three

Nancy wished she could get over the niggling unease coursing through her as she got ready for her date with Bert Conway. She should have canceled. Would have, if it hadn't been for the play. She'd promised Brent she would be there, and if she didn't go with Bert, she wouldn't have a ticket.

Her heart told her she needed to give him another chance. Her gut, however, told her she was making a big mistake.

She brushed on a hint of blue eyeshadow and enhanced her lashes with mascara. She'd never been one for false eyelashes, but then, hers were so long and dark, she hardly needed makeup of any kind.

Her hair had become longer. Time for a trim. It was easy to forget when she kept it up or in a ponytail the majority of the time. Tonight, off-duty, she decided to skip the ponytail and leave it down. A hundred strokes with a brush every night kept it shiny. Mom called it her "crowning glory" from the time she was four. She loved it long, but, at some point, she stopped wanting people to see it. Didn't want it to be misunderstood.

There was a reason for the idiom, "let your hair down," and the shame that went along with the idea had taken hold of her as a teenager. After Danny said she'd asked for it.

Was she ready to share her "crowning glory" with the world again?

Maybe she needed to prove to herself there was nothing sinful about letting her hair swing free. After all, wasn't that the style these days? She'd even known of girls in the dorm at Auburn who took their clothes iron and straightened their long locks. She'd never had to do that.

But then, after her last date with Bert, did she really want to test her theory?

She put a hairband in her purse, just in case.

Her face? Eh, she'd seen better. Style and appearance hadn't been a priority for her since she was a teen. Her mind drifted back to another time she primped in front of a mirror. She'd kept her hair long that night.

She had found Mom's pouch of makeup in the bathroom closet. After Mom died, neither Nancy nor her dad had the nerve to dispose of Mom's things.

That night, she'd experimented with eye makeup. She still remembered the magazine she had opened to the image of Elizabeth Taylor and the interview in which the movie star explained her makeup regimen to achieve her famous sultry eyes.

Mom didn't have some of the cosmetics listed in the article, but Nancy had made do, and upon completing the look copied from the magazine, she'd been proud of herself. At sixteen, she could have easily passed for twenty or more.

Nancy closed her eyes and slammed the makeup case closed. She would *not* revisit that night. Some old memories are good. Some change your life, and not for the better.

There. She gave herself another critique. Not bad. She heard a car pull into her drive and was ready when Bert knocked.

"Hey, beautiful."

She cringed inwardly and hesitated at the familiarity of the greeting. It jarred, but she dismissed it and smiled, clearing her face of any unease. It would be fine. Bert was an upstanding citizen. A nice guy. They'd gotten off on the wrong foot the last time they went out.

Everyone deserved a second chance. Didn't they?

"Hi, Bert."

"Are you ready?"

Eyes all over her, he was chomping at the bit, making her glad she wore one of her most conservative outfits. High neck top with long sleeves, a vest, and a matching midi skirt. She felt … safe.

"I am." Rather than invite him in, she pulled the door shut and allowed Bert to open the car door for her.

"My assistant, Brent, is in the play. I'm glad it worked out for me to go." She smiled, hoping it didn't look false.

"Me too." He winked at her. "I don't think I've ever seen you with your hair down." He reached over and touched it as it fell in a silken sheet over her shoulder. She flinched in surprise. Hand pulled back, he chuckled. "Hey, it looked so soft, I had to touch it."

She tried to tamp down her internal dialogue. The bud of panic inside her tempted to change her mind, but surely she was overreacting. Bert was an adult. He wasn't Danny. He wouldn't let his desperate teenage hormones get the best of him, then blame her and cause her to blame herself for his lack of character. Surely after their last encounter, Bert remembered she wouldn't stand for any funny stuff.

Nancy didn't say anything, just stared out the front glass. She could endure this. Her mind went in forty different directions. The time spent at her dad's house last weekend had all the events in her life showing up in Technicolor. Then, unbidden, the thought of a pair of brown, almost black, eyes swam into her thoughts. MC. Why now?

She was attracted to him, yes, but he had his issues, and, while she might be more adept at hiding them, so did she. What would happen if those two sets of issues collided?

They might explode.

The steakhouse on the edge of town exceeded expectations and was far enough out that it might not contain all of Park Haven, unlike the diner in town.

Come to think about it, maybe the diner would have been a better choice.

Overreacting again, Nancy.

The dim lights were an attempt at a romantic atmosphere, but Nancy's annoyance grew when Bert asked for one of the round booths. Putting her purse between them, she made it clear she wasn't in the mood to be crowded. He should have learned from the moment he touched her hair. She did not want him to touch her, and so far, he hadn't tried again. She hoped it would last.

After a good meal and pleasant, general all-purpose conversation, Bert glanced at his watch, then signaled the waiter for the check. "I would offer dessert, but if we stay for that, we'll miss the beginning of the play."

"I'm too full for dessert, anyway." Nancy finally relaxed. A full stomach and anticipation of the theater performance lulled her into a better mood. She had to stop thinking the worst of people.

Nancy didn't notice that the car stopped in front of the high school auditorium entrance.

"We have arrived."

She shook herself. She shook herself. In the course of the ten-minute drive, she'd talked herself into and out of giving Bert the benefit of the doubt. She'd landed on ambivalence. Plastering a smile on her face, she nodded brightly. "So I see."

Bert came around and opened her door, holding on to her hand long enough to tuck it in the crook of his arm.

Much, much too close. She stiffened. What might seem to some as a throwback to gentlemanly behavior, was outdated and unwelcome. Finally, they reached the door. She pulled her hand away, entering in front of him. He tried to regain her hand, but she pulled away, ostensibly to look for something in her purse.

They were seated toward the back of the auditorium.

"Great seats, huh? I figure if it starts going long, we can skip out under cover of darkness."

"I plan to see the whole play."

"Of course, I thought ..."

"I appreciate you bringing me here." She pretended to read the program, not taking the bait. "See, here's Brent's name."

Bert situated himself in his seat, leaning into her shoulder. Still wary, she didn't have room to avoid contact in the crowded auditorium. It didn't mean she wouldn't try.

Chapter
Thirty-Four

Nancy evaded Bert the length of the play, noticing with annoyance, toward the end, that his hand across the back of her seat kept inching down to her shoulder and neckline.

Upon leaving the school parking lot, he put his brand-new Buick Gran Sport in drive and turned left. Not right.

"My house is the other way."

"I know, but there's something I wanted to show you. Relax."

She cut her eyes toward him, trying to get a read on his intentions.

"I'm really tired, Bert. I'd like to go home, please." She spoke carefully, weighing her words, all the while, the skin on the back of her neck prickled.

"Aw, this won't take long. I found a place where you can see the stars perfectly. The constellations are easy to find."

Bert Conway, an astronomy buff?

"How long have you been interested in astronomy?" Maybe if she kept the conversation light and calm, he would get her home sooner rather than later.

Forgiveness, Nancy Jean. Forgiveness.

He smiled in the darkness, and the shadows on his face made her tense up. The green glow of the car's dash lights gave him an eerie countenance. Her gut tightened. This wasn't right.

"Probably since high school."

Did Bert have more in common with Danny than she thought? Did every man have it in him to have their way with women? Nancy kept an eye on the side mirror, to see if any cars came close, but Bert drove fast, on a mission. No cars would catch up to them. Could she possibly jump from the vehicle? No, she'd end up injuring herself. But then, if she stayed, she might be hurt too. All possible scenarios flashed through her mind, none of them good.

Bert turned down a familiar gravel road. He had to slow down now. Wouldn't want his precious car to get a ding from a piece of gravel. She could jump at this speed, but the gravel would make for a dicey landing.

As if reading her mind, he peered over at her moving farther and farther away on the bench seat. Taller and much stronger than she, he pulled her closer to him. She shouted. "Let go of me!"

"Ah, Nancy, you know you wanted this. Why would you go out with me if you weren't looking for a little action?"

"I wanted to go to the play. I thought maybe you'd gotten the message last time."

I'm trying to forgive you.

"Oh, I did. Loud and clear." He laughed sharply. "The voice says 'no,' but the heart says 'yes.'"

This was almost word-for-word her thoughts, earlier. *Are you there, God? I want to forgive him, but I can't trust him. Does that mean I can't forgive him?*

She searched the interior of the car. What could she use as a weapon? The pocketknife in her purse was just out of reach. She couldn't reach her bag on the floorboard now that he'd pulled her to the center of the seat. His fingers bit into her arm like a vise.

If only she had her vet bag with her. The scalpels and scissors she carried there would do some damage. Anesthetic. The small vial of Ketamine would drop him. But then, if he overpowered her, he could turn it on her. No need to dwell on that.

"Come on, relax." He loosened his grip, but only to caress her arm. "We won't do anything you don't want to do. We can look at the stars, then I'll take you home. Deal?"

What if I don't want to look at the stars?

She couldn't trust him, and she could kick herself for not talking to Mary Ann about him before tonight. When she'd gone out with him before, she and Mary Ann barely knew one another. Mary Ann hadn't said anything, but she did not have a poker face. Every expression told volumes.

Nancy was angry with herself. God gave her good sense and discernment. Why didn't she listen? Why did she think that it was up to her to force Bert to *ask* forgiveness?

As landmarks sped by, she realized where they were. In the dark, everything appeared different and dangerous, but she'd been here before.

The Dunne farm. Hope.

As they passed the farmhouse, she tried to get her hand to the steering wheel. Maybe if she honked the horn, or jerked the steering wheel, Mr. Brendan or MC would hear them and come out to help her.

Bert scoffed as he grabbed hold of her left hand. She'd been so careful, but he was alert. On a mission. Dunne Farm retreated into the rear-view mirror.

"We're almost there."

They got to a clearing, and the moon and stars were brilliant. Bert was right about the view of the stars, if only that were his goal.

He kept hold of her, putting it in Park with his left hand while holding Nancy tightly against his side. She wasn't going to make it easy for him.

"We're going to get out of the car now, and look at the stars."

"Bert, you don't need to do this. I'm sure somebody else—"

"I've had my eye on you since you arrived. These women around here? They're old hat. Same old, same old."

"Let's talk about this."

He narrowed his eyes at her. Was he making his plan of attack? She shivered, and if his lecherous smile was any indication, he noticed. It only seemed to encourage him. "On second thought … I think we'll stay nice and cozy here in the car. I'm tired of talking."

Not good. She couldn't get away. The car was a trap, and she was the prey. His hand still held her tightly, but now he reached farther and grabbed her arm, pulling it behind her back.

"No!" She could feel the muscles and tendons straining as she struggled to get away.

He shook his head, still holding her arm like a vice. "You're just making it worse."

His mouth came down on hers harshly. She tried to turn her head away, but he was too strong. He lost concentration for a moment while he ripped the top buttons off her shirt, and she screamed.

Screamed bloody murder.

Why didn't that stop him?

"Bert. Bert." She tried to get his attention, but he was intent on getting what *he* wanted, what, in his opinion, she'd denied him.

"Relax, sweetheart."

God? Where are you? Do you hear me?

Nancy froze, much like her adolescent encounter with Danny.

Danny didn't have the experience, or the adult strength, that Bert had. Her brother Steven decided he wanted sodas, so he went to the market, leaving Danny in front of the television, and Nancy in her room, unaware she was there with him, alone. He was cute, and she'd always had a little crush on him. But she knew, when he came into her room, that something didn't feel right.

He stole a kiss, which was nice, she thought, at first. Exciting. But in the back of her mind, she knew she hadn't asked for it. When he tried to explore the bare skin underneath her top, she was completely out of her depth. She was terrified and confused. He carried it too far.

The moment Danny wrapped her hair around his hand, pulling it, hurting her, she'd gone crazy on him, biting, kicking, and screaming, finally using a move she'd seen in the movies, with her knee, and it disabled him, temporarily. He'd cursed her, threatening her if she told anyone, and left the room before her brother, Steven, came back. She never said a word.

Danny was an adolescent. Bert was a grown man who should know how to treat a lady.

Nancy couldn't fathom that a man, one who respectably walked the streets of the town, whom everyone thought was a decent guy, would do this. So, maybe it *was* her fault?

Had she done something to entice him? Had she led him on?

"Come on, honey, don't tell me you don't want me." He fisted her hair.

That was it.

No.

Please, God. Please.

She wouldn't be a victim.

I am a treasured child of the Most High God.

Words from scripture came back to her, *I have told you these things, so that in me you may have peace. In this world, you will have trouble. But take heart! I have overcome the world.*

She had to fight back, and barring physical strength, which Bert held over her like the Sword of Damocles, she had her mind, and she had her voice.

Even if nobody heard her, God would hear her. *He* was her only hope.

And so, she screamed. How she screamed.

Chapter Thirty-Five

T he evening was still, not a cloud in the sky. Even the crickets and frogs were confused by the brightness of the moon. MC decided to take a long walk before going to bed. Maybe it would relax him enough to sleep.

Rusty barked before he left the cabin. He usually only did that if a car went by, but if one had, MC didn't notice it.

Not unusual. MC's thoughts could easily block everything else out. More like blanked out, not noticing anything around him.

His first instinct was to not bother with a flashlight since it was so bright, but he grabbed one anyway. The woods could be black as pitch, the shadows sucking up every bit of light from the full moon.

He sauntered down the lane, Rusty jogging along beside him. It amazed him how quickly animals healed as opposed to humans. Except for a slight limp, you'd never know Rusty had recovered from a fractured leg.

As he got closer to the clearing, there the chapel stood, a sentinel in the bluish light.

"Are you here, God?"

Nothing. Not a sound.

And then the sounds were everywhere.

A piercing scream, and then another, ripped the silence.

MC felt the scream down to his toes, and couldn't get to the cemetery fast enough. A woman in distress, somewhere. Nearby. He had to find her. In his hurry, a distant memory kept going in and out of his mind. He found himself in two different places at the same time.

It's not real.

He and his unit were hiding in the jungle, carefully, silently watching a known Viet Cong encampment. After a few hours, some of the guys were getting antsy. Gunnar helped him to stay still. That dog could be on alert for eight hours if needed.

About the time they were going to ambush the camp, a woman screamed. It sounded terrified, and, to be honest, terrified him. He couldn't tell where it came from. Instinct kicked in, and he started running toward the tent in the direction the scream came from.

He threw open the flap of the tent to meet with the muzzle of a Type 56 firearm, the Viet Cong equivalent of an AK-47.

The screaming woman in question stood behind the gunman, laughing, screaming again for good measure.

It had been a trap. He ducked out of the tent, and the bullet missed him. He'd thrown himself down the embankment nearby, into darkness and safety.

A trap? MC paused, and scanned the area. No. There was the chapel in moonlight, shining bright as day. He had to get in the shadows, or they would see him. Shaking his head to get his thoughts together, he rounded the corner to see a car parked between the chapel and the cemetery, sounds of shouting, and a woman screaming, "No!"

He recognized that car. Had complimented Bert Conway on the new vehicle the last time he ran into him.

Another terrified "Help" ripped through the night. That's all it took. He rushed to the car and pulled the door open to see Bert manhandling Nancy, and he lost it. MC pulled Bert out of the car by his collar, paying no attention to the choking sounds as he threw him against his precious car. The hood might have a dent in it, but MC didn't care.

His vision clouded and MC's strength grew as the Viet Cong operative in his hands tried to fight back.

After a few minutes of his hands around "Charlie," the enemy in his grip, MC heard Gunnar's bark. At first, it was far away, but as it got closer, he realized that someone pulled at his arm, saying "Stop! Stop! You'll kill him!"

He dropped the man in his hands and drew back to hit the enemy trying to get in the way of doing his job—protect and serve the United States of America, win or lose.

As he turned, MC's vision cleared to see a horrified Nancy within striking distance. He peered down at the almost-limp man at his feet. Bert Conway. Part of him wanted to continue, finish the job, but seeing Nancy's face, realizing he almost hit her, doused that desire like a bucket of cold water thrown on him.

NANCY REACHED out and touched MC's arm, the corded muscles were tensed, ready to fight. She knew how adrenaline worked. His still worked overtime.

"It's okay, MC. It's okay."

MC's eyes were wide as he turned toward her, the whites almost glowing in the moonlight. Nostrils flared, and she thought of a bull ready to fight. She watched as reality eventually broke through. Recognition pulled at him.

"Are you all right?" His voice ground out the words.

"I'm fine. Just scared." She shrugged and tried desperately to smile. "I'm glad you were here."

She minimized the effects of the situation to calm him, she most definitely was not fine. Traumatized like before, with Danny. Only back then she had to fight her battle alone.

"You're sure?"

She nodded silently.

MC stared at her. In the wake of his flashback, did he have a sense of what happened? She had to wonder what could have happened if she hadn't got through to him.

After a few moments suspended in time, MC took a deep breath and peered down at the frightened man at his feet.

MC kept Bert pinned to the ground with his look. "Nancy, get your things." She almost didn't recognize his voice, but, saying nothing, she obeyed. Her hands shook as she went around the car to get her purse. He lifted Bert by his shirt front, high enough off the ground that he had to balance on tiptoes.

Getting in his face, MC spoke low, slow, and menacing. "If I ever catch you so much as looking at a woman in this town in a way I might construe as objectionable, I will kill you. Do. You. Understand?"

"MC." Nancy came up beside him and laid her hand on his arm. "I'm okay."

Was her voice getting through to him? At this point, Nancy could tell MC wasn't thinking about whether or not she was fine. His anger pulled the man up higher, making him strain to keep from dangling in the air. Nancy didn't know where his strength came from, but she observed the results of adrenaline surging through his body at an outrageous speed.

"MC, put him down." Her voice sounded strange, even to herself. Nothing could still the quiver.

Lowering Bert to the ground, MC bent, nose to nose. "I'm not kidding."

He led Bert to the driver's side of his car and threw him in. "Go home, and don't forget what I said. I'll be watching."

Bert slammed the car door closed and started the car. In the safety of his vehicle, he blustered. "I'll call the sheriff. You're crazy."

"You really want to do that? Go ahead. Call the sheriff so we can have you arrested for assault." MC glowered at the bully who'd met his comeuppance. "Might, anyway."

Bert's Adam's apple bobbed as he swallowed nervously. He got in his car and turned it around as quickly as possible, throwing gravel all along the road to the highway.

In the stillness of the night, Nancy could hear Bert's tires squeal as he sped onto the highway.

MC closed his eyes. She knew that the adrenaline that pumped through him before was beginning to ebb.

Nancy trudged over to the steps of the chapel and dropped her head into her hands, letting the tears fall. No way she wanted him to see her fall apart. She tried to breathe slowly, and get her heart rate down before facing him.

She was so afraid. Not of Bert, and certainly not of MC.

She was afraid of herself. Afraid of her future.

Chapter Thirty-Six

Only three events in Nancy's life terrified her this much.

The last time her dad hit her and knocked her unconscious. She stayed at home from school the next day, nursing a headache and visible bruises.

The encounter with Danny. He didn't get far, but he could have, easily.

The other terrifying event in her life? The death of her mother.

She hadn't been prepared. Even knowing it would be the outcome, no one ever taught her how to react as the most important person in her life died, leaving her to a grieving father and two brothers with lives of their own.

But this? This was premeditated. Bert didn't lose himself in the moment. He planned it. He meant to have his way with her, no matter if she were a willing subject or not.

There was no repentance, no admission that he was at fault. She'd thought it her duty to forgive him for the way he behaved months ago. But tonight. How could she forgive that?

Nancy took the hair band in her purse and with shaking hands, finger-combed her hair into a ponytail. Security. Control.

While beating Bert, Nancy saw a wildness in MC's eyes she hadn't seen before. More than anger, it was as close to wrath as she'd ever seen, and she prayed she'd never see it again.

Her whole body shook, but the solid rock step she sat on grounded her. Safe. Secure. Just like God. She might be unstable, frightened, and wrong, but God loved her anyway.

And, He loves Bert.

The first charge Jesus gave was to love, as He loved us. Maybe the most loving thing she could do would be to hold Bert responsible. That was too deep to consider at that moment.

She tried to straighten her spine and stifle the attack of emotions, but even while she sat there, silent tears coursed down her face.

She was embarrassed, preferring to show her strength, not her weakness, and yet, here they were. A part of her wanted to be angry with MC for ordering her around like an underling. Like a child. But she couldn't.

She'd never cried like that in her life that she could remember. Why? It wasn't as if this were worse than other things that happened. It was him. MC. His gentleness, his sensitivity to her feelings held her captive. As if he reached in and took out her bruised heart and observed it, then carefully tucked it away where he could find it later.

MC GLANCED OVER AT NANCY, slowly falling to pieces on the front stoop of the chapel. He should go to her, but how? He'd seen the utter terror in her eyes. Terror directed at him as he narrowly missed laying her out with his fist.

His heart broke for her. He'd ordered her around like a child, no better than Bert and so many men he'd known all his life. Bullies. That's all they were. In Basic Training, they'd been taught the fine art of intimidation, and some soldiers were natural at it. At this moment, he could identify. He wasn't proud of it.

He closed his eyes, shuddering.

A tiny thought crept into his brain. Had she, somehow, enticed Bert? Asked for it?

Before the idea could take hold and start to grow, he shook his head, hating himself for even thinking it. Her face said it all. The buttons ripped from her blouse. The utter terror in her eyes. Not guilt for something she'd done. Complete fear of what could have, and had happened to her.

What if he'd hit her? Even accidentally, he could have injured her. He couldn't be trusted with someone weaker than himself. Anyone in his vicinity had to be prepared, aware of the possibility that he would lose it at any given moment. Had to be able to deescalate a situation.

But she'd done that. Her voice and her touch stopped him from killing Bert. Would he have snapped out of it for anyone else?

He walked over to her and sat quietly on the step beside her.

Tears. They were hard to take from anyone, but from someone you love?

Did he love her? Terrifying, but yes, he was pretty sure he did. He could never tell her, though. Because she needed someone whole. He'd never be that.

As she lifted her face to his, his heart almost stopped. Right now, at this moment, she had nobody else.

MC sat there, on the step, unsure of what to do. She looked up, saying nothing. He couldn't meet her gaze.

What could he say? He was out of his depth. War? Battle? As life-altering as those events were, suddenly, he knew that what she'd gone through—what she *could* have gone through, was an entirely different level of trauma.

He finally took in her tears flowing. It was his undoing.

He put his arms around her and pulled her close, cradling her head to his chest. He tightened his hold as she released great, gulping sobs.

Maybe this was all he needed to do. Hold her.

After a while—it seemed like an hour, but in reality, a few minutes —she lifted her head, and he loosened his hold, allowing her to pull away.

He grazed her cheek with the back of his hand. In the moonlight, MC could see the tear stains on her face, but even then, she was beautiful. When he held her close, it amazed him how she fit, perfectly, in his embrace. If only she could stay there, never leave it.

He needed her more than she needed him.

When he touched her face, she shivered.

"Are you cold?" He shed the jacket he'd grabbed on his way out for his walk.

She shook her head. Why did she suddenly have trouble meeting his gaze? He'd frightened her. What were the odds that she wanted to have anything to do with a boor who wanted to fix everything with violence? A man who could, with his bare hands, kill a man in a fog of anger and disorientation?

"Sorry."

She gaped at him, startled. "For what?"

Maybe he wasn't crazy. "For almost hitting you."

Her lip turned up on one side. "That was the least of my worries, believe me."

"I could have hurt you."

"But you didn't. You protected me. You saved me from Bert."

He lifted an eyebrow. "From a 'fate worse than death?'"

"You could say that. I needed you, and you were there."

MC scoffed. "Good thing I have insomnia, huh?"

"This time? Yes. Although I think you could have heard me scream all the way to Nashville."

The grim reality of what happened sobered him quickly. "I'm sorry you had to endure that."

Nancy tilted her head, gazing at his face as if she couldn't quite make sense of it all. "I'm sorry you had to endure what you did too."

He ducked his head. Beyond his closest family, she was the first person to acknowledge the effects his wartime experience still had on him. The first person to really "see" him for the broken man he was.

"We're a fine pair, aren't we?" He put his jacket around her shoulders, holding it there for a minute. Someday she would decide he wasn't worth it, and he would remember this moment of being able to touch her, even through the layers of a jacket.

Chapter Thirty-Seven

MC rose to his feet and held his hand out to help Nancy up.

"Are you ready to go home?"

She hesitated, catching her lower lip between her teeth. "Honestly?"

"Honestly."

"No, I'm not. I'm not ready to be alone." She rummaged in her purse and pulled out a handkerchief, blowing her nose. "Sorry."

He chuckled. "Never apologize for blowing your nose." He narrowed his eyes. "Or for not wanting to be alone."

She nodded, wanting so badly to burst into tears again.

He gestured to her to follow him. "Come on. I'll show you the inside of the chapel."

"I'd like that." No pressure. Just relief.

He took her hand and squeezed it, then turned and opened the door. He went in ahead of her and lit an oil lamp on the wall and some candles at the altar.

She walked down the aisle, gazing at the architecture. "It's beautiful."

She turned to him, and he nodded. "My great-uncle and Grandpa built it in the twenties."

"Why did they build it?"

Why, indeed? MC paused, frowning. "Uncle Patrick said God told him to build it, so he did."

"A leap of faith on his part, especially this far from town." She wandered around the small sanctuary, running a finger along a smoothly-polished pew back.

MC nodded. "Grandpa and Grandma were married here."

"I'd love to see it in daylight."

He smiled, the candles softening everything around them. "It's a sight, especially when the stained-glass window is in."

"Is this it?" She pointed to a large piece of plywood cocooned in paper and cotton wool, laying on top of the front pews. "Did something happen to it?"

"Age, termites. We picked it up a few days ago. I figure we'll try to put it in tomorrow."

"I hope I can see it someday."

"You will."

His simple words were heartfelt and drew her attention back to him.

"I need to get you home." MC sounded as though he didn't want to say it. It wouldn't be proper for her to be here any later.

Times had changed, but attitudes among good people were still conservative. "I'm ready."

He nodded and blew out candles. "No electricity here."

"It doesn't need it. The candles fit the chapel."

"So they do."

They walked down the hill toward the cabin and farmhouse.

Suddenly she became aware of the awkwardness of the situation. What would people think if they found out she'd been here, this late, alone, with MC? And what if they found out about Bert, and what he'd tried to do?

"Will it wake Mr. Brendan when you start your truck?"

"Probably not. He's known for his snoring." MC glanced down at her with a smile, almost magical in the moonlight.

"Good. I'd hate for him to know what happened tonight."

"If anyone would understand, it's Grandpa." He opened the truck door and settled her in the passenger seat, then went around to the driver's side. As soon as he got in, he grabbed the keys from above the visor. "Not much call for security around here."

"After tonight, you might want to revise that statement."

Keys in hand, he turned toward her. "A-are you sure he didn't hurt you in any way?"

She shook her head violently. "Just my ego." She sighed. "I went out with him once, not long after I moved here. He didn't go that far, but he did get a little 'handsy,' if you know what I mean."

"I do. Why did you go out with him again?"

"I don't know." Even in her frustration, she couldn't tell him the reasons she went out with Bert—that she needed, for her sake, to forgive Bert because she'd been forgiven. And, that she was lonely, and she'd given up on MC and decided to take her chances. "I guess I thought after last time he'd learned I'm not that kind of girl." She shrugged. "I guess I didn't get the idea across as well as I thought I did."

"Guys don't always catch on to cues."

"No kidding."

"Something tells me he won't be asking you out again."

"Thank you, Lord." She raised her eyes Heavenward, then turned to him, shaking her head. "I get the feeling he might be crossing to the other side of the street when he sees me—or you—from now on."

"That's fine with me." MC scoffed, looking at her as he turned the ignition. "Bert and I have never been what you'd call buddies."

"I think I like you even more, now."

"Good to know." He chuckled.

Nancy reached over and touched his arm. "Really, thank you, MC."

The intensity of the look he sent her way in the dim light of the dashboard instruments stole her breath. "At your service, ma'am."

∼

"YOU DIDN'T HAVE to walk me to the door." Nancy struggled with her keys. Was she nervous, standing on the front porch with him? He held out his hand and she gave them to him, no questions asked.

MC opened the door with ease.

"I want to check the house before I leave if you don't mind."

"You don't think …?" Nancy's eyes flashed to his, fear on her face.

Bert was angry, but to what extent? Who knew? Didn't matter. He was going to make sure if only to make himself feel better.

"Probably not, he's too lazy, but you never know. I don't want you to take any chances with that guy."

He'd protect her at all costs.

"MC …"

"May I come in, please?" Did she think he would take advantage of her, as Bert had? Her smile was a relief. She trusted him.

"All right. But I'll be fine." She grinned at him. "I keep a baseball bat next to the front door and a flashlight on the nightstand."

A chuckle bubbled out of MC. "Far be it from me to discourage your security system, but I'd like to see for myself if you don't mind."

She opened the door and turned on the light, waving him inside. Did she worry that her neighbors were up and looking toward her house, seeing her allow a man into her home?

He searched closets, and behind curtains, checked her window locks, and met her at the front door.

"Satisfied?"

"Not entirely, but I'll have to be." He nodded his head toward the back entrance. "Did you know you have a cracked window on the back door?"

"Yes. It's been that way for two years." She raised an eyebrow. "I'll be fine. I may not sleep well, but then we'd be even, right?"

His lips twisted in a lopsided smile. "I guess we would."

MC couldn't help it. He had to touch her cheek one last time. He grazed his knuckles across her cheek, much as he had earlier. He'd done it under the pretense of wiping away her tears, but he simply wanted to touch her. Her involuntary shiver made him drop his hand quickly. The last thing he wanted was to make her feel uncomfortable or frighten her.

"Goodnight, Nancy." He turned to the door.

"'Night, MC."

She whispered, causing him to turn. Maybe she wasn't afraid of him.

Grabbing his hand, she paused, as if waiting for his full attention. He looked into her eyes, happy to give it to her. "You did a good thing tonight. You saved me, protected me, and now you've made sure my home is secure. I can't begin to thank you for that."

"No need."

"I know." She raised herself on her tiptoes and kissed him on the cheek. "But I appreciate it, anyway. It means a lot to me. Goodnight, MC."

Nancy double-checked the lock and then leaned on the door, sliding down to sit on the floor when her knees threatened to buckle with the aftermath of emotion. She listened as his truck started, backed out, then left her driveway. Loneliness enveloped her. That truck held a very special man.

He didn't see it. Clearly.

Oh, God, help him. Help him to see how valuable he is. You sent him. Help him to see that too.

She wasn't surprised that tears trickled down again. Wrapping her arms around herself, she thought she'd cried more in the last few months than she had in her entire life. Everything bad that happened in her lifetime threatened to close in on her.

Did MC feel like his experience in Vietnam entrapped him, even here at home?

To be honest with herself, before MC arrived and pulled Bert off of her, she could easily have lost herself in the past. The night Danny assaulted her.

She'd never mentally slipped into the horror before, but it was there, on the edge of memory, triggered by Bert's unwanted touch. She realized the strength of Bert's determination. That frightened sixteen-year-old girl was inside her, hiding, and with this assault, it was right there in front of her, in stark relief.

To lose control because of an event that you couldn't avoid, for it to happen again and again? That would be enough to drive a person insane. Would there be a point at which there's no coming back? When your mind stayed in the past while your body was in the present, confused?

She saw that tonight.

Her heart hurt for MC.

Chapter Thirty-Eight

MC woke to the rooster crowing. He'd been asleep an entire two hours this time.

Disgusting.

At this rate, he'd go crazy from sleep deprivation.

After he got home the night before, he walked, getting back to the cabin around 3 a.m. By then, too physically and emotionally exhausted to change, he'd kicked off his shoes and fallen into bed. He must have shoved the blanket off at some point—or had he gone to sleep without covers?

It didn't matter. The images and impressions swirling through his brain made him wish for the pills he'd been accused of taking to end his own life. Pushing the heels of his hands into his eyes, he had no choice but to endure. He didn't want to die, but he did want the hurt, the trauma, and the loneliness, to go away. To stay away.

Nancy. Did she sleep, or did she relive the horror of the night before? He didn't want her gratitude. He was there at the right place, at the right time. What man would walk away from a woman fighting off a beast? Nobody he could imagine.

She'd fought. The idea made a smile tug at his lips. She was strong, determined, and beautiful.

He closed his eyes and winced. He couldn't think of her that way. He'd already decided that he had to stay away from her. If that meant moving to Fort Benning, Georgia, he'd do it.

She deserved more. More than he could ever give her, because part of him died in Vietnam, and the rest had been drifting away ever since he got home.

A knock at the cabin door got his attention. He was thankful for the distraction.

"MC? Son?"

Grandpa. MC walked through the kitchen-living room combination and pulled the door open.

"Are you all right?" Grandpa's wrinkled brow indicated his worry.

"I'm fine." He narrowed his eyes at Grandpa. "What's up?"

"Apparently you, in the middle of the night."

"How did you …"

"Nancy called to see if you were okay." Grandpa tilted his head, looking at the side of his face. "Looks like you've got quite a shiner."

MC touched his left cheek. Sure enough, it smarted. He hadn't even noticed last night. Adrenaline?

"Yeah … had a little altercation with Bert Conway."

"Bert?"

He wasn't about to tell Grandpa what prompted the fight unless Nancy said something. "What did Nancy tell you?"

"That you saved her life."

MC looked down, trying to get the lump in his throat to go away. He was tougher than that.

Wasn't he?

"I don't know if I'd go so far as that, but she was in danger, yes."

Grandpa nodded, looking at him gravely, and patted his shoulder. "You did the right thing, son."

"Thank you, Grandpa. I did what any man would have done."

"Not necessarily." He shook his head, frowning. "Where did all this happen?"

MC respected Nancy's privacy. "I'd rather not say, but I'm surprised you didn't hear me drive Nancy home."

"You know me. Once I'm asleep, I'm dead to the world." Grandpa grinned. "You sure you don't need to see the doctor?"

"What would he do? Tell me to put ice on it. Take an aspirin? I can do that on my own. Besides, I don't want to drive to Nashville for a black eye."

Grandpa chuckled. "It won't be black long. I'm already seeing shades of purple, yellow, and lime green. It's gonna be a doozy." He turned back to the door. "Well, glad you're okay. I thought I'd better check on you after Nancy called. Want some breakfast?"

"That would be great."

Grandpa nodded and opened the door, stepping out on the porch. "Good. I'm making waffles, so come on pretty soon. You want 'em while they're hot."

"Yes, sir." MC stared after the old man as he walked briskly back to the house, long arms swinging, whistling.

Grandpa always tended toward the "sunny side." How? He'd been dealt more than his share of blows, and MC didn't even know the story of some of them.

Mostly an open book, sometimes MC had the feeling some bad things happened to Grandpa in the distant past. What brought him to Tennessee? Who were these mysterious relatives in Illinois? How did he get over the death of Grandma, the woman he referred to as "the love of his life?"

And if, as Grandpa told, he and Grandma had a rushed-up wedding, how did they have their wedding here, in the chapel?

One of these days, he wanted to get the whole story, if Grandpa would tell him.

For now?

Now he'd enjoy a waffle—nobody made them like Grandpa.

The morning was gathering steam. Steam rising from the pond, from the dew burning off the ground. It was going to be a hot day. Walking down the path to the chapel, MC was lost in thought. Thoughts of the night before, of Nancy, of the job ahead of them.

MC and Grandpa uncovered the repaired window, and stood,

looking at it, in awe of the craftsmanship both of the old artisans who built it, and the new craftsmen who repaired it, making it look like new.

"The only thing that would give it away is that crack." Grandpa pointed out a piece of translucent blue glass on the edge. "They couldn't find a match, so I told them to use the old glass. We're all a little cracked here and there, aren't we?"

"Yes, sir, we are." MC sent Grandpa a half-smile.

Grandpa nodded. "Listen, I don't know what happened last night, but I get the feeling Nancy needs you right now."

"One of your gut feelings?" He wanted to deflect, to avoid the subject if at all possible.

"More like a Holy Spirit feeling."

MC scoffed, and stared at the window, pristine right now. How long before it started collecting dirt and cracks? To protect it, they had to maintain it, and that meant keeping an eye on it.

He'd protected Nancy last night, but he almost hurt her in the process. Honestly, he didn't think he could face her.

"I don't think she would have called me if she didn't need a strong shoulder to lean on." Grandpa glanced at his watch. "While I'd love to put this window in today, I have a couple of errands to run."

Earlier in the week, Grandpa was chomping at the bit to get it installed. Now he had errands? Just as well. His arm was stiff after the altercation with Bert. They'd waited this long, what're another few days?

MC nodded, saying nothing.

"I hope you'll think about what I said." Grandpa winked at him, patted his back, and left, leaving MC to ponder the best course of action.

The best course? Get as far away from Nancy Jean Baker as possible.

But the course that would fulfill something he hadn't realized he needed?

Going to her. Now.

～

NANCY STIFFENED at the deep purple bruise on her left arm.

Bert.

She'd been bruised before. Her dad had inflicted bruises on her. She wasn't sure if he'd been careful to avoid hitting her where it would show, or if she was careful in selecting her clothing to cover them up.

In her encounter with Danny, as a teen, she remembered being bruised in several places.

She pulled on a sweater over her short-sleeved blouse. Thank goodness for Saturday. She didn't feel like facing anyone this morning.

After letting her dogs out, she called Mr. Dunne. Shouldn't she have called MC directly?

For some reason, she couldn't make herself dial his number. Embarrassed? No, not so much embarrassed as disconcerted. Unsure of her feelings bouncing around.

Did her feelings for MC stem from the fact that last night he acted as her protector? No, she'd been thinking about him before that.

She poured herself an additional cup of coffee and sat at her table, chin in hand. Over and over, she played the night before in her mind. What did she do, or say, that made Bert think she welcomed his advances?

Could she have stopped it before it started? Shouldn't she have been able to take care of herself?

Maybe she could have, but she thanked God she didn't have to. In sheer size alone, Bert could have seriously injured her—even killed her, if that had been his goal. MC appeared, sent, she was convinced, by God, who loved her and wanted the best for her.

She prayed through her tears.

Thank you, Lord. Thank you for Your protection and for sending help. I made a bad decision going with Bert. You said to forgive, but you never said we had to wipe out all that happened before. Only You can do that. I can forgive the person, but not the action. You've given me the discernment to know whether or not I can trust people. I can trust MC. Oh, God. Help MC to see how important he is to You, and how much You love him. Help me to follow You, and only You, in all aspects of my life ...

From experience, the events would replay in her mind at the oddest times. She'd already experienced that.

It would be so easy to be bitter. A part of her was. She tried so hard to give that over to her Heavenly Father, but it still cropped up. It made her think about MC.

Did he relive the horror of what he encountered in Vietnam? Her experience was horrible, but she couldn't imagine, couldn't perceive how a person could come back from the atrocities of war. If part of her healing depended on forgiving those who hurt her, where did that leave MC? How do you forgive a nation? A war?

When it was over, and Bert left, MC distanced himself from her. He apologized for almost hitting her.

MC apologized. No

How could they get past their individual traumas?

She dropped her head into her hands and groaned.

Oh, MC, what are we doing?

After puttering around in the quiet, the knock on Nancy's front door startled her. She'd just taken the kettle off the stove to make herself a comforting cup of tea. She glanced at herself in the mirror by the front door and sighed. Awful. She'd cried on and off all morning, wore no makeup, and the look of dejection on her face would worry her if she observed it on anyone else.

The tall shadow at the door made her pause until she realized who it was.

"Hi MC." She unhooked the screen to let him in. "Come in."

She could tell he didn't want to make her uncomfortable. "Are you sure? If you'd feel better, we could sit on the porch."

His care almost broke her again. She shook her head. "No, come on in. The mosquitos have arrived with a vengeance."

He came in, seeming so much taller in her small house. She hadn't noticed it the night before, but today, he was larger than life.

Not a bad thing when you need a protector.

"Grandpa said you'd called this morning." His dark brown eyes drew her in, and while she wanted to look away, she found she couldn't.

"I worried you'd hurt yourself more than you realized, last night." She tilted her head, looking at the spreading bruise on his face. "Looks like I may have been right."

"You could have called me." That half-smirk grin widened, slowly, on his face. He had a slight dimple on the side that went up naturally. His eyes sparkled, showing the life inside him amidst the trauma he'd experienced.

Her face warmed. "I ... I couldn't find your number right off hand."

Liar.

"I wanted to check on you too." The smile was gone, the serious look taking its place. "Do you want to press charges against Bert Conway?"

The mention of his name was like having cold water thrown on her. She could, but did she want to? Would it be better for Bert if she held him accountable?

"I hadn't thought about it." If she did, everyone would have to know what happened. Could she face that?

"Just know it's an option and might put some fear into him, legally, that I couldn't put in him, physically."

Now her lips tugged in a grin. "I have a feeling you put plenty of fear into him last night."

"I hope so."

Nancy bit her lower lip, trying to find the right words to explain what was going on in her head. "Do you think it would help Bert if I did press charges?"

MC's brows rose in surprise. "How do you mean?"

"Actions have consequences. When you punish a child for something they did wrong, it reminds them not to do it again. When someone breaks the law, they have to pay for it in some way, hopefully deterring a repeat offense." She tilted her head and shrugged, uncertain.

He stared at her, his eyes softening. "I'll have to think on that one. It's your call."

She nodded, knowing that the subject was closed, for now. Come back to the kitchen. I'm making a cup of tea. Want some?"

"Uh, sure."

He sat at one of the two dinette chairs she'd found at a second-hand store.

"What's Mr. Brendan up to?"

He frowned for a few seconds. "Honestly? I'm not sure. He said he had some errands."

Nancy poured the steaming water into a mug and dropped a tea bag into it, watching the liquid darken with flavor. She took the tea bag out of her cup and measured out a spoon of sugar, stirring longer than necessary.

"Are you okay?" MC had a troubled look on his face.

"I'm fine." She stared down at her cup, both hands wrapped around it.

He didn't say anything, and the silence between them grew. "You don't have to deal with this alone."

Her head whipped up. "Neither do you." The tears she thought were surely spent were threatening to resurface, this time not for herself, but for him. How could she ask anything of him? He must hurt as much, if not more, than she.

"Nancy …" MC reached across the table and tugged her hand into his, examining it, rubbing her palm with his thumb.

Words escaped her, but at this moment, she didn't want to be anywhere but here, her hand in his.

He stopped, looking up at her. "I want you to feel safe."

"I do." Her eyes met his, and once again, she shivered. He pulled his hand away, but she held on to it. "I feel safe because I'm with you."

A tear made its way down her cheek, and MC caught it with his other hand.

# Chapter Thirty-Nine

MC's brain whirled in confusion and want. A lifetime ago, he'd thought himself in love with Rebecca. But when she ended it, he gave up. After that, he stopped planning for the future. His future became uncertain.

But the feel of Nancy's hand in his sparked something in him he'd never experienced, even with Rebecca. He'd thought he loved her. A nursing student, he thought she'd make the perfect "Vet's wife."

He couldn't have been more wrong. Nancy brought on only one thought—hope. Hope, and a future.

"I thought you were going to install the window today."

He glanced down at their hands. She said she felt safe with him. Hard to accept when he didn't feel safe with himself.

"I think Grandpa invented some errands so I'd come to check on you."

Watching the color rise on her face affected him in a way he hadn't been in a very long time.

"I can't argue with his logic." Nancy squeezed his hand and smiled at him.

A thought flitted into his mind, but he was afraid to ask. Would she? He didn't want to leave her. It was assuming a lot, but …

"Would you like to come back with me? Maybe Grandpa is back from his errands, and we can slip the window in place."

"You make it sound like no big deal." She chuckled, her color still high.

He didn't want to ever do anything to take that look off her face.

~

MC AND NANCY drove up to find Grandpa back at the chapel.

He kept an eye on her for signs of stress. Would being here trigger the memory of last night?

"Are you sure you're okay … being here, I mean?" MC hadn't thought of himself and his afflictions since last night.

She nodded, looking toward the place where it all happened, then aimed for the front porch of the chapel. "I need to be here. To see it in the sunshine. Otherwise, I might always be afraid, and I don't want that."

"I get it." He took her hand and led her up the steps and to the door, only letting it go with a squeeze as they went in.

"Well, hello there, you two." Grandpa stood on a ladder nailing some trim around the windows on each side. So far, he'd finished two of the six.

"I wasn't sure if you'd be back from your 'errands.'" MC smirked.

"Ah, yes. Had to get some more nails."

MC's brows went up. There were three boxes of nails on the window sill. "I'm still game to install the window if you are."

Grandpa frowned. "Are you sure? I don't want you to strain your shoulder."

"If Nancy can help us balance it, I think we can." MC raised his eyebrows at Nancy, who nodded.

"I can't wait to see it in place."

That's all it took.

"Before we can do that, I want to replace some of the sill."

MC went to the porch and pulled some lumber to reinforce the window frame. As he took out the old sill, he found the stud behind the wall spongy with dry rot, so he went down farther.

"Grandpa, could you come over here for a minute?"

MC held a small cardboard box in his hand. As soon as Grandpa recognized it, he stopped, a smile blossoming on his face.

"I'd forgotten about our 'time capsule.'" Grandpa walked over and took it from MC, the small box that had contained nails back at the time they were building the chapel. They opened it, and rather than nails, there were two objects—a locket and a pocket watch.

"This certainly brings back memories."

Grandpa pulled a handkerchief out and wiped his nose. "Can you read what's written in the box?"

Nancy took it and held the box top up to the light. "A three-fold cord, forever strong." She gazed up at him, curious. "And then, BD and EGD."

"Grandma and Grandpa's initials." MC stared at the faded script.

Grandpa smiled, fingering the delicate gold chain on Evangeline's pendant. "That day, we put the past behind us and decided to consecrate our marriage to the Lord. From that point on, we put our trust in God for everything we needed. He blessed us beyond measure." He shook his head. "What a time."

While Grandpa moved his ladder out of the way, Nancy and MC moved the sawhorses closer to the opening. They'd lay the window across them, then raise it up and into the frame.

MC took down the plywood covering the window opening. As soon as he did, light poured into the sanctuary.

He glanced over at Nancy, and she smiled at him. A genuine smile.

A smile that made him want to be a better man.

It was trickier getting the window placed in the opening than they thought, but there it sat, in all its glory, sun streaming through the colors making the room look like a kaleidoscope.

Looking closely, Nancy examined the shattered-glass pattern of the cross surrounded by a serene blue—peace amidst chaos. The intricate knot pattern around the cross ended with a three-petaled flower. Symbolizing a cord of three strands, perhaps?

"It's beautiful."

Grandpa stood next to her. "It is that. I hope it never gets in such bad shape again."

"Somebody will have to take care of it." She side-eyed MC, who raised his eyebrows. "I guess that would be you?"

"I think I'd like to put the box back in the space underneath the window." Grandpa examined the hole in the plaster. "We can drywall it in afterward."

"Good idea. Someday someone will find it and wonder."

"Maybe someone in our family." Grandpa sighed. My Evangeline and I had such plans. We wanted a big family. Lots of kids, lots of grandkids." He beheld MC with fondness. "Instead, we were blessed to raise your daddy as our son, and then we had you."

Nancy laughed. "No pressure, MC."

"Your grandma and I wouldn't have changed a thing."

MC went to him, hugging him tightly. Grandpa loved kids. Will thought of him as Grandpa, and there was no relation there except through Mom. All the kids at church were aware he carried peppermints in his jacket pocket. He wasn't buying their affection, more that the kids were comfortable coming to him, and he loved it.

To be the single grandchild in such a family? He understood he'd been spoiled. Not in the way that ruins a kid, but rather in that God had blessed them so much that the blessings ran over and touched him too.

That's what he used to think, anyway.

"I'm going to walk up to the house and get some tape. Fix this box before we fix the wall." Grandpa nodded absentmindedly. "I may want to put some more stuff in there."

"We don't have to put it in today. There's plenty of time."

"I reckon so. This one hasn't seen the light of day in nearly fifty years. A few more days won't make any difference."

After Grandpa left the chapel, the atmosphere changed. MC was uneasy. He was falling for her. Hard. He thought, hoped, Nancy's feelings were along the same lines. What he didn't know was what he needed to do about it.

Rebecca had made it clear she didn't want any part of a guy who *might* get killed in action. It didn't matter that they had formed a physical bond that should have waited. A bond that should have been saved for the confines, the blessings, of marriage.

Why would Nancy want a man who may as well have been killed? A man who could hurt her in a fit of blind rage? A man who didn't wait for his one-and-only?

He raked his hand over his face, staring at the window, knowing she watched him. Unable to stand the inactivity, he cleaned the worksite of the shims, scraps, and packing material they'd taken off the window. He put the tools back in the toolbox.

With no other tasks, he turned to her. "So. Now you've seen the window."

"I have." Nancy regarded him tenderly.

As much as she needed to be loved and cherished today, after what happened last night, her open gaze twisted something in his heart that confused him.

He wanted to pull her to him and kiss her. That part of him, he understood. The other part? The other part told him to run as fast, and as far as possible.

For her own good.

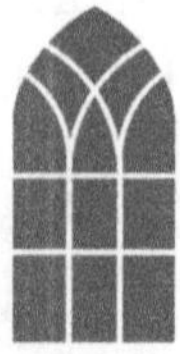

Chapter Forty

She needed time. Time alone to figure things out. Something was happening, had happened, between herself and MC.

Nancy took Major and Biddie on a short walk after church. The air had a softness to it, but the July heat was rising, which felt good to her sore joints and muscles. When would her physical body stop reminding her of the ordeal of Friday night?

She chose a route that led to the park and not through a neighborhood that would require a lot of interaction. The tiny park in Park Haven covered an entire city block—a Park Haven city block, at least. To get in a mile, she would have to go around it at least five times.

Church had been harder than she thought. Her mind kept telling her "They're looking at you" and "they know what happened." As if Bert's attempt to violate her was her fault. When she was invited out for lunch, she tried to beg off, citing the need to walk her dogs, but Marjorie told her there was no hurry. Walk the dogs, then come over. Maybe she wouldn't stay long. Maybe come home right after lunch.

She needed to think.

It would make sense, after the experiences she'd had, that she would shy away from men in general.

Her track record was horrible. At one point, she wondered if all men were animals because the men in her life were destined to disappoint her in some way, large or small.

Going back to her father, at one time, she thought all fathers must be like hers. That didn't make sense when she observed other fathers at her friends' houses.

After Danny assaulted her, she thought all teenage boys were degenerates. She dismissed that because, as far as she was aware, at least hoped, her brothers were not like that.

In college, she simply didn't date. She avoided social activities to graduate early. It wasn't that she wasn't interested. She'd had her fair share of crushes once she realized all men weren't created equal.

In Park Haven, she had two totally different dating experiences. She went out with Bert when she hadn't lived here long. What sane woman would put herself in that situation twice? There was no excuse.

Will, on the other hand, never gave her pause. Why couldn't she have fallen in love with him?

Then, she met MC.

Finally.

Why had they never met at Auburn? Neither of them had mentioned remembering the other. Did he wonder, as well?

She thought about clean-cut MC versus the current war-weary version. Maybe it was a sign of her bad judgment, but in school, he was the big man on campus—at least in their department. Top of his class. She was glad they weren't in the same one. She remembered a young lady with blond curls who hung on his arm any time she saw him on campus, and the ripple of surprise in the animal science department at the news that he'd put his doctoral program on pause and answered the call of the draft.

He hadn't needed anyone or anything back then. His life appeared to be perfect.

Now? Now he needed her, or at least someone who could listen and understand the aftermath of trauma.

She stopped in the middle of the path that ran through the park. He was strong, a protector. Why would the thought even come to her mind that he might need *her*?

Was she attracted to men who needed her?

Nancy found a bench and sat, dog leads around her wrists, head in her hands. No, no, no, no, no.

Nancy didn't want a guy she needed to "fix."

God, where are you leading me? Have you been preparing me for this all my life? Why can't I have a normal, safe, happy life?

She paused, convicted.

Forgive me. You never promised easy, did You? It's for sure Jesus didn't have it easy, or You, either, having to watch Your Son die in my place.

Nancy looked down at the eager faces of Major and Biddie. They were constant, didn't ask anything of her other than her time and basic care, and they were always overjoyed to see her, no matter what mood she was in.

A grin formed on her face. She could feel it. Looking toward the sun, she closed her eyes, drawing in the light and heat. *Thank you, God.*

As MC FINISHED out the trim on the stained-glass window, a strange noise surprised him. Grandpa had gone to church that morning, and MC had, once again, sidestepped the invitation.

He was alone. So what was that sound?

After a moment, it came to him.

He was whistling. How long had it been since he'd done that?

Did it have anything to do with the fact that He'd spent yesterday with Nancy?

The corner of his mouth rose. He didn't think about the horror he'd seen or the deaths he'd witnessed when he was with her. What could he do for her? How could he protect her, make the way smooth for her?

Love her.

He squeezed his eyes shut. Pain seared through his head.

This was new. He'd had numbness and tingling in his arm, but this? Sheer pain. It hit him like a ton of bricks.

He needed to get down. Dizziness and trying to stand on the fourth rung of a stepladder weren't a good combination. Slowly, he rubbed the area on his head where the pain concentrated. It was tender, but where did it come from?

He'd been shot in the shoulder, but that didn't hurt. Sitting on the front pew of the chapel, he took in deep breaths. Rusty came up to him, wagging his tail, checking on his master. Maybe if he could relax. That's it. Get rid of the tension creeping up his neck and into his head. It had been a rough week.

Maybe … if he laid his head back for a few minutes …

"MC!"

His world shook when the sound of his name being called broke through the fuzziness.

Grandpa?

"What?" MC jerked up from where he'd been leaning back on the pew.

Mistake. His stomach and his head were at battle with one another, and neither was winning.

He'd closed his eyes just a minute ago, hadn't he?

"You okay?"

MC frowned. "Yeah. A little headache, maybe."

"Are you dizzy?"

"I was a little woozy earlier. Got off the ladder."

"That's good thinking." Grandpa peered at him strangely. "I came down here to get you so we could go to Connor's for lunch, and Rusty met me at the door." He scrutinized him more closely. "Your eyes don't look right."

MC stood quickly, again regretting the movement. Had he whacked his head on a brick wall? "Ouch." Hand to head, he sat back down, eyes closed.

"Yeah. I think you need to see the doc."

"It's Sunday. I'm not ready for another trip to the emergency room." If he did, would people think he'd tried to hurt himself again? He was almost a doctor—for animals, anyway. "You said my eyes don't look right. What do they look like?"

"Pupils don't match."

Red flag. Man, dog, the eyes could tell you a lot about their health. "Do you have a flashlight down here?"

Grandpa went to the toolbox and pulled out the antique Ray-o-vac flashlight.

"Shine it in one eye at a time and tell me what the pupils do."

"The eye that's bruised all around it isn't moving as quickly as the other one."

Great.

"Sounds like I've got a concussion."

Grandpa nodded. "Not much we can do for that, is there?"

"No. I think we'd know if it was serious." MC shook his head in disgust. "I'll stay off the ladder for a few days." He closed his eyes tightly. "Got any Tylenol?"

"Yep. Doc got me off aspirin when my blood pressure pills stopped working for me." Worry etched Grandpa's face. "You feel like going to your mama's?"

"Yeah. She'd worry if I didn't. Don't say anything about it—she'd start hovering and want me to stay there."

"I'll keep my mouth shut." Grandpa quirked his brow. "I think she may have invited a few others too."

MC closed his eyes again after getting up from the pew. "Figures."

"I don't think you'll mind." Grandpa chuckled. "It's Nancy.

NANCY HAD EATEN Sunday dinner at the Dunne's house before, but this time was different. Before, MC wasn't there. Now?

Now, he was there. And how.

As soon as MC walked in the door ahead of Mr. Dunne, she immediately saw something was wrong.

He was perturbed about something. Maybe he didn't want her there, in his parents' home. Too much of a good thing … if he considered her a good thing. No, his eyes, to her, anyway, seemed to light up when he saw her. She felt the flush roll up her cheeks. Hopefully, no one would notice.

Wait. His color wasn't good.

MC walked right up to her and smiled at her, his concern evident. "How are you?"

"I'm fine. What about you?" She narrowed her eyes at him, then widened them. "Oh …"

"Fine and dandy." He shook his head and turned, giving her the signal to not say anything.

Marjorie bustled between the kitchen and the dining room, so she hadn't had time to notice and worry about him. Mr. Dunne and Connor were in the living room reading the paper.

MC took her hand and pulled her to the screened-in porch in the back.

"You've got a concussion." Nancy made the statement. She touched the bruising on his face, feeling flush as he took her hand and pulled it away. "Do you need to go to the doctor?"

He shook his head, wincing. "I've got one in front of me, haven't I?"

"I'd be more likely to give you a correct diagnosis if fur covered the bump on your head." Nancy twisted her lips in a wry grin.

"I'll be okay. I guess Bert's right hook packed more of a punch than I thought." His dimple came out on his left cheek. "I made it through two tours in Vietnam. I think I can heal up from Bert Conway without any issues."

"I don't doubt your toughness." She smirked at him. There was nothing wrong with his swagger.

He squeezed her hand, and she returned the pressure. They had a secret. It felt good. Intimate. Exciting.

Especially when he couldn't seem to take his eyes off of her.

"Your hair looks nice."

Nancy didn't want Bert Conway to be the reason for anything about her, especially her hairstyle. She touched it self-consciously, not sure about the half-up, half-down style she'd tried out. "Thank you."

"I always wondered what it would look like, down."

She raised startled eyes to his. "When …"

"When we were at Auburn." His grin reached out and touched her heart.

"I didn't think you remembered me."

"You're hard to forget."

"Lunch is ready." Marjorie's voice floated through the double doors to the porch.

"I should have been in there helping her." She couldn't seem to escape his gaze, but she was self-conscious.

"I think she has it under control." He rubbed the inside of her wrist with his thumb, as he had the other night, comforting her.

Comforting, and at the same time, scintillating.

Chapter Forty-One

Monday morning dawned bright and clear, and MC had slept. Really slept.

It was amazing what a decent night's sleep could do for one's outlook.

Nancy once again broached the subject of his working at the clinic. Mary Ann's maternity leave was permanent. Except for the residual headache that reminded him he wasn't 100 percent, he could almost see himself doing it.

What came next?

He'd been living day by day without a plan ever since he got home. The only thing that kept him going was the people he loved, and he endured life for them. Not for himself. He'd have been fine with dropping dead then and there, if not for them.

The guilt he still carried for the losses he'd seen tended to revisit him at his lowest points. The work with Grandpa, on the chapel—especially the stained-glass window—helped to block the images and memories out of his mind.

For a while, anyway.

With Nancy, the budding hope continued to grow.

He'd spent too much time telling himself he couldn't have what regular guys had—a home, a family, a normal life. Over and over. He didn't deserve it. He couldn't maintain it. He would be too dangerous to be around Nancy or anyone else. What if he cracked?

The farther he got from the horrors of war, the more he considered a whole new life available to him.

Sure, he could take the job at Fort Benning, or he could go back to Auburn and finish his degree.

Were those his only options?

He wasn't sure. Did God figure into all this?

Good question.

He noticed a stack of papers on the table. Grandpa had brought him his mail on Friday, and he hadn't dealt with it. Rifling through it, he pulled out the junk mail and sale bills and put them straight into the trash.

There were three other pieces of mail: a formal letter offering the K9 training position; a letter from Shorty McGuire, the youngest of their group and one of the last remaining guys in his unit. According to the return address of Detroit, Michigan, he was home. The last piece of mail caught his attention, the beautiful script handwriting familiar. All too familiar.

Rebecca.

MC placed the letter on the table next to his easy chair and walked around it all day.

Grandpa brought over some soup and ate lunch with him. MC thought he recognized the tune he was whistling as he headed down to the chapel afterward—"What a Friend We Have in Jesus."

Still a little on the dizzy side, MC decided to take it easy. Part of his reasoning, concussion-related. The other part? That letter.

What could she want? She'd shown herself unwilling to sacrifice her happiness for others.

Maybe he'd been too hard on her. It made him angry. For weeks, he read her "Dear John" letter over and over, trying to make sense out of the swift kick in the gut. Did it make him more reckless? Maybe. After that, he started taking more chances. Started not caring if he came back or not.

He hadn't considered how he would feel if Gunnar didn't come back. His dog had done nothing to deserve the end he had.

MC, however, had given up on a future.

He picked the letter up and sat down, pulling the chain to turn on the lamp in the increasing dusk. There was only one way to find out what it said.

Open it. Read it.

He reached for the letter opener on the table next to him, and he used it to carefully slit the top of the envelope. The embossed stationery was classic Rebecca Randall. Light blue, with lacy cut-paper edges.

He shook his head. No postcard for this lady.

He unfolded the one-page letter and took a deep breath.

Dear MC,

I heard you were home and that you sustained injuries while you were in Vietnam. I'm so sorry, and I hope you recover soon.

Are you going back to Auburn, as you'd planned? I've had you on my mind lately.

I'm living in Auburn now. I married the man I wrote you about …

That was a stab in the gut.

… and he got drafted soon after …

So much for avoiding the war, eh Rebecca?

… The last I heard, he'd been captured.

I moved back in with my parents. I have a little boy— he's three and into everything—and I needed their help. They were disappointed in me for breaking it off with you, but there's no going back now. Clint was a good daddy to my son. He took care of us.

An odd turn of phrase. Why wouldn't a man take care of his wife and son?

My mother passed away, suddenly, of a heart attack, soon after I came. That was hard.

I'm sorry I hurt you. I realize, now, how selfish I was. I hope to be able to make it up to you someday. Now I'm in a holding pattern, waiting to see if I'm a widow or not. Maybe Clint and I should have waited to get married, but we didn't, and it is what it is.

I hope you can forgive me. If I'd never written you that letter, we would be together today, I think.

I hope your recovery goes well. Say hello to your family for me.

Sincerely,
Rebecca

It hurt to read, but not for the reason he would have thought.

Yes, she'd been selfish. And yes, she'd broken his heart. At the time, her letters had been a lifeline to home and hope—until that last one.

He had to think that, all in all, they weren't meant to be. Reading it didn't make him desperately unhappy, as he would have thought a few months ago. He was over her.

If they'd married, he had a feeling they would have been relatively happy, but would it have been a good fit, once he got home? Would her voice, her touch be the one that could soothe him at the times he wanted to jump out of his skin?

MC folded the letter and stuffed it in a drawer. He was sympathetic to the loss of Rebecca's mother, and he didn't wish bad things for her, or her husband, either.

She had a son.

Could he forgive her?

Yes, he could. His thoughts shifted to Nancy, asking if she should press charges, hoping it would help him. She would forgive this man for hurting her, even though he didn't think he'd done anything wrong.

Rebecca knew. She took full responsibility for hurting him. She had a son without a father.

He frowned, thinking, and then dismissed it. No, she just happened to meet Clint very soon after he left. Still, odd.

God, bring that man back to his family.

He hadn't talked to God in a while. It was the first time his prayer hadn't been about himself longer than he could remember.

Nancy glanced up at the clock. Three o'clock. Brent would be there in the next fifteen minutes.

Thank goodness.

It had been a busy day. Not just busy—crazy busy. Fortunately, she'd found a young mother to cover the desk for a few hours a day. It had been the best decision she'd made in a long time.

Laurie Pike's husband served as a Marine overseas, and her two young children were both in school. She said it gave her something to do besides worry about him.

"Here's the mail that came today." Laurie handed her the envelopes. "I culled out the junk mail."

"Thanks, Laurie." Nancy shrugged. "Somehow, I always think I might need to look at the junk, so I put it in a pile. After a while, the pile gets so big I can't face it."

"I get it." Laurie chuckled. "I get magazines I never open." She perked up. "Hey, would you like some in the waiting area?"

Nancy nodded. "That would be great."

"I can fix you right up with *Good Housekeeping* and *Field and Stream.*"

"*Field and Stream?*" Nancy laughed. "Tell me that's Robbie's subscription."

"It is. He started getting it before he left, and I mistakenly renewed it instead of canceling it." She shrugged. "Never been read."

"Thanks. Our male pet owners will appreciate it."

"Glad to get some piles of magazines out of the house."

"How's he doing?"

Laurie reached up to finger the heart pendant she wore every day. Her voice was intentionally light, probably practicing for when she was at home with her girls. "I wish I knew. I talked to him last month. He didn't say directly, but watching the news makes me think he's in Cambodia." She glanced up, a sheen of tears in her eyes. "I can't watch the news if the girls are up, so I wait for the ten o'clock news."

"That's rough."

How would she react if she had a husband thousands of miles away in a place where thousands of our soldiers were being killed or wounded?

MC had been wounded, but so many weren't lucky enough to make it home.

Not lucky. Blessed. How she wished MC would realize how blessed he is to have a second chance at life, and that he is not to be blamed for surviving.

God's got a plan for him. She had faith.

Chapter
Forty-Two

I t got harder and harder to watch the news. Cambodia had been invaded. The president promised to send troops home by the thousands. College campuses erupted in violence.

Was the world falling apart, shaking the confidence of the nation?

The headaches subsided after a few days, and MC resumed work on the chapel. He liked working with Grandpa. They talked when necessary, and if not, they didn't. The silence wasn't awkward.

These days, even Grandpa was quieter than usual. They were a pair.

Rebecca's letter had thrown him for a loop, but in some ways, it propelled him to think more about the future. It would help if he could stop reliving the past.

"What about the hole in the wall under the stained-glass window?"

The two men stood in front of the window, sunlight streaming through it, spreading shards of color everywhere. As the sun moved in the sky, so did the beauty of the Irish work of art. The cross motif had always intrigued him. It was what made him choose that pattern for his tattoo. Sometimes he regretted the permanent reminder of his time in Vietnam, but he was stuck with it now.

Grandpa stood there, hands in his pockets. "I think I need to talk to you and your dad before we close it up. Might want to put some other things in there."

MC watched Grandpa, thinking about the times, recently, that he'd appeared troubled about something.

"Anything you want to run by me, first?"

Grandpa shifted, glancing away for a moment. "No. I think Connor needs to hear it the same time you do."

"Okay." MC hesitated. "Grandpa, can I ask you something."

"'Course you can, son."

"How do you know, really know, that God's there?"

A slight smile graced the older man's face. "Because if He wasn't, there would be no hope." He blew out a breath. "There have been a lot of times I've wanted to turn my back on God. In my younger days, it would have been easier if I had. Then, at the time your Grandma died, it just about finished me. I wanted to lay down and die with her."

"But you didn't."

Staring at the window, Grandpa shook his head. "Your Grandma made me learn this verse soon after she got sick. You know how she was."

"I know. She didn't brook any arguments."

Grandpa smiled. "She did not. Here it is, straight from Jesus. *'I have told you these things, so that in me you may have peace. In this world you will have trouble. But take heart! I have overcome the world.'* There's no peace to be found in this world, only trouble. The only peace we have is in Jesus Christ. The only hope we have to survive this crazy life? Jesus. He's got plans for us, MC."

MC said nothing. He wouldn't argue with Grandpa. Grandma didn't have the market cornered on stubbornness.

MC and Grandpa worked quietly, clearing up little jobs here and there. The stepping-stone path leading to the front door of the chapel was disappearing into the earth, so, one by one, they dug them out, put sand and gravel in the hole, and replaced the stones, bringing them to ground level.

While MC finished up the landscaping work, Grandpa focused on refinishing window frames and fixing loose spots on the pews inside.

MC heard a truck drive up. He straightened and waved at his dad. "What's up, Pop?"

Connor Dunne walked to the chapel, looking around at the work that had been done, both inside and outside.

"Inspecting our work?" MC smiled at Dad.

"Nah, I just thought I'd check y'all out, see the progress." He put his hands in his pockets. "Grandpa inside?"

"You wanted to see the window, didn't you?" MC followed him inside and to where he stood, gazing at the window.

"You found me out."

Dad choked up, taking in the beauty of the window that had seen so much.

"Thought I heard you drive up. How are you?" Grandpa walked over to stand between his son and grandson, putting a weathered hand on each man's shoulder. "It's something else, isn't it?"

"It is. Seen a lot of life." Dad smiled at Grandpa. "Marjie said you'd called."

MC wondered if they would finally get some answers.

"I did." Grandpa cleared his throat. "I've intended to talk to you for a long time but kept putting it off. I'm not getting any younger, and losing Evangeline has reminded me there's no time like the present to get things out in the open."

"Pop, I know I'm adopted, and I know where babies come from." Dad grinned.

Grandpa chuckled. "Yes, and you're the spitting image of my brother, your father, James."

"I've seen a few pictures." Dad sat down next to MC, Grandpa across from them, taking a deep breath as if he were settling in.

"Ah, James. A good-looking young man." The half-smile on Grandpa's face indicated his thoughts going back to earlier days. "Good-looking and charming, but a rascal."

Did he hear a slight Irish lilt on the American-born man?

"I kinda figured that, since my mother, Nora, raised me." The look on Dad's face was one MC had seen off and on throughout his life. Sadness.

"I know, son, I know. I've wished time and time again that you could learn more about your mother's side of the family. How much do you remember before you came to us? You were upset, understandably, when you arrived, so we didn't talk about it much." Grandpa shook his head. "My Evangeline and I were so young, we didn't know anything about raising kids."

MC looked from his father to his grandfather. "I think you figured it out pretty quickly."

Connor smiled at his son, then frowned. "I remember when I arrived, I was angry. Angry at Ma for dying, at you, at Mother, Uncle Patrick. Angry with grandparents on both sides who didn't want me."

MC could see tears glistening in both the older men's eyes, and emotions threatened to overcome him as well. "Did you ever know your grandparents? On either side?"

"I was blessed to know my adopted grandparents, the Moores. They tried to be both sets of grandparents. I remember, before she died, asking my mother about her family. She never talked about them. If I asked, she got a pained look on her face that made me decide it wasn't worth hurting her. I asked about my father." Connor looked up at his dad. "It didn't take long for me to figure out he must have been involved in illegal activities. I caught her reading a letter—I think it was from her mother—and she was crying. She didn't know I was there, and I heard her say, 'We don't need your help.'"

"She wouldn't tell me much, but after she died, I was sent to a mansion in the old part of Chicago."

"Mother and Father's house." Grandpa's countenance was that of heartbreak. "Most Irish children would have called their parents 'Mum and Da,' but not us. Father wanted to be American, and formal, at that."

MC couldn't help feeling sorry for him, dredging all this up. And yet, he wanted to know. Had to know.

"I gathered that. I knew there was a lot more to the story than she'd shared. She always said she'd 'not speak ill of the dead.'" Connor scoffed. "When I got to the house, I never met the owners of the house, just the housekeeper. Seemed that she'd had a letter from my mother telling her to send me to you."

Grandpa cleared his throat. "Back then, folks didn't share the skeletons in their closets. It's not the right attitude, because those skeletons are people. Situations between people. God's grace covers it all, if we let Him." He shook his head. "Those situations are what brought us here. Home."

"During Prohibition, Chicago became a crossroads for the country —especially in the liquor trade. As a child, all I understood was we had money, and a lot of other people didn't. I didn't know that my father, Sean Dunne—" Grandpa pierced Dad with his eyes. "—your grandfather and the owner of that big mansion—was the boss of the largest Irish organized crime family in Illinois."

Dad leaned forward, a frown on his face. "How did I not know this?" He blustered, angry, confused. "I knew something was off, and Ma would never tell me more than my father's name, and that she'd made a bad decision. She mentioned once, when she was getting sicker, that her sins would probably be visited on me." Dad let out a breath, his eyes on the floor. "I haven't thought about that in a long time."

"I know, son. I know. You didn't know because your mother and I were ashamed. I freely admit it."

MC was stunned but curious. "So, were you …"

"I met your grandma in Harrisburg, after Father tasked James and me with enlarging our territory, so to speak."

MC shook his head. "Okay, let me get this straight." He swallowed thickly, then looked his Grandpa in the eyes. "You were a criminal?"

Grandpa nodded. "I guess I was." He considered his son and grandson. "It was our way of life. I wouldn't have chosen it, but James, Father's favorite, reveled in it. The night James died, Evangeline was seen with me. When I found out he blamed me for not protecting James, I knew he wouldn't hesitate to have us killed. He turned his back on me. We had to leave Harrisburg under cover of darkness. We were both in danger."

"Your own father would have killed you?" Dad's eyes bulged, then, shaking his head in disbelief, he scoffed. "That explains why my mother was afraid, but that doesn't explain …"

"How we got to Tennessee?" Grandpa smiled, then. "Your Uncle Patrick, Father's brother, escaped the 'family' years before, but not before he had a big influence on me in spiritual matters. My parents kept up the appearance of religion for business purposes. They had everyone fooled.

Dad and MC stared at one another. "So, were you and Mama …"

"Your grandfather, the judge, married us before we left Harrisburg. I was already smitten with her, and we'd started courting. To protect her reputation, her father and I decided we should marry. I convinced him I would love and cherish his only daughter."

"Knowing Mother, I can't imagine she went along with that, but by the time I came, you had patched things up. Although," Dad scoffed, "I can see her eyes flash, now."

"Oh, mad as an old wet hen, was my Evangeline. In her heart, she comprehended we had to leave, for our safety, but her head wanted to stay angry forever. She had to leave behind her whole life, and maybe would never see her family again. Having been raised in a well-to-do Christian household, she knew her reputation was ruined in Harrisburg, and the worst thing for a lady of breeding was to have anything embarrassing in their past, and a rushed-up wedding usually meant only one thing. She was young and thought better of herself. Didn't want anyone to think she was misbehaving."

"I get that." MC understood. When he and Rebecca's relationship got too serious, even though it wasn't planned, the last thing they wanted was for their parents to find out. They thought they were pretty smart. Now, the very idea that his friends and family could think he would commit suicide was part of what kept him on the farm, away from as many people as possible.

It was pride, pure and simple.

Grandpa looked at MC with love. "I know you do. And we all know that "pride goeth before a fall."

"The only place I could think of to go and hide out was Park Haven and Uncle Patrick. By the time we got down here after driving all night, your grandma decided she was angry with me and wouldn't have anything to do with me."

"But …"

Grandpa waved his hand. "She finally came around. I came to the conclusion I'd have to court her all over again, so, because she held my very heart in her hands, I did." Grandpa paused, rubbing his ear, looking embarrassed. "The wooing delayed the honeymoon somewhat, but it was worth every minute. We got to know one another. Gave her time to fall in love with me, and cement what I already had committed to."

The love of his life. Nancy's face flitted through MC's mind, causing him to smile.

"I know what you're thinking, young man." Grandpa quirked his eyebrow, and MC simply nodded. "I can't say I was always happy about it."

Grandpa's gaze swept around the chapel. "Uncle Patrick had started on the chapel, and my attitude made me wonder why—kind of like you, MC. I was pretty angry, myself, that my beautiful wife seemed to change into someone I didn't know after we were married. Anyway, I helped him, and we installed that window right there." He pointed to the heirloom window.

"Did it really come from Ireland?"

"It did. Just before Father and Uncle Patrick immigrated from Ireland, what was left of the castle chapel was about to be razed, so Uncle Patrick asked for the window. He was the sentimental of the two. That's why we still have it today." Grandpa shook his head. "I'm not sure how old it is. I just know that it was instrumental in convincing your grandma to trust God, even when we, in our humanity, think it's wrong. He can use us wherever we are, and in whatever situation we find ourselves."

Dad sat there, stunned. "So, basically, I'm the son of an Irish mobster."

Grandpa's eyebrows shot up. "Well, I guess so, but then, so am I." He chuckled. "It's taken a long time for me to get over the stigma of being part of a crime family. Like I said, I was young. I wanted to put the past behind me and pretend it never happened. Uncle Patrick had left years before, when I was a lad. After he became a Christian, he wanted to change the business, and Father refused. Said Uncle Patrick dishonored the family by refusing to cooperate. He was in danger the same way my Evangeline and I were."

It explained a lot. The time MC had made the crack about extorting money, Grandpa lost all color in his face. And no wonder. There had been other reactions over the years that were confusing, but he'd written them off as unimportant.

"It's always fascinated me, MC, how much you look like Uncle Patrick and me, and you, Connor, look like James."

Dad smiled. "I remember my mother had light hair like you've described my father."

Grandpa nodded sadly. "They were so young. Nora, the daughter of the head of a rival family, and James, the son of the other. Romeo and Juliet. Chicago in the twenties. James loved her, I believe, in his way, but he couldn't bring himself to buck Father's power over him. He'd been tagged as second-in-command, after all. Father's favorite." He shook his head.

"The two families tried to keep them apart, but the day Nora's family found out about her and James, and her carrying James's baby, they turned her out, and Father made sure James never had another opportunity to see her. From that point on, James was even more focused on pleasing Father. On the job. He took his anger out on everyone who crossed him."

"What happened then?" MC was enthralled. He'd heard bits and pieces over the years, but this, hearing it from the beginning, was more than he expected. This was his regular, boring, normal family. But then, what was normal?

"As soon as I got to the Dunne house, Mrs. Higgins put me on a train to Harrisburg, to Judge Moore. She protected me from even meeting your father, Dad, which I didn't understand. I'd never had grandparents, but I knew kids who did. What grandparent didn't want their own flesh and blood? I was one angry little boy, wasn't I?"

Grandpa smiled. "You were, but we loved you anyway. The only thing that could have made raising you better would have been for your parents to have come down here with us, changed by the Lord Jesus. I tried, son. How I tried."

"How have you kept this to yourselves all these years?" MC's mind reeled at the story. Even more amazing, Dad never told him his part of the story.

"Not much to be proud of. It was a long time before I could forgive the family for what they'd done to my mother, and to me. I soon found out, though, that I couldn't be the man I wanted to be and not move forward." Dad leaned forward, clasping his hands in front of him. "Your mama's family prided themselves on being very strait-laced." Dad looked closely at MC. "Your Grandpa Morgan would never have let your mom and me go together if he had a hint of my pedigree—and I didn't know about the Chicago crime connection, then. Beyond forgiving, I knew enough to keep my mouth shut." He grinned. "He died not knowing the checkered past of his son-in-law's heritage."

"I'm sorry, Dad. I'm just surprised."

"Life can be surprising, can't it?" Grandpa snorted. "It's for sure it's not pretty, much as we'd like it to be."

No, it wasn't pretty. But it was real.

Chapter Forty-Three

MC sat in the chapel after Grandpa and Dad left, still stunned at what he'd learned about his family. Grandpa had broken the cycle of crime and violence. As a result, the Dunne family became the family he'd enjoyed all his life.

A life of love, faith, and gratitude.

Gratitude. He'd almost forgotten what that felt like, and he was ashamed. Now, knowing what Dad and Grandpa had gone through and survived, guilt rattled him.

Why had he been blessed, and protected, and others, not?

It wasn't fair, but then, whoever promised fair?

That verse Grandpa mentioned, saying the world is full of trouble. As a teen, he'd memorized a lot of scripture, and he remembered this one. It hadn't meant much then, because he hadn't faced real trouble.

Now? Now he wanted, desperately, to hang on to the part of the verse that says, *"Take heart! For I have overcome the world."*

Could he trust God? Grandpa did. Dad and Mom? They did too. Dad had every reason not to.

What about Nancy? She went to church—he knew that much.

MC had been drifting even before he went to college at Auburn. He and Rebecca never talked about spiritual things, and he was keenly aware, even then, that to create a household of faith—one like he'd grown up in—God had to be at the center. In the months before he shipped out to Vietnam, they'd gotten ahead of themselves, physically. They thought they were wiser, smarter than their parents, than God, about what was best for them. Modern thought prevailed. They thought nobody would know. Maybe Rebecca could convince herself of that, but MC, deep down, was grounded enough to know it was wrong.

He told himself he'd convince her, later. They'd make up for it once they were married. He never got the chance.

Faith. Could he possibly get back to the belief and faith in God he had before he encountered the horrors the world? Would God even want him, when he'd dismissed his Creator so completely?

He wasn't sure. He could write it off now and not look back, but something kept tugging him back. Rebecca's letter still puzzled him. Could her son be his?

He raked his hand over his face, trying to wipe the thought away. No, she would have told him. Surely.

Something was pulling on him, gently. Sometimes not so gently, but always with love.

From experience, he recognized that tug. Knew it intimately. The Holy Spirit. The Spirit who indwelled him the moment, at a young age, he accepted Jesus as his Savior.

That gentle beckoning, tender, yet strong. Similar to the way he wanted to deal with Nancy. She'd been hurt. He wanted to care for her —but he wanted her to desire it.

Did she? He thought so, but considering his track record with women, maybe she was blowing smoke.

No. He'd seen genuine affection on her face and in her actions. She'd picked up on his concussion as soon as she saw him. Because of that, he'd been able to keep Mom from knowing about it. No point in worrying her—plus, Nancy did not need her business brought out unless she wanted it so.

Could he return to his faith for Nancy?

He could, but what would be the cost? God was a jealous God.

God must be number one. To be worshiped simply because He was

God, not because MC wanted peace in his life. He'd messed up on so many levels.

Immaturity focused on God as a vending machine that dispensed blessings and curses, hoping to hit the right button and get the good stuff.

He was the Father, the Son, and the Holy Spirit, three in one, God Almighty.

MC admitted his fear. Could he maintain a relationship with God any more than he could maintain the one he'd had with Rebecca? Getting to know Nancy made him realize he'd forgiven Rebecca.

That night, sleep evaded MC, as usual. Exhaustion claimed his body. So tired, while his mind whirled.

He wanted to talk to Nancy, but wanted to figure some things out first. He had to make sure of himself before he dragged anyone else into his life.

Bits and pieces of individual scriptures about faith drifted through MC's mind. He couldn't remember the chapter and verse references, but they revealed themselves to him, one after another, in no particular order.

Now faith is confidence in what we hope for and assurance about what we do not see.

For we live by faith, not by sight.

Because you know that the testing of your faith produces perseverance.

For it is by grace you have been saved, through faith—and this is not from yourselves, it is the gift of God—not by works, so that no one can boast.

Therefore, since we have been justified through faith, we have peace with God through our Lord Jesus Christ.

Peace.

Peace only came through faith in Jesus, through knowing that He is the only path to salvation.

MC sat on the porch of the chapel in the dark, pondering the words that flew through his brain.

God had a plan. He understood that now. His plan might be for him to become a veterinarian, but it might not. God was in control, and if MC wanted even the minimum of peace in his life, it could only come through his personal relationship with Jesus Christ.

~

Nancy was surprised when MC showed up at the clinic Wednesday morning, bright and early. Had he changed his mind, or did he want to see her for other reasons? A smile threatened to blossom at that last thought, but she put on her professional face and greeted him.

"Good morning, MC. How are you today?"

"I'm good." He noted the absence of patients in the waiting room. "Have I come before appointments started?"

"Yes, your timing is perfect. What can I do for you?"

He paused, looking everywhere but at her. Did he have his hair slicked back a little? It was still long, but he had tried to up his professionalism.

"I … I wondered if you still needed an assistant?" Did he mean it? As soon as she met his gaze, she was caught, much like an insect in a spider web. What did he say? Oh …

"Yes, I do." Awkwardness came over her. She didn't know what to do with her hands. Smoothing her hair, she found it still neatly coiffed and sprayed, relieved that nothing was out of place.

But it was early, yet.

"I would like to try it, if you're still willing to take me on."

His eyes. So, so dark. So probing. So serious. She could see the hurt lingering behind them, but today she detected another aspect to his countenance. Hope?

"I am." She wanted to say more but kept it simple.

He nodded, looking away for a moment. "I can't promise you I will stay."

"I understand."

His eyes drew Nancy in, forcing her to stop evading his gaze.

She did understand. She perceived nothing but honesty and compassion in his eyes. And maybe something else she wasn't prepared to acknowledge yet.

"When can you start?"

"Tomorrow?" When he smiled, she couldn't help smiling back.

"I can do tomorrow."

Nancy took a deep breath. "Perfect. Brent is taking summer classes at the community college, and I would be without an assistant. Laurie is great with the office stuff, but she's no vet tech."

"Good timing?"

She breathed out a small chuckle. His face softened to the point she almost regretted agreeing to work alongside him every day.

"More like God-timing."

That's what she needed to know. Could she count on him to stay focused? Could she separate her attraction to him from her desire to live in a way that would honor God?

With God's help, yes.

The back door to the clinic opened with a gust of wind. A feminine voice came from the back room. "Whew!"

"That would be Laurie."

"That wind is something else." Laurie stopped, realizing she and Nancy weren't alone. "Oh, hello."

"Laurie, this is MC Dunne."

Laurie smiled. "Ah, the illusive Mr. Dunne."

MC twisted his lips. Was that a grin threatening to come out? Could he see the furious blush Nancy felt invading her chest, neck, and face? She had a distinct dislike of her easily embarrassed complexion. But wait. Was there a tinge of red on his well-tanned face?

Maybe it wasn't just her.

"Call me MC." He held out his hand, and Laurie shook it.

"MC's going to be working with me while I try to find a replacement for Mary Ann."

"Talk about good timing, with Brent finishing up this week."

Nancy and MC eyed one another. Were they thinking the same thing? His slight wink told her yes.

It wasn't good timing, it was God-timing.

Chapter
Forty-Four

MC's first day at the clinic challenged him. True to her word, she didn't ask him to accompany her to the large-animal calls on the schedule, but he'd already decided the next time she went out he would accompany her. He hadn't told her, yet.

He pondered the future. K9 training? Vet school? Nancy?

At least he'd marked "disappear" off his list.

He drove up to the cabin to see Grandpa walking toward him.

"Did you have a good day?" Grandpa was pleased with his decision to accept Nancy's offer.

"I did. It's a busy place."

"That it is, that it is."

He held up some envelopes. "Got your mail. You saved me from leaving it in the door."

"Thanks."

In the days since Grandpa let him and Dad in on the story of their family's past, Grandpa's countenance was more relaxed. Relieved?

As good as the relationship was between himself, his dad, and his grandpa, it had grown closer with the shared knowledge.

Grandpa told MC that he regretted, as soon as MC left for Vietnam, not telling them the truth about the Dunne family story.

After that, MC asked questions from a more informed perspective, about life, love, and faith. Grandpa figured out MC's feelings for Nancy. Some, he guessed, and some MC had to tell him to ask for advice. He didn't give him any details about the night of the attack. It wasn't his story to tell.

He didn't tell him about the depth of his hurt at the time Rebecca broke it off. The past could stay in the past. He counted on God throwing his sins as far as the East was from the West.

MC rifled through the paper, stopping. Another letter from Rebecca. He hadn't answered her last one. Didn't know what to say to her. He had to consider how far he'd come. When he first came home, her first letter would have sent him flying into a rage, or perhaps made him gloat that she'd made a mess of her life.

Now? Now he had not only love but also compassion for her. She'd tried to run her life to make her way smoother and instead made it more complicated by bringing marriage and a baby into the mix.

Studying the envelope, the handwriting was different, but it had the same return address.

Dear MC,

I found your address in Rebecca's things and wanted to let you know that she died in a traffic accident last week. I know she let you down, and I'm sorry for that. She had a good heart but could be selfish. I guess that was our fault.

I tried to get in touch with her husband, and I found out he'd been captured, then died in captivity. I started searching for him about the time they were gearing up to let Rebecca know she was a widow.

She told me she'd written you, but didn't have the heart to tell you that right after she married Clint, she discovered she was going to have a baby. You have a son, raised as Clint's.

MC stopped right there. He turned the paper frontwards and backward, trying to make some sense of this.

Wait. Rebecca? Dead?

And then, the kicker. The nugget of truth that had niggled at his mind ever since he received the first letter. He had a son?

I love my grandson more than life itself, but I'm in no shape to raise a two-year-old without Rebecca or my wife.

I hope your tours didn't leave you permanently disabled. I understand you were recovering from a gunshot wound. We have some relatives who will take little Michael if you aren't able, but I felt beholden to you for what Rebecca did in not telling you.

I've told myself to be angry with you instead of Rebecca for a long time, but I don't have the energy anymore to carry the burden. I never would have thought about Rebecca going behind our backs and getting in trouble. I know it happens, and I know we neglected to see that she knew the importance of following God's path instead of her own. I guess what I'm saying is that I'm sorry. We knew better.

She'd named him Michael.

MC sat there, holding the letter until darkness crept into the cabin. The lamp next to him put out a small light, but his thoughts were like the darkness that surrounded him.

He didn't know at what point he'd cried, but there were tears on his face. The shock of knowing he had a son put him into a stupor for a time.

How could he offer himself to Nancy, knowing he had a son—a part of himself that he created with someone else—and that he needed to take responsibility for his actions?

On top of that, how could he care for a small child? Loving him wouldn't be a problem. Knowing what to do with him, the caring and feeding of a child, made veterinary science look like a fun hobby.

He couldn't do it on his own, and he wouldn't ask his parents. He'd messed up, he'd clean it up. Like Nancy said—actions have consequences.

The more he went around and around in his head, the fuzzier

everything around him became. He had nothing to offer his son except his name and his love.

After Grandpa's revelation, he couldn't help but think about his biological grandfather, James, and "the sins of the fathers."

For weeks now, MC had prayed for peace and forgiveness. Peace in his heart, his mind, his world. He'd found that much of the peace he craved only came with trusting God. Trusting that God loved him and wanted the best for him.

And for his little boy.

NANCY ANTICIPATED mornings with MC in the office. She made coffee, and they sat in the office, going over appointments and activities of the day.

It was nice. Domestic. Made her wonder what a future with him could look like.

As far as she was aware, he hadn't had an episode with hallucinations and nightmares in a week or so. Maybe he was better … maybe being here helped him.

He still hadn't asked her to go on a date with him. Nancy worried she was reading too much into the budding relationship. It wasn't so much that she wanted to date, period. General all-purpose dating had never appealed to her.

No, she simply wanted to spend time with him. She had confidence in her abilities as a vet, but when he was there, things felt right. Like that's the way it should be.

Nancy lost track of time, daydreaming. Laurie came in, and it surprised her. MC always beat her there. How else could they have their morning ritual together?

"Hey, Dr. Baker."

"Hi, Laurie, I've lost track of time this morning." She was flustered. Her day started wrong, somehow.

"Where's MC?"

"I guess he's running late." She looked at her watch and frowned.

As if on cue, the phone rang. Laurie answered. "It's for you."

Nancy took the receiver. "Hello?"

"Nancy …"

"MC? Are you all right?" He didn't sound right.

"I'm fine … I will be. Hey, I'm going to have to be off today. I'm sorry to leave you in a lurch, but something has come up."

"That's fine." She swallowed, then cleared her throat, waiting for him to say something else. He didn't. "MC—"

"I'll talk to you later, Nancy. 'Bye."

And he hung up. Dread rose in her. Dread, doubt, a little fear, and anger with herself for counting on him for more than assisting at the clinic.

"MC, I presume?" Laurie tilted her head curiously.

Nancy nodded, her mind trying to decipher the phone call. She didn't want to say anything else until she talked to him face-to-face. Nancy checked her watch and then back up at Laurie. "Would you call my morning appointments and reschedule them?"

"Yes, ma'am." Laurie pulled out the appointment book and the Rolodex with all the patients' phone numbers. She glanced back up at Nancy. "I hope everything is okay."

Nancy took a deep breath and expelled it slowly. "I do too."

The bright light in the chapel hurt MC's eyes after the sleepless night he'd spent tossing and turning. He'd hoped to break his record of three nights in a row of sleeping. Instead, he'd walked the property half the night, finally falling asleep in his chair around 4 a.m.

The nightmare came back, the one where he's being pulled out of the swamp, comrades falling left and right, and both Gunnar and Rusty being killed. Halfway through the dream, there was Rebecca. She called to him, and then she slowly disappeared into the mist. In the end, as usual, he rode in the claustrophobic Medevac chopper, Nancy caring for him, telling him it would be okay. This time, she wore her hair down, and she caressed his face. Then, about the time he would have liked the dream to continue, he woke up.

This time, however, his heart rate didn't take as long to slow. He could remember the end of the dream.

Peaceful.

Loved.

God had a purpose for him, but could he meet the challenge?

At that point, he'd missed his opportunity to have his first cup of coffee sitting across from Nancy in her tiny office.

She sounded worried. He needed time to think things through. He compared the last few years to a merry-go-round that he'd jumped off of at its highest speed. It wasn't pretty.

He'd grabbed the bottle of pills and taken them with him, placing them on the altar.

So, he sat, looking at the cross on the stained-glass window they'd replaced, amazed at its beauty. It was stunning. As a child, he appreciated its beauty, but now, knowing its history, it meant more. It told the story of a part of his family. An outward symbol that Christ was, or at least should be, the center of their family, and their faith.

Grandpa and Grandma had suffered. They wanted a child and couldn't conceive. He had no thought of having a child, and he discovered a child of which he knew nothing. Like his biological grandfather and Dad. He and James Dunne each with a child out there with no knowledge of his father.

He had to figure it out, so he stared at the colors, and the prism effect on the walls as the sun continued to rise higher in the sky.

The altar was right there. Right in front of him. As if God spoke audibly, he groped at these words: *I have overcome the world.*

"It's a good thing, God, because I don't have a clue. I don't think I ever did."

He knelt at the altar a few feet from the window, and bowed his head, not knowing what to say, except "take over," "help me," "guide me," and "forgive me," over and over—not in that order.

As he bent his knee there at the altar, he sensed someone in the room with him. There was Grandpa, preparing to kneel next to him.

"Thought you might like some prayer company."

Neither of them prayed out loud, but Grandpa laid his hands on MC. Sometimes prayers are "groanings which cannot be uttered." When you don't know what to pray, give it all to Jesus.

After a while, Grandpa got up, leaving him there at the altar. He heard the door open softly, and taking Grandpa's place, instead of manly hands on his shoulders, a small, soft hand reached for his.

He turned, facing her, not caring if Nancy saw the tears in his eyes. Pulling her hand to his lips, he kissed it.

Did he have his answer?

But she doesn't know.

Yes, God had forgiven him. But Nancy? How could he tell her he had a son?

Rising from the altar, he took her hands in his, not quite meeting her eyes. Her clear gaze went too deep.

"Are you …"

"I'm fine." MC took a deep breath and looked up at the ceiling, and then at her. She looked confused. And why wouldn't she be? He was too. A kick in the gut couldn't feel any more unexpected.

"Sit."

She obeyed without question, looking up at him as he paced up and down in front of her. Words. That's what he needed. Words.

The right words.

God? Are you there? I need you, and I have a feeling Nancy will, too, before it's all said and done.

He finally stopped walking and knelt in front of her. He'd been on his knees before his God today, and now, he was on his knees before the woman he loved. The woman he wanted to keep from hurt and harm. The woman he had to hurt right now.

"MC, you're scaring me." She reached out and put her hands on his cheeks, forcing him to look at her. "Is it the pills?"

She'd noticed them on the altar. If only.

He shook his head. "No."

"Then, what?" She tilted her head, worry rolling off her.

"I got a letter a few weeks ago."

"Okay. From?"

"Rebecca."

Nancy stiffened. "What did she want?"

If he weren't so beaten down at that moment, he could have enjoyed the idea of Nancy being jealous. Like she had any reason to be.

"Nothing. She'd heard I got home, and wanted to let me know she was sorry, and that she was married and had a baby."

Nancy broke eye contact. "Are you … sorry she's not available."

MC grasped her hands tightly. "No."

Her head shot up, a look of hope in her eyes. The glint of tears made him want to pull her into his arms, and she would have gone, he was pretty sure. But now wasn't the time.

"MC, what is wrong?" She was begging, now.

Closing his eyes, he paused to listen. *God? Are you there?*

Tell her the truth.

Was that God, or was it simple human reasoning?

Or, maybe simple human reasoning could *be* God sometimes.

"Nancy, I got another letter, yesterday, from Rebecca's father." He swallowed deeply. "Rebecca's dead."

Nancy's eyes widened.

He closed his own to her, grinding out the words between clenched teeth. "And I have a son."

~

"I ... I CAN'T."

MC was not the man Nancy thought—wanted him to be. Sure, he'd had trouble adjusting to life after Vietnam, but this had nothing to do with it. *This* happened before he left. He'd taken for granted that life would return to normal.

What even *was* normal?

The shock nearly brought her down.

He told her he had a son, and she pulled away. Everything around her went fuzzy, much like after her last episode with Bert. The image of Rebecca while they were at Auburn came to her. She'd had MC's child.

Had he forced himself on her? Was he not the hero she'd built him up to be? Was he an abuser too? She had been beaten by her father, by Danny, by Bert, and now, differently, by MC. She was defeated.

The look on his face almost finished her, almost making her soften. Almost. What would this do to him? Would he have another relapse? What if he tried to hurt himself again?

Then the anger came back. No. It wasn't her problem. There were consequences to sin.

Why, God, do things have to be so complicated? It wasn't fair. Why couldn't she just drift into a warm, fuzzy relationship with a normal guy? A stable, loving guy who had morals that matched what she tried to live. Somebody more in tune with God than she was. A man she could follow in faith.

It made her furious.

Why now? She and MC had each worked through their issues, both knew that God was in control, not them. She was well on her way to falling in love with him.

Scratch that. She had been in love with him since the first time they met. Now?

Now, she didn't know what to think. Maybe it was her fault. Had she committed some sin that made God angry with her? Something she should have been smart enough to catch in time to ask forgiveness for?

Could she, if things progressed with MC, raise another woman's child? It was one thing to raise an orphan, but this? This was asking too much.

Her heart stirred within her at the thought of a little boy who resembled MC, but what if he was blonde, like his mother, and not dark, like MC?

No.

Walking out of the chapel was the hardest thing she'd ever done that she had control over.

She couldn't do it. She would go into self-preservation mode even if it meant she would remain alone for the rest of her life. If she stayed away from relationships, she couldn't get hurt, right?

As soon as she got to her truck, she put it in gear and sped down the lane, throwing gravel as she entered the highway. She let loose the tears that had started as soon as he tried to take her hand. She had to let it all out.

MC PICKED up the bottle of pills that were still there, on the altar, where he'd placed them that morning.

The bottle seemed to stare at him, asking him what he was waiting for. When Nancy ran out of the chapel, he wanted to empty the bottle of pills into his hand and throw them down his throat. It's what he deserved. He'd hurt too many people. They would all be better off without him.

He should have been man enough to wait for Rebecca. In Vietnam, he should have been able to save Gunnar and so many others. He should be able to handle dreams and hallucinations. He should be able to reintegrate into normal life like a real man.

He should, he should, he should.

If he came across the word "should" one more time, he would lose it.

Coward.

He had to make a decision. Did he start over and follow God the right way this time, or did he throw away all he'd learned about His love and forgiveness?

His instinct told him to throw it all away. Not worth it.

Before he left for Vietnam, everyone thought him an exemplary example of manhood. Good student, athlete, church-goer, all-around-nice-guy.

Those were the ones that would get by you every time.

The window they'd installed only days before taunted him. He'd been close to the top of the world that day. Life could turn on a dime.

He didn't expect Nancy or his family to understand. Telling Nancy made him want to die. Imagining the faces of his parents almost finished him. Maybe in some families, this was acceptable. In his? As much as he knew they loved him, the image of their disappointed faces haunted him.

Now faith is confidence in what we hope for and assurance about what we do not see.

He didn't see a way out of this. Through it? He couldn't see that direction, either.

His confidence was nil, his faith shaken.

<h1 style="text-align:right">Chapter Forty-Six</h1>

"So, you weren't the paragon of virtue you were believed to be?"

"No, and I guess I never was." He picked up the amber bottle of pills and studied them.

Grandpa came back when Nancy left in a hurry. He gave MC a sad smile but grasped his shoulder. "We learn a lot more from mistakes than we do while things are going our way." He fixed MC with his eyes. "Give her time. She's hurting and disappointed. That doesn't mean she won't come around."

He didn't see how. God had left him again.

Wait. Had God left, or had MC sidled away the moment things got tough again?

Didn't matter. The amazing news that he had a child was overshadowed by the moral implications that shook him to the core.

He didn't see a way past this one.

NANCY KEPT DRIVING. She didn't care where she went, but eventually, she came to herself and checked the gas gauge on the truck. She wouldn't get much farther without filling up the gas tank.

It was busy at the truck stop twenty miles out of Clarksville.

Travelers stopped and visited the Stuckey's confectioner store that sold more cheap souvenirs than candy.

After paying the pump jockey for her gas, she pulled the truck up to the front door and got out. She needed something to drink, and according to her watch, she had missed lunch by two hours.

Laurie will be frantic.

Digging in her purse, she found a dime and entered the phone booth. She closed the folding door, letting the quiet envelop her. She closed her eyes and stood there for a moment before inserting the coin and dialing the phone.

Deep breath.

Dial the phone.

One step at a time.

"Laurie? This is Dr. Baker."

"I've been worried about you. Are you all right?"

Nancy closed her eyes, tears threatening, but she swallowed them. "I'm fine, just had an unexpected … had something come up."

"I rescheduled the rest of the appointments for today. Are you sure you're okay?" Laurie's voice lowered.

Laurie had to hear the quiver in her voice. "I'll be fine. See you in the morning."

She hung up the phone and checked the change slot out of habit, but no spare change.

Wandering the aisles of the store, she found herself beginning to stabilize. An older couple at the soda counter caught her eye. She could tell they had been together for many years. The smiles, the touches, the relaxed way of interacting with one another? It was nice to see. In the souvenir part of the store, there was a mother and two small children, a girl probably four or five years old, and a little boy around two, with black hair and deep brown eyes.

Is this what little Michael looked like? Hanging back in his mother's arms, Nancy could tell he was heavy for her. The young boy didn't notice, and the mother didn't fuss. He turned toward her, and in a moment that stood still, he smiled at her, reached out to her, and said, "Hi!" Nancy automatically smiled back and waved at him.

The boy's mother turned and smiled at Nancy. "He never met a stranger."

"He's cute." Nancy turned and went to the truck as quickly as possible, her mind racing. What if MC's son had been an orphan? Could she love him then? Take care of him? Stopping to think, she realized it had nothing to do with his son. Could she accept the fact that MC had a relationship before her, making her jealous of a dead woman?

Jesus said when we do things for the least of these, we're doing them for Him.

Her heart and her mind were negotiating as she drove back home in the lengthening shadows of evening.

Nancy was nearly back to Park Haven. A cough, then a sputter, followed by a full-on stall. Not the carburetor again. She worked the steering wheel, maneuvering the truck to the side of the road before losing the steering completely.

She sat there a minute, basking in the way this day had gone. Basking being a very ironic way of describing a day that if she could start over, she would.

Looking around, she recognized her location.

About a quarter-mile from Dunne Lane.

She hit the steering wheel a few times and then shook it. Not that it would do any good, but it made her feel better to be a little violent to her faithful steed.

She tried the ignition switch again. Sputter, sputter, sputter, wheeze.

All she gained was a flooded engine. Only one thing to do.

Walk to Brendan Dunne's house, right next to MC Dunne's cabin, the last place she wanted to be, and the first place she probably needed to be.

Lord, what gives? She raised her gaze skyward to the headliner of the truck, then put it in Park and exited, grabbing her purse and the flashlight she kept behind the driver's seat. Maybe if she left the keys in it, someone would steal it. Of course, they'd have to get it started, first.

Darkness hovered, especially under the canopy of the trees just before the house. There were lights on at the house, but none at the cabin. Would MC be at his grandfather's house?

She hoped not. She wasn't ready.

Walking onto the porch, she rapped on the screen door, immediately hearing someone come near.

"Nancy." Mr. Dunne raised his eyebrows. "What can I do for you?"

"My truck stalled out down the road. Pretty sure it's the carburetor, but I fix animals, not trucks. Can you give me a ride home?"

"Of course. Let me get my keys." He turned, then turned back toward her. "MC said you talked earlier."

She grimaced. "He talked." Looking up at him, her eyes filled. "I ... I walked out."

He nodded. "Nobody would blame you."

"I can." She shrugged and turned toward the cabin. "How is he?"

"I left him at the chapel a couple of hours ago. Haven't seen him come back to the cabin." He scanned through the trees toward the chapel. "Looks like he's lit the lantern or some candles."

She was torn. Conflicted. As if she had to make a decision now, and if she didn't, it would be too late. Not sure why, but she did. Suddenly, she needed to see MC. In the depths of her soul, seeing him, talking to him, was crucial.

"I'm going down there." She put her purse on the rocker next to the door and turned on her flashlight. "I need to see him."

"I'll be here if you need me." He held up a finger. "Hold on." He went back into the kitchen and gave her two napkins containing biscuits and bacon. "MC will be hungry, and I have a suspicion you are too."

A flicker of life came back into her. Sometimes the little things meant the most. Tears threatening to fall again, she pulled together a wobbly smile and reached out to hug Mr. Dunne. "Thank you."

Nancy found MC where she'd left him, hours ago. He didn't turn as she walked in the door, so she took the box of matches she'd noticed next to the lantern and lit some more candles, then turned up the flame on the lantern.

That got his attention. "Nancy?"

"Listen. Don't talk. Just listen, okay?" She had to get through this without crying because the look on his face gutted her. Hopeful, but scared out of his wits. Did she want the kind of power he appeared willing to give her?

"I'm sorry."

He opened his mouth to speak, and she held her hand up. "Nope, I said don't talk."

He made the motion of locking his lips and throwing away the key, which sparked a slight smile on his face, and she could feel herself beginning to relax, as well.

"MC, when you told me about Rebecca, and Michael, I didn't know how to respond. I was prepared for the issues you had from Vietnam, but … this was different. This was personal."

She held up her hand when he would speak, and he stopped, gazing into her eyes.

"And you know what? Life is personal, and it's messy." She swallowed, not sure where she would land with this, but she sent up a quick, silent prayer that God would help her figure it out as she went. "I went to Stuckey's earlier this afternoon."

"Stuckey's?" His eyebrows quirked up in surprise.

"Yes, Stuckey's." She held up her hands. "Stay with me, here. My whole childhood, I used to beg to stop there. Today, there was a little boy there, who, honestly, could be you as a toddler." She wiped her tears on her sleeve. The likelihood of finding a tissue here was doubtful. "I realized something. It wasn't a child who made me angry."

"It was me."

"It was you." She paused, tilting her head, gazing into his eyes. "And I have no right to be angry with you over something that happened before we even met each other.

He didn't say anything. He watched her, waiting.

Nancy took a deep breath, hoping she could get through reliving her past. Somehow, she knew that if she was to know his experience, he needed to know hers.

"I'd like to tell you a little about me if you don't mind."

Chapter Forty-Seven

They sat on the pew and talked until the stars came out and the moon rose in the black velvet sky. The crickets and frogs in the nearby creek serenaded them.

After the initial shock of hearing the story, now that she'd had time to digest it, Nancy's heart felt free in a way it hadn't in a long time. He told her everything, and in return, she told him about her father and Danny. About how she blamed herself for so many things, including her thought that somehow it was *her* sin that caused this heartache.

He grabbed her hands again—he'd done that several times throughout the conversation—and stared at them, before catching her gaze again. It continued to amaze her how, with this particular man, she could read his emotion in a simple look, gesture, and smile.

"I had the dream again last night." He'd mentioned nightmares in passing, but he'd never told her about one particular dream.

"Rebecca was there, but she disappeared." He gave her a crooked grin. "You were there too."

"Really?" Was she wrong to be slightly pleased to be represented in his nightmare?

He nodded. "You've been in it for a long time. It's usually as I start waking up. You're telling me it'll be okay."

"That's a good thing, right?" Her self-confidence was still a little shaky.

"Very." He surveyed the moonlit landscape. "Let's take a walk."

"It's dark."

He pulled her up. "I've walked this property in the full moon and in the new moon. Tonight will be easy." He grasped her hand. "I won't let you fall."

He kept hold of her hand as they walked down the hill. She could hear a creek gurgling. Would he bring her here one day?

"Nancy?" He stopped her and faced her, his hands brushing her upper arms. "Can you forgive me?"

This was a moment she could make or break whatever their relationship was beginning to be.

How could she not forgive him? God forgave her of so many things, not the least of which was her distrust of Him. She didn't give her earthly father the forgiveness he begged for. She'd waited until it was too late.

That wasn't going to happen with MC.

After a moment of looking into MC's eyes, she nodded solemnly. "No one is righteous. Only God."

She put her hand on his cheek, and he closed his eyes for a moment before he pulled her closer. He wrapped his arms around her much like he had after her encounter with Bert. She wanted his protection, and held him closer, sharing some of her tiny amount of courage at the same time.

He leaned down and touched her lips with his. Their first kiss. She smiled into the kiss, responding in kind.

"Is it too soon to tell you that I love you?"

Nancy's heart was in her throat. "I'm not sure what the timetable is supposed to be on that." Her words came out raspy.

He chuckled, then groaned, humility pouring out of him. "I mean it." He shifted his eyes away from her. "At one time I told Rebecca I loved her too."

"I know."

"How?" He eyed her curiously.

"Because I know you wouldn't have committed yourself to her if you didn't think you loved her."

"I didn't know what it meant, then."

"You made a mistake. I get it. I love you too."

Her heart pounded as his countenance brightened and he pulled her up in his arms, kissing her as if he would never let her go.

Which would have been fine with her.

Chapter Forty-Eight

"Hello there, Michael."

The two-year-old boy stared at MC, thumb in his mouth, big brown eyes giving nothing away. His world had been turned upside down, and he couldn't comprehend why his mother wasn't there.

MC knelt on the floor next to him. He'd seen baby pictures of himself, and, yes, Michael looked like him at that age. He couldn't take his eyes off him. His son.

Rebecca's father, Victor Randall, wiped the moisture accumulating in his eyes. MC understood. There was some moisture in his, as well. "We've called him Mikey since he was a baby. Not sure why. I guess it's not too late to start calling him Michael." Victor smoothed the boy's dark hair. "I'm not sure just how I can let him go."

MC looked up, then. "I understand, sir. Can I just say ..." He wanted to apologize. Beg his forgiveness for the sins he and Rebecca had committed. Let him know how sorry he was that he hadn't been there.

Victor shook his head. "You don't owe me any explanation." He blew his nose noisily. "When Rebecca left home for college, we didn't feel good about it. Didn't feel like we'd finished our job of teaching her about the world and about how to stay set apart from the world, but we thought maybe having her in church was enough. When she brought you around, we felt pretty good about her."

"Mr. Randall …"

Victor held his hands out in front of him. "MC, you aren't perfect. Rebecca wasn't perfect. This little boy, here?" He chuckled, looking at him with eyes full of love. "He's pretty close to perfect, but even he has his moments. I blame his mama and my wife—and myself—but he probably has some of your imperfections too." The older man smiled. "I think it's time Mikey knew his daddy. Time he had somebody besides an old curmudgeon chasing him around."

One of the things that he always liked most about Rebecca was her family. Looking back, that might have been part of what drew him to her—the idea that they could have a similar life to that of his parents and grandparents.

It wasn't enough, though. If what they had didn't measure up to what he felt for Nancy, then it wouldn't have worked. Maybe on the surface, but would they have always wondered if there was someone else out there that would make them happier? That they could bring happiness to.

MC looked up at Nancy, who knelt next to him. Mikey immediately crawled into her lap and hugged her, stroking her hair gently. The tears in her eyes as she squeezed his son sent a ripple of astonishment through his body that surprised him.

And didn't, at the same time.

MC felt his ankle begin to give way, so he stood.

"Sit, sit. Can I get you something to drink? I have some sweet tea in the refrigerator."

"That sounds good, Mr. Randall."

"Please. We're family. Call me Victor." He hoisted himself up. "We've got this boy drawing us together. I hope you'll let me see him as often as I'm able."

"Mr. … Victor, you can rest assured you'll be in Mikey's life as much as you want to be."

"I appreciate that." Victor looked down at his grandson, then at MC. "He sure does look like you, doesn't he?"

Nancy laughed. "I think the Dunne genes are very strong."

MC looked embarrassed. "Yeah, there's a lot of black-haired Irish in the family. Me, my grandfather, my great-uncle."

"I'll get that tea now."

"Thank you."

Nancy got up, picking Mikey up as she stood. Standing next to him, the boy reached out to MC, who instinctively caught him as he lunged.

"Whoa, there, cowboy!" MC laughed as Mikey pulled at his over-long wavy hair. "You've got a much better haircut than your daddy, don't you?"

Nancy rubbed the boy's back. "Remember when I told you about the little boy at Stuckey's?"

"I do."

"God sent me there, just then, so I'd see a boy who looks so much like Mikey." She looked up at MC. "I like calling him Mikey, don't you?"

MC grinned, shifting his precious burden as he sat on the nearby sofa. "Mikey it is. Something tells me that eventually, he'll want it shortened to just Mike or Michael." He put his face down even with his son. "What do you think?"

"Mikey." The child spoke, poked himself in the chest, and brightened when they laughed.

Victor came into the room carrying three glasses of tea. "That's what we've needed around here."

"What's that?"

"Laughter."

"I'll do my best to make him happy, sir."

"I know you will. Between the two of you, I think he's in for a treat. How long have you been married?"

MC and Nancy looked at each other wide-eyed. Nancy spoke first. "Um. We're not …"

"We've only known one another since March," MC added, hoping that the additional information would explain the situation. Seeing the red creep up Nancy's cheeks tickled him. If he had his way, they would get married soon.

But there was still a lot to consider.

The veterinary clinic.

Raising a child. A ready-made family. Was Nancy prepared for that? Was he?

What about his career?

It was happening too fast.

God? Where do we go from here?

"Yes, sir. I understand, sir."

Being on only one end of a conversation was frustrating.

MC put the phone back in its cradle carefully as if it would break.

"Well?" Nancy couldn't tell, from MC's expression, what the result of that conversation was.

The genuine smile that bloomed on his face almost took the stuffing out of her. She wanted to melt into his arms, but she wanted details, first. MC had other ideas. He pulled her close, and she could see the excitement—in anyone else, she'd have called it "giddy," but not this man. Maybe in years, months, weeks, and days, they hadn't known each other that long, but in depth? Spiritually? In that way that you only know the one person you love? In all the ways that count, Nancy knew him well.

"They want me to come down to Fort Benning and look the program over."

Nancy bunched the fabric of his shirt sleeves in her hands. "So ...

"I've got the assignment if I want it. It would be an automatic bump in rank, and I'd be working nine to five, five days a week—unless things escalate, and they call for more trained dogs."

"And do you want it?" Fort Benning wasn't exactly a hop-skip-and-a-jump from Park Haven. It would be an adjustment for both of them. They'd just found one another. Could their new relationship handle the distance?

MC narrowed his eyes. "Honestly?"

"Please." Nancy took a deep breath, trying to be patient.

"I'm not completely sure. Am I ready for that kind of responsibility? Can I do it?"

The vulnerability of his words pierced her heart. She didn't say anything for a moment. Just stood there, looking deeply into his eyes. "*I* know you can, but do *you* know you can?"

"There's a program that would let me finish my DVM through the Army. With my service record and the amount of schooling I already have behind me, I could have it done in two years. There's a catch, though."

She tried to contain the huge sigh that threatened to erupt from her. *Here we go. There's always a catch.* "I hate to even ask."

MC pulled her closer, squeezing her, kissing the top of her head tenderly. "I'd have to sign up for a two-year active-duty military vet assignment—which includes the handler assignment—and five years of Army Reserves."

Nancy pulled away, her eyes wide. His brow was clear. He looked more relaxed than she believed she had ever seen him. "But … those are good things, right?"

He smiled, nodding. "It's the best of both worlds. I can get my training and fulfill my obligation to Uncle Sam, and at a discount."

She snuggled into his arms, her head resting on his chest, underneath his chin. "So …"

"With my combat experience, if this war lasts a while, I might be deployed again, but this time as a veterinarian instead of a scout." He paused. "What does this mean for us?" He tilted her chin up and kissed her lips softly, then gazed deep into her soul. "Are you prepared to be an Army wife"

Wait. Army *wife*? It wasn't the first time she'd thought about marrying him. It was, however, the first time he had put into words the idea of them spending their lives together.

She tilted her head and stared into his eyes, trying to see inside his head. *Was he ready for a commitment on this level?*

Then there was Mikey to consider. MC had brought him home to his parents' house and moved back in with them until his future was decided. The cabin was empty again, but MC liked to go there to think. And pray.

The idea of mothering his son tugged at her. The idea of adding brothers and sisters to Mikey's world made her smile.

"I take it the idea isn't objectionable?"

"Not completely." She didn't want to show all her cards, so she twisted her lips, not meeting his eyes. She played with one of the buttons on his shirt. When she peered up through her lashes, instead of the humor she expected, she saw vulnerability and the light of love in his eyes.

She felt his body relax, and yet hold her tighter. He let go of the breath he'd been holding and threaded his fingers through her loose hair. She was glad she'd left it down today. Somehow, with him, she didn't think of her hair as an "enticement," but when he touched it, it was her crowning glory. Dipping his head down, he tilted her head so he could capture her lips. He didn't tease, didn't overstep, but instead let her know that she was beautiful and desirable. She was respected and loved.

Epilogue

September

The drive from Park Haven, Tennessee, to Auburn University, in Alabama, usually took seven hours. This trip took four days.

As honeymoons went, it was different. They meandered through the outskirts of Nashville, made stops to visit Aunt Jean and Richard, and then every historical marker and tourist attraction they could find.

It wasn't often that a honeymoon netted a young couple a two-year-old child, but this time, it did. Mikey rode in the back seat with a basket of toys and kept them laughing with his antics. When Mikey was sleepy, he slept on a blanket in the back seat. When he was hungry, they ate. When he was tired of riding, they stopped for a while.

MC missed the dogs. Grandpa was caring for all three until they had a place to keep them. As part of his job, he would have with him a K9 trainee, so they wouldn't be completely dogless.

Mikey was in the back seat, sound asleep, and Nancy sat in the center of the bench seat of their new-to-them 1965 Ford Galaxie 500, her left thigh lined up with his.

This. This was peace.

"I miss your curls." She'd been running her fingers through what was left of his black hair.

"I can let it grow."

"I don't think the Army would appreciate that." She sighed and traced the bottom half of the tattoo on his arm, visible under the short-sleeved shirt. "I was just getting used to the long hair."

"Are you trying to distract me?"

"Why, Mr. Dunne, whatever gave you that idea?" She examined the tattoo closely, smiling at the knowledge that now she knew what it looked like. The intricate lines mimicked the cross in the stained-glass window they'd faced during their wedding ceremony.

He turned to see her batting her eyelashes at him and laughed. "I love you, Mrs. Dunne."

"And I love you, Mr. Dunne."

"Won't be long until we can call ourselves 'Dr. And Dr. Dunne.'"

"I suppose." She rested her chin on his shoulder. "I hope this works, you going to school and working at Fort Benning. It's a lot to take on."

MC detected a note of worry in her voice. "You're the one making the sacrifice. What about your adjunct teaching at the university? It won't be easy, but we can do it. What's got you worried?"

Her laughter bubbled up. "Nothing to do with that. What if I'm not a good mom?"

Looking ahead, a sign announced a wide spot in the road with a picnic table. Perfect. He swung the car in and parked under a tree with leaves just beginning to turn, rolling down the windows with the touch of a button. As soon as he put it in Park, he turned to her, pulling her close.

"You? You will be the best mom in the world."

"I think you're exaggerating a little."

"Nope. And just so you know, I want at least five kids."

Her eyes rounded. "Five? At least? Counting Michael?"

MC shrugged. "I don't know. How many were you thinking?"

"Uh, two or three?"

He scoffed. "That's for wimps. We've got to make up for so many one-child generations in the Dunne family. Time's a ' wastin'! After all, who's gonna take care of the farm when we're old and gray? And the chapel will need work again, eventually."

"This from the guy who used to say he was the end of the Dunne family line. Sounds like you've got big plans."

He laughed. "Just putting it out there." He looked up. "Hear that, God?"

"You're awful."

"And you love it."

A soft breeze blew through the open windows. They rested in comfortable silence for a while, Nancy dozing on his shoulder. He could stay like this forever.

MC felt her stretching next to him, waking. She looked behind her at the sleeping boy and sighed, continuing the conversation as if twenty minutes hadn't passed with them all sleeping.

"I guess we should do our part to keep the chapel up. It was so pretty for the wedding, wasn't it?" She relaxed, melting into his arms at the thought of their August wedding. The flowers were perfect."

He had no idea what floral varieties his mother had picked out of her garden, but he'd admit, it was pretty, if not as pretty as the bride. "You were perfect." He laughed as she rolled her eyes.

She blushed. "Please."

Her just-above-the-knee white lace dress suited her perfectly, he thought, hugging her curves just right, and showing off her waist-length brown hair.

Nancy's sister-in-law had come up to act as her stylist and be her matron of honor next to Mary Ann and Laurie as her bridesmaids. Her brother, Richard, walked her down the aisle. The moment Nancy told her niece, Lisa, that she could wear a tiara, she was all in for being the flower girl.

They weren't entirely sure young Mikey could handle the responsibility of ring-bearer, so his new cousin, Ryan, was tasked with wrangling not only the toddler but also the three dogs who were part of the ceremony. If a red Border Collie could blush, everyone would have seen Rusty's embarrassment about having flowers attached to his collar.

Rounding off the wedding party were young Jason and his sister—the princess—making their way up the aisle to drop rose petals, preparing the way of the bride.

MC chose Dad as his best man and Grandpa and Will as groomsmen.

They'd decided to place the time capsule back into the cavity under the stained-glass window as part of their ceremony. They soon found that a larger box was needed. Grandpa had written out the story of himself and Evangeline and their trip to Tennessee.

MC wanted to put his Purple Heart medal in the box, but Nancy wouldn't let him. She wanted him to save it for his son. In the spirit of the original offerings, MC placed his wartime Army-issue wristwatch and Nancy a charm bracelet that she'd discovered in her mother's jewelry box, along with their own love story and a current family tree.

Yes, the wedding was perfect, and his wife, Nancy, was perfect.

She laid her head on his shoulder and was quiet for a moment. MC thought she was beautiful when she was thinking. He turned, pulling her head down to his chest, wondering since Mikey was still sleeping, if another nap might be in order.

The gentle breeze blew through the car windows as they rested, simply enjoying one another's company.

Nancy's voice broke into his semi-sleep state. "I wonder who will find the time capsule in the next fifty years?"

"That will be up to our kids, I guess."

"Our kids." She turned, leaning her chin on his arm. They were nose to nose. Well within kissing distance. "It could be Mikey."

"Maybe. Who knows, it could be one of our other eight kids."

She stiffened, eyes flashing. "Eight? What happened to five?"

He waggled his eyebrows. "Thought I'd see if I could sneak some in. Who knows—it might be our grandkids. We should have plenty with ten children."

She swatted at him, and he caught her hand, pulling it to his lips.

Laughter bubbled up inside him, and at the same time the desire to hold her as close as possible. When MC saw her eyes soften, he glanced back to make sure his son was still asleep and took full advantage of the situation. After the trauma and abuse she'd suffered, MC knew she had been afraid that physical contact would be difficult, but just as she had the power to calm him and bring him back to the present during an episode, she welcomed his touch.

"Do you think Doc Phillips will be okay?"

MC shook his head. Nancy did her level best to worry about everything possible, including what they'd already given over to God. Their family, their vet practice, and their future. All were important. But mostly?

Their service to Him.

He'd tried to assure her many times, but one more wouldn't hurt. "His heart doctor gave him a clean bill of health. Brent will be there in the summertime, and you have Laurie trained to take care of the office. Plus, we'll get down there during breaks. It's two years, then we'll be back to open 'Dunne and Dunne Veterinary Clinic.'"

"The name sounds very industrious. I like it." She winked at him, then shivered with excitement as his lips touched hers. "I'm glad Laurie wanted to stay."

"Mary Ann coming back part-time was a God-send, too, so yes, I think Doc Phillips will be fine."

"What about us? Will we make it?" The words were whispered. She had less confidence than him. Conversely, other than his dependence on and recognition of the Holy Spirit working in his life, most of his confidence came from her.

"We will."

He pulled her closer and held her, eventually kissing away her fears. They were an hour from Auburn, where they would pick up the rest of Michael's things at his grandfather's house. After that, they were going to move into an apartment to begin living as a family of three.

She pulled back. "You know, as soon as I met Mikey, I saw you." She touched his hair gently and shook her head. "That hair."

He grinned. "I wish you'd known Uncle Patrick. He was another one of us 'black-haired Irish' guys. He had hair almost as dark as mine at age 85."

"I wish I'd known him, but I feel like I do, a little."

MC pulled his fingers through her long hair, massaging her scalp and smiling when she relaxed in his arms.

She'd been leaving her hair down, long and free, but she usually had a hair tie handy, just in case. Sometimes vet work and long hair weren't a good combination. He'd gotten his cut short for Uncle Sam, and hers kept getting longer and longer, and he didn't mind. She finally appreciated her "crowning glory."

"You had the dream again last night, didn't you?" He could see the shadow of worry in her eyes. From the state of the bedclothes, he knew he'd thrashed around in the night.

"Yes, but waking up, I wasn't in distress. That hasn't happened in a while." He still worried that one night he'd have it bad and somehow hurt her. "If I ever act violently while I'm asleep, leave the room and lock the door."

"I know. You've told me." She frowned. "That seems a little excessive."

He shook his head. "No, I mean it. We have Michael now, and my main concern is the safety of the two of you … and whoever else we might bring along."

She swatted at him. "Way to turn a serious conversation into a pickup line."

"I'm getting good at that, huh?"

Her smile grew. "Very." He could see her attention fixed on his lips, as his were on hers.

"Come here."

He hoped no Alabama State Police officers pulled over to check on them, because he wanted to well and truly kiss his wife. For an undisclosed number of times.

Because with Nancy in his arms, there was peace. They'd been blessed beyond measure.

Life would never be perfect for a Vietnam Veteran or for a victim of abuse, but with God's help, they would endure. They would understand the peace that passes understanding in Him.

In this world you will have trouble. But take heart! I have overcome the world.

"Daddy? Mommy?"

A sweet, sleepy little voice interrupted the quiet, causing MC and Nancy to turn toward the back seat.

Mikey was quietly playing with his toes. When he saw he had their attention, his face broke out in a grin.

MC answered him. "Yes, son?"

"I wuv you—and I'm firsty."

And so, it began.

THE END

Discussion Questions

1. When the story begins, MC Dunne is on a bus, returning from Vietnam in 1970, after two tours of duty. Why was the "coming home" experience different for Vietnam veterans as opposed to WWII?

2. Nancy Jean Baker left home as a teen because of an abusive parent and became driven to excel as a student, compartmentalizing her personal life and her professional life. Do you ever compartmentalize your emotions concerning certain areas of your life?

3. During this time in history, at the end of the conflict overseas, service animals that saved thousands of soldiers' lives were listed as "surplus equipment" and either euthanized or abandoned. Do you think that would be acceptable today?

4. Flashbacks and hallucinations by day and nightmares by night haunt MC, striking when he least expects it, but in 1970, PTSD hadn't been named and had not been studied to the extent it has today. Most doctors told soldiers to "suck it up" and go on. Was he right in refusing, for a time, to work for Nancy at the Animal Clinic? Why, or why not? Could it

have helped him? Why is it important for all of us to understand something about PTSD?

5. Nancy misses a chance to forgive her estranged father on his deathbed but learns that he had become a Christian after he died. How would that change the way she feels about missing that opportunity?

6. MC's dad, Connor, had always known he was adopted by Brendan and Evangeline Dunne when his mother died and that James Dunne was his father, but he didn't know that Brendan and James' father was a mob boss in Chicago. How difficult do you think it was for Brendan to share the story of how he came to Park Haven? Why?

7. While clearing out their father's house, Nancy and her brother discover evidence of another sibling that died in infancy. The only living person that knew was their Aunt Jean, who was also estranged from her brother, their father. In the 1940s, people didn't talk about their feelings— especially men. How could sharing the pain of losing a child, rather than self-medicating with alcohol, have changed the landscape of their family when death touched them later?

8. MC has insomnia because he's afraid to sleep for the nightmares that plague him, and he's lost his faith in God. On the night Nancy is attacked, he is there to help her, but he nearly kills her attacker in a fit of blind rage. Do you think God was preparing him for this time, or do you believe in coincidences?

9. When Nancy learns of MC's illegitimate child, she runs away from him. Why? What changes her mind? Have you ever been blindsided by news that could change your life?

10. MC must choose between two excellent positions upon his medical release: Service dog trainer or finish veterinary school. He wants to follow God's leading and be in His will. How does a person choose between two excellent options? Pray? Make lists? Consult family? What do you think MC did?

Regina Rudd Merrick started her journey as a lifelong lover of reading in first grade, and eventually parlayed that love of literature into a degree in library science, with stints as both elementary and middle school librarians, and later as a public library director.

After finding the enjoyable world of reading and writing "fanfiction"--original stories based on characters from familiar stories, television shows, and movies--she realized that for some reason, God had given her the ability to weave a story, whether it be in this online community or with her own original characters.

Her first novel, Carolina Dream, was the winner of a publishing contest with Mantle Rock Publishing, LLC (now Scrivenings Press), and her writing career was born. Now the author of six novels and a contributor to four novella collections, Regina writes about people like all of us who sometimes struggle with their faith and trusting God and recently added editing to her resume.

Regina loves chocolate, the beach, playing keyboard and vocals in her church's praise band, historical homes, watching other people renovate on HGTV, and Hallmark movies. She and her husband of nearly forty years are empty nesters in rural western Kentucky and are the proud parents of two grown-up daughters and a son-in-law, along with the family's fifteen-year-old Schauzer-mix, Cedric.

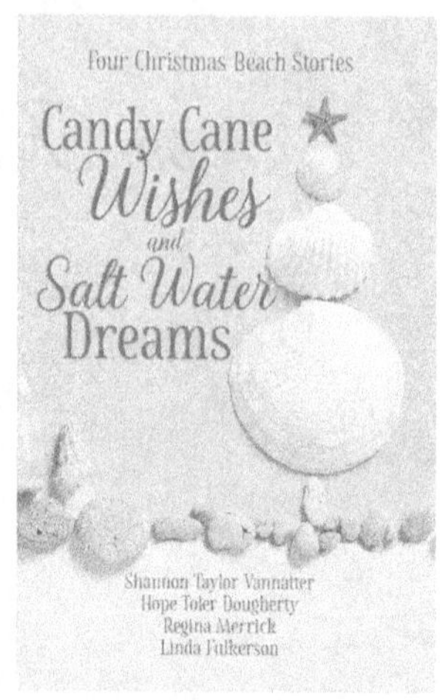

Candy Cane Wishes and Saltwater Dreams:

A Novella Collection

https://scrivenings.link/candycanewishes

A Southern Breeze Series:

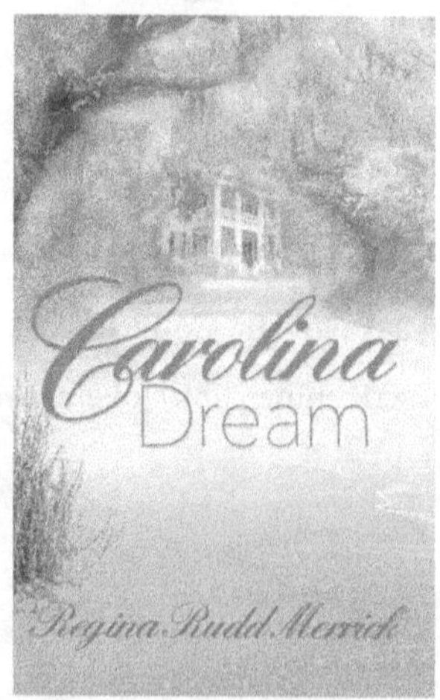

Carolina Dream

A Southern Breeze Series: Book One

*More Historical Romance
from Scrivenings Press*

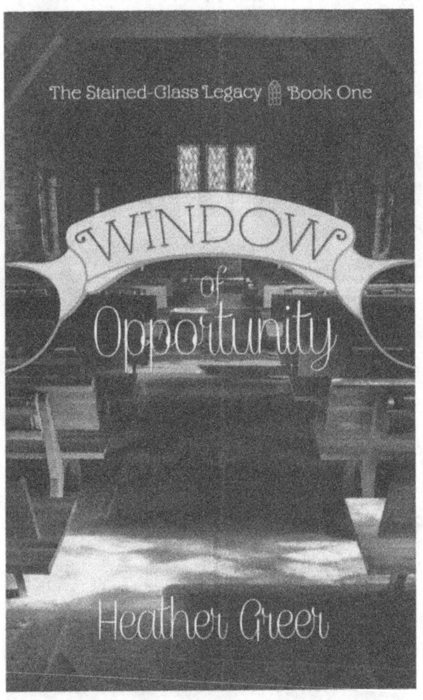

Window of Opportunity by Heather Greer

The Stained-glass Legacy Series—Book One

Faith and duty drive Evangeline Moore to protect her father's pristine image
as a judge in Harrisburg, Illinois. Her resolve's biggest test? Dot, her childhood
friend. With Evangeline beside her, Dot's desire for the Roaring Twenties' glitz
and glamor leads the pair into questionable situations.

Born into a Chicago mob family, Brendan Dunne understands duty, but faith
puts him at odds with his father's demands. Even when his brother James's

propensity for trouble lands them in Harrisburg, the truth is undeniable. To their father, the lines he won't cross mean Brendan will never measure up.

When circumstances push Brendan and Evangeline together, unexpected events create opportunity to break free of family expectations. Will they be brave enough to forge their own path before the window closes on their chance to change?

Get your copy here:

https://scrivenings.link/windowofopportunity

~

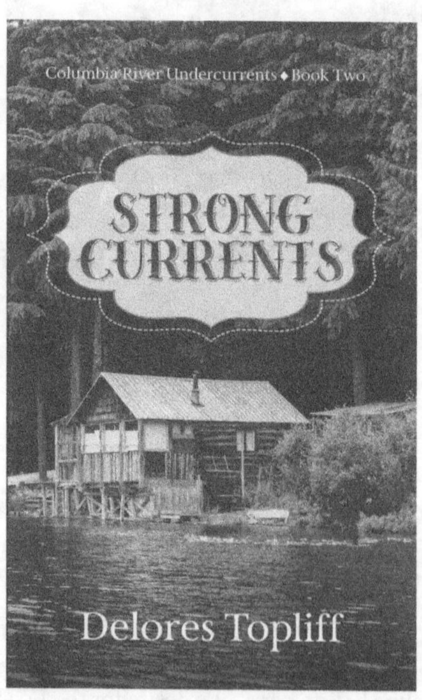

Strong Currents by Delores Topliff

Columbia River Undercurrents Series—Book Two

Erica Hofer, a young German Christian woman opposes Hitler and flees to her uncle in America but encounters suspicion, rejection, and attempts on her life.

Josh Vengeance, a pastor's son joins the US Navy to become a hero but gets invalided home, crippled in body and spirit.

During world war, is any price too great to pay for love and freedom?

Get your copy here:

https://scrivenings.link/strongcurrents

~

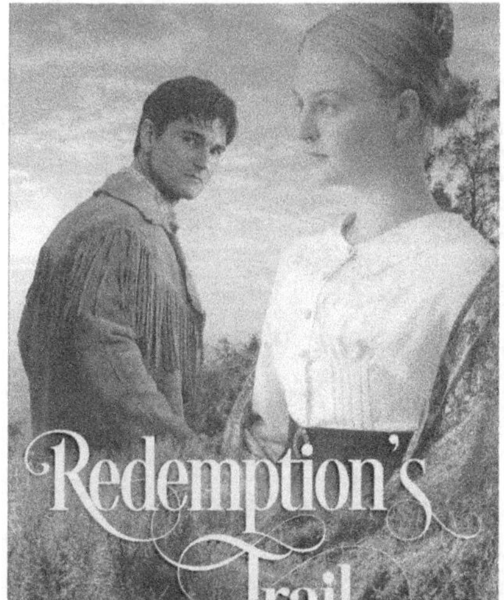

Redemption's Trail by Betty Woods

Trails of the Heart — Book Two

Newly widowed with her second child due in a few months, Lily Johnson has nowhere to go until Toby Grimes, her late husband's boss, asks her to stay on as housekeeper at his ranch. Remaining in the house Mr. Grimes built for her and her husband is an answered prayer. But malicious gossips see her godsend job as a ruse for a sinful dalliance since her employer is a nice-looking, single man.

God and a lot of others turned their backs on Toby during the war, so he returns the favor by keeping to himself. Yet the need to care for and protect Lily overwhelms him. The way she tugs at his heart scares him more than going into a losing battle.

Unwilling to allow anyone to destroy a fine woman's reputation, he proposes a marriage of convenience. After much prayer, Lily accepts. Her first marriage was a love match made in heaven. The second leads down a trail only God knows. The peace she has concerning a marriage to a troubled man she doesn't love begins a walk of faith to a destination neither she, nor Toby, can guess.

Get your copy here:

https://scrivenings.link/redemptionstrail

Stay up-to-date on your favorite books and authors with our free e-newsletters.

ScriveningsPress.com